KIRS

BRIGHT

THE
TITANIUM
TRILOGY

YIELD

WE MUST EVOLVE IF WE WANT TO SURVIVE

YIELD
The Titanium Trilogy: Book 1
By Kirsty Bright

Copyright © 2022 Kirsty Bright
ISBN: 978-1-7399978-0-9
Published through Untuned Publishings Ltd

First Edition: August 2022

Book and Cover design by Untuned Publishings Ltd

For information contact:
kirstybrightauthor@gmail.com
Or visit
www.kirstybrightauthor.com

UNTUNED
PUBLISHINGS

To Mum-

For teaching me that my only limit is the one that I set for myself. Thank you for always supporting and believing.

To Dad-

For teaching me the importance of perseverance and determination, and for making story time so exciting as a child. The dog says bow-wow.

To Kas-

For always being there. I'm lucky to have a sister like you.

To Ryan-

For everything.

To Demi, Meg, Freya, Chloe, Clodagh and Charlotte-
For always supporting my endeavours.

I love you all.

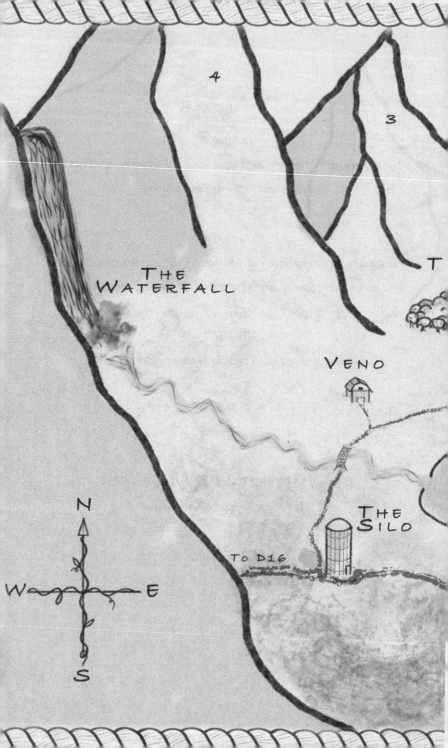

To those who feel as though they don't fit in.

Your difference is your superpower.

Use it.

PROLOGUE

HIM

The Farm was left to me in my parents' will, alongside the hidden world that lay beneath it, decades of research, and the burden which it carried.

Their every moment had been injected into the project and as a result, my life had been an extensive training program, learning the ropes so that one day I could pick up where they left off. They died seven years ago, and since then I'd continued as they wished, making a few changes here and there.

Above ground, there was 185 square miles of open space, fields upon forest, streams, and more field. It was very scenic, especially at this time of year; the sort of place I could imagine on a postcard.

It was a mountainous area, creating a bowl-shaped landscape. The trees slowly started to change color; various oranges and reds amongst the yellowing greens. We found that colors played a crucial part when testing the animals.

The animals were let out once per day for training purposes, but it was crucial that they didn't mix for their own safety. The barns were marked 'Titanium' and 'Veno' to keep the animals in the correct place.

The silo is where I kept the supplies; food, training equipment, and various other things; situated in the middle of The Farm, facing the guesthouse (where the farmers lived), and also the gates.

The land's perimeter was marked by a tall wire fencing which made me feel imprisoned as a young child; before I was introduced to what The Farm really was; before I understood the impact of The Farm's findings, and what it would mean for the future.

Nobody could get in.

But more importantly, nobody could get out.

It was crucial that the animals didn't escape, and that nobody knew what really happened inside the fence. The location was key to keeping it a secret. The only thing connecting it to the rest of the world was the single road which meandered for miles until it reached a village that most people hadn't heard of.

Most people turned around after following it for more than a couple of minutes due to how rural it was, whilst others were put off by the signs reading *'Military Zone - Danger of Death'*. In the seven years that I had been in charge, nobody had yet reached the gates; ten feet tall and armed by gunmen. I hoped for their sake it remained that way. If The Farm was exploited to the world then the program would surely have been ceased.

That is why it was so important that nobody could enter The Farm.

But most importantly;

Nobody could escape.

Phase 1

METAMORPHOSIS

"noun,

-a change of the form or nature of a thing or person into a completely different one.
-(in an insect or amphibian) the process of transformation from an immature form to an adult form in two or more distinct stages."

- Oxford Dictionary

CHAPTER
ONE

ARES

The tingling in my feet woke me from a heavy sleep. My toes twitched with anticipation, it had been a long time since I'd last moved them, if ever?

It was the pins and needles sensation I recognised as it slowly crept up my legs, heavy against the mattress I lay on. The old springs dug into my back. The fabric itched against my skin.

It all felt so familiar, yet foreign at the same time.

At some point, I started to notice the sounds around me. Birds chirped in the distance, and water tinkled through a slow-moving stream. I felt thankful for the muted tones. Anything too loud would have increased the throbbing pain in my head.

A soft autumn breeze brushed my skin. I inhaled deeply, enjoying the clean air in my lungs.

I lay there for a few minutes. Listening. Absorbing.

After so long, I opened my eyes. The morning light burned at my retinas and blurred my vision.

I rested my eyes again and this time welcomed the darkness.

I felt drugged.

Time passed as I faded in and out of consciousness, and I became one with the breeze, neither coming nor going.

"Get up!" The voice cut through my sleep like a knife, sharp and demanding. It was accompanied by the shock of cold water.

My legs swung over the side of the bed, and I was sitting before I even had time to register what was happening. My eyes scanned the area; a small room with wooden panels and barred walls. A man stood on the other side of the door with a hose in his hand, aimed in my direction.

I studied his shaggy hair which continued as stubble across his weathered face. Small wrinkles dragged at his eyes making him appear older than he actually was.

"Lunch." He shoved a small tray onto the ledge with his free hand, dropped the hose with little care to the noise that it made upon landing, and crossed his arms, tapping his index finger against his rain jacket. It was a small gesture but the sound echoed in my ears with clarity. He looked at me, and then at the tray, and back to me. "I don't care if you eat or not. Just take it."

I struggled to find balance on my feet. I moved like a newborn horse; all legs, gangly and weak.

"Well, would you look at that? It walks."

My body felt like jelly, and lifting one foot off the ground resulted in the other straining beneath me. It took me a while, but I made it to the door and reached out for the tray.

"Welcome to The Farm, Ares. Let's hope you live up to your name," he mocked and I stared in confusion. "Keep to the rules and you'll get along just fine."

And with that, he left.

I stood in the doorway, following him with my eyes as he walked down an open corridor and through the large double doors.

'Barn.'

The word crossed my mind without any explanation, and I questioned what a barn was. Looking down at my so-called lunch, I picked up the bacon wrapped in bread and studied it slowly. Was this a barn?

No. That didn't sit right somehow.

I looked around again, noticing that there were many more rooms like mine. Stalls. The building was a barn. The food in my hand was a sandwich.

I nodded in satisfaction and then retreated to my bed, feeling a little more steady on my feet now.

As I ate, I questioned how words formed in my mind. How did I know this language? I searched for memories, yet I found nothing before this day.

I concluded that I must have experienced memory loss, as I was sure that this wasn't my first day on Earth. I hoped that I would be able to make more sense of my situation as the drugs wore off.

The sound of shoes on gravel distracted me from my sandwich. The main doors screeched open to let somebody in and then closed again behind them.

"Ares." Another male stood behind my door. He was unlike my first visitor; kind and approachable. "My name is Dr White. I'm not going to hurt you, please don't be alarmed." He held his hands out in surrender before reaching for my door and slowly cranking it open without taking his eyes from mine. I didn't notice that he had a companion with him until the door was fully open, and he was gesturing for me to step out of my stall.

I felt as though my safety blanket had been ripped away. Was it the idea of leaving the stall which scared me?

Or the fact that Dr White's not-so-friendly companion was holding a gun?

The doctor said something quietly to his friend, and the man with the gun stepped aside. "I'm sorry about him. I know how this must look." He held the door open slightly wider now. "It's just a precaution. I assure you that no harm shall come to you, so long as no harm comes to me."

I understood the warning.

I had no intention of bringing harm to Dr White or his friend, and I complied without any more persuasion.

Dr White walked beside me whilst the bodyguard trailed behind. I peered over my shoulder and felt something nudge into the sensitive spot between my shoulder blades.

"Move," the man grunted.

Dr White shot his bodyguard a look. "Please, he's not going to hurt me."

"How can you be sure after what happened to the last one?"

Dr White shook his head. "Ares is different than the others."

I didn't know what he meant by his words but it seemed to reassure the guard enough, and the gun disappeared from its resting place against my back.

"Well, it's your funeral," said the guard.

"Yes," Dr White sounded unimpressed by his friend's concern. "Thank you, Tim…"

The doors opened for us, and we stepped out into a chilly but otherwise beautiful day. The sun's rays reflected off a lake which shimmered in the light wind, inviting me to jump in. It must have been several miles long; surrounded by a forest which whispered the secrets of autumn.

Tucked into the trees just above the lake sat a large house. It was big enough to sleep 15 guests and was in desperate need of renovation. Yet, it seemed to fit right in.

Far beyond the lake, a tractor pulled a kind of mechanism which chopped the yellowing grass as it moved. I found it peaceful to watch as I walked, and I realized that the beauty of The Farm brought me warmth and comfort. Happiness. I felt comfortable blanketed in nature. I ran my hands through the long grass and forgot all about the shifty man who lingered close behind.

I could see another barn far to my right, mirroring the one that I had been in, and a tall vintage silo stood before me. The hatch at the bottom had been replaced by a door which opened as we approached.

Dr White held his hand out as if to say *'after you'*.

I hesitated for a second, wondering what we'd possibly be doing in a silo, then entered through the steel door.

It was a lift.

Tim shoved me inside and Dr White followed, pushing the top button which read '-1'. The lift lurched into action. I stumbled and fell into Dr White, and as I tried to correct myself I felt Tim's hands pull me back.

"I'm sorry, it was an accident," I said. My voice felt rusty as I spoke. My words were barely audible. How long had it been since I last used my voice? I held my hands up in apology in case they didn't understand.

Tim did understand, although he didn't seem to believe me.

I once again felt the pressure of the gun against my spine as we sunk slowly into the abyss of the unknown.

The lift came to a steady halt and the doors opened to reveal a large cavern. Spotlights circumferenced the floor, shining against the rock of the walls, and casting unusual shadows against the ceiling.

I expected it to smell damp. Instead, I was greeted by a

fresh breeze and air so clean I felt as though I were deep into a rainforest.

Acoustic guitar played through the speakers as we descended the stairs of the oval room. It looked like the waiting area of a luxury spa. Curved sofas, coffee tables, drinks dispensers, and a large rug; so far from the run-down farm above us.

"Welcome to the common room." Dr White gestured for me to try out the sofas and offered me a drink whilst I studied the fish tank on the far wall. "These are the farmers." He pointed towards the people dressed in gray armored vests standing next to the lift. "You will get used to seeing them around The Farm. Please make yourself at home, and I'll be back in a short moment."

He marched down one of the tunnels that branched from the common room, leaving me with the mountain that was Tim.

Tim didn't make small talk, which I was thankful for. Now and then, I would sneak glances at him and try to work out what his job on The Farm was. His physique, as with most of the other farmers I had seen, was muscular. Something about the shape of his neck reminded me of a bull. I guessed that his strength would come in handy when lifting heavy hay bales.

We waited in silence for a couple of minutes and I fanned through a couple of books on the shelf. I could read rather well.

"Global Warming, Animals of the World," I read the titles out loud, getting used to the way that the words sounded in my mouth. I spent the remaining time sipping from my water bottle until Dr White finally returned and motioned for me to follow him back through the tunnel.

The room at the end was locked off by a door, and the inside was much like a building; the cave walls were replaced by breeze block and painted white. Everything in the room was white, for that matter, which was a harsh contrast to the tunnel. It was sterile. I never imagined a room this far underground could be so completely dirt-free.

The doctor took a seat on the chair behind a desk and pressed the computer monitor to bring the screen up.

"So, how are you feeling, Ares?"

I stared at Dr White for a few seconds. The words *'lost'* and *'scrambled'* came to mind.

How was I supposed to feel? "My head hurts," I replied simply.

The doctor nodded and reached into the drawer beneath his desk. "It's not unusual to experience headaches after you wake from hibernation. The medication is still in your system, and it might make you a little drowsy and confused. Take these." He placed two small pills into a plastic cup. "And make sure to drink plenty of water."

"Hibernation?" I questioned.

Dr White nodded. "You've been asleep for a very long time, Ares. Fourteen years, three months, and eight days to be exact."

A slight ringing in my ears caused the headache to implode

and my brain felt as though my skull was shrinking. Something didn't seem quite right.

"Why don't I remember anything from before?"

"The hibernation removes all personal memories for your own sake. You didn't have a good childhood, and helping you forget is the first step we take into safeguarding your future."

I shook my head. "But I don't remember anything at all."

Dr White shrugged. "You remember the important things, like walking, talking-"

"But I don't remember me! Who am I?" I yelled and surprised myself with the outburst. I didn't expect it. I recalled the long grass swaying in the breeze which calmed me, bringing me back to a place of control. I steadied my voice. "I'm sorry."

"It's quite alright." Dr White's brows knitted together, then he crossed the room and pulled back a curtain to reveal a large mirror. "Although, I've never seen anyone act this way after hibernation before," he stated.

Curiosity took over and I followed him, not recognizing the person who stared back in my reflection.

My voice had led me to believe that I was coming to the end of my teens, but my appearance showed that I was several years older. I pulled my wavy brown hair back so that I could study my face. Very small freckles spotted my nose, distinct jawline, and fair brows, but my eyes were the thing that caught ahold of my attention; an unusual shade of silver.

Dr White pointed with his pen as he spoke. "Your eyes are

quite exquisite. They've certainly changed over the years, a side effect of the metamorphosis."

"The what?"

"The metamorphosis," he replied without further explanation. "You are twenty-three years old, but your mind isn't quite so developed yet. The hibernation slows down the mental ageing process."

I frowned at him as he continued back to his desk; so many questions whizzing around my mind.

"I understand that this is a lot to take in." Dr White pulled out a folder and started sifting through the pages it contained. He finally found the one he'd been searching for and opened the binder to pull it out.

I walked over as he held it in my direction and quickly skimmed over the writing.

"This will tell you everything that you need to know about yourself. You can take this back to the barn, read through it, and become familiar with yourself."

"What if I want to know something that isn't on here?" I asked.

He cocked an eyebrow. "Then you don't need to know it."

NAME: ARES
SEX: MALE
DATE OF BIRTH: 01 MARCH 2052
HEIGHT: 5FT 9IN

DAYS IN HIBERNATION: 5212

CATEGORY: TITANIUM

GENERATION: 2

PACK: E

HYBRID BASIS: ARCTIC WOLF (23%), TITANIUM FROG (18%), FENNEC FOX (6.2%), RAVEN (1.7%), ELK DEER (0.2%) LEAF CUTTER ANT (0.2%), FALSE WIDOW SPIDER (0.07%)

"What- What is this?" I stuttered. "Hybrid basis?"

"As you have probably already realized, this is no ordinary farm. That is your genome. Whilst you were in hibernation your body has been changing, evolving, becoming stronger, and more alert. Ultimately, becoming a hybrid," he said.

I looked back to the sheet of paper in my hand, reading over the list of animals and percentages.

Somewhere in the back of my mind, the ringing and fuzziness that I had felt since waking cleared, and everything started to make sense.

Red vignetted my senses. The hairs on the back of my neck raised.

"You've been... experimenting on me?" It wasn't a question because I knew the answer. I read over the hybrid basis once more for good measure.

Something dark stirred inside, an emotion I didn't recognise. It swept over me and grew with my anger, eager to surface and take over.

Dr White sensed the sudden shift in my mood and rushed to press what I guessed was a panic button under the table. "Experimenting is not what we like to refer to-"

I beat him to it.

I didn't recall moving. But, with the adrenaline pounding through my veins, I moved faster than I believed could be possible.

I pushed him against the wall, letting the anger take over. I couldn't have held it back if I wanted to. I was no longer in control of my own body, and the more confused and angry I became, the stronger the animal fought.

Muffled noises in the corridor alerted me that Tim was on his way to save Dr White from my grasp. I heard the footsteps approach long before they arrived.

I knew that I should have backed away, but something kept me there; that same something pressed me to take his neck in my hands and squeeze. Tunnel vision zoned in, lighting the doctor up like a target. I saw the fear take over in his eyes, and for some twisted reason, I fed on it, lifting him off the ground. He started to panic, trying to wriggle free of my grasp; a fly trapped in a spider's web.

The human inside begged my body to stop.

The animal inside pushed for the kill.

And then a sharp volt of electricity zapped through me, vibrating my bones.

My body fell limp, and the world turned from red to black.

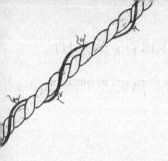

CHAPTER TWO

ARES

I awoke sometime later on the bed in Dr White's hospital room, staring at the ceiling, and trying to ignore the strange itch underneath my skin.

Dr White sat at his desk, typing at his computer screen as though I hadn't just tried to kill him. The only evidence that it had happened at all was the red handprint around his neck which would surely turn purple by morning.

My stomach twisted.

I did that.

I had wanted to hurt this man; I could have easily killed him. The thought made me feel queasy. The guilt overwhelmed me, and I quickly escaped from the bed to vomit into the nearby bin.

Dr White gazed briefly in my direction. "I was about to ask how you are feeling, but I needn't ask any longer." He continued to type as he spoke.

I reached for the tissues, not understanding why my body had reacted in such a way. I never intended to hurt the doctor. He had been the only one to seem half approachable, and I certainly didn't want him dead.

There was a long silence and it hung in the air like a bad smell. "I'm sorry."

Dr White nodded. "Not to worry, it's an occupational hazard." His uncaring approach led me to believe that this wasn't the first time he had been attacked by someone like me. "Please tie the bag in a knot and take a seat." He gestured to the chair in front of his desk.

"But what if-"

"It won't happen again. There's a taser built into your suit that can knock you unconscious until I'm ready for you to wake. I'll activate it as soon as I see you lose control," he said, picking up a remote from his desk and waving it in my direction as he spoke.

I was uncomfortable with the idea of another controlling my state of consciousness, but I pushed the thought back in fear that it might spark anger.

I couldn't let myself get angry again.

I did as he asked and moved towards the chair, not trusting myself to get too close.

"It will take a while to control the animal within you. I like to explain it as though you have mild Multiple Personality Syndrome. It's a desired side effect of the genetic engineering. It can be unpredictable to start with, but one day it will become your greatest weapon. Right now you are in your human state of mind. When angered, you might find yourself slipping into your mutated state where the animal hormones take over and consume you, as they did earlier. The hormones enhance your abilities, but you're not so easily able to control them."

I'd already figured as much.

"There is a third state too, we call it evolving. This is when you find a middle ground between the animal and human states, giving you the physical capabilities of the mutant but the control of the human."

He looked up from his computer and noticed my blank expression. It was bad enough having one alter ego, never mind two.

"I know that it can be a lot to process, but we will do our best to guide you. Over the coming weeks, you will undergo a series of challenges to help you understand these new emotions and learn to control them."

"What sort of challenges?"

Dr White smiled. "Now that would ruin the fun, wouldn't it? Best to leave you to find out for yourself. I think that you are ready to take a shower, head back to the barn, and meet your fellow hybrids. Enjoy the rest of the day before the hard work begins."

I guessed that this was my queue to leave, but when I stayed seated he continued, "Unless you have any further questions?"

I had plenty of questions.

Too many questions.

"Why?" I asked.

"Ares, I'm clever but I'm no mind reader. You'll have to be a little more specific."

I gestured to the room and everything above. "Why do you do this? Experiment on people, lock them in barns…"

He ran his hand through his thinning gray hair and replied, "You won't remember, but you signed a contract, as did your parents, agreeing to this." He mimicked my gesture, pointing to the room. "The world outside of this farm... It's not a nice place to be living. War broke out many years ago. And it's a war that we're not winning. It's violent and it's cruel. But we have high hopes that you and the other hybrids can change that."

"You're turning us into weapons?"

"Some may call you weapons." He tilted his head from side to side. "I prefer the term warriors."

"And what if I don't want to be a warrior?" I referred to my discomfort.

"Then you can leave the program. But I highly recommend that you should stay for a few days and get a feel for your new life. Try to enjoy your time on The Farm, make friends, and train hard. Just follow the rules and don't take anything for granted.

Although sometimes you may hate life here, remember that it's better than what is going on outside the fence."

I tried to remember what life outside The Farm looked like but the mental block stopped me. "You mentioned earlier about my parents. Are they still outside?"

Dr White sighed. "Rule number one... don't ask too many questions."

"Please," I begged. "Just this one question and then I'll leave."

He looked down at the folder in front of him and paused. For a while, I thought that he was going to turn me away without an answer, but reluctantly he replied, "I'm sorry Ares, but we're not permitted to give out that sort of information." When he read my unamused expression, he looked back to the folder. "You've been in hibernation for fourteen years, and with the war going on outside... I hate to say it..." he paused as though it pained him. "But they're most likely dead."

I looked to the floor, now understanding why he'd tried to keep this information from me. My parents sent me here to save me, to keep me sheltered from the war whilst I was defenseless, and to learn how to fight back when I became old enough.

They'd made that decision.

They had sent me to The Farm knowing that I would become a science experiment. That was the *better* decision. They'd rather me go through this ordeal than allow me to live through the war.

It made me wonder how bad life outside the fence could actually be?

I needed to trust my parents' judgment.

"I'm ready now," I informed.

Dr White raised an eyebrow, almost as though he found something amusing. I didn't understand his reaction.

"The showers are back this way." He began to retreat down the tunnel towards the common room and then paused to let me pass. "Tim will escort you as I have a lot of paperwork to do. I'll catch up with you later."

The doctor returned to his room and lingered by the door as I walked away, watching until I was out of sight with a strange expression. I wondered if the shock had worn off and he'd suddenly become aware of the attack my mutant self had forced upon him.

I continued forwards, thankful that the drugs were finally fading. My mind seemed clearer.

Tim was waiting for me on the sofa in the common room. As soon as he saw me, he began to march in my direction. He stayed close, with no respect for personal space, as though he expected me to flip at any moment. He didn't trust me.

I didn't trust myself either.

Not the mutant side, anyway.

Tim lead me down another tunnel which branched out from the common room. This one was a lot longer, probably a two-minute walk instead of the fifteen-second one to Dr White's room, but it seemed to drag on forever.

"How long has the war been going on?" I asked Tim. I didn't expect a reply, I just wanted to break the silence.

"Rule number one; don't ask too many questions."

I paused for a second. "Cool, so that's like a written rule then? 'Cause I thought Dr White said it as a joke."

Tim stared at me, leaving the thump of his feet to do the talking.

I continued after him, having to stride out to keep up.

As I walked, I looked back to the paper in my hand and read over the section that stated my hybrid basis was almost a quarter wolf. "Am I a werewolf?"

I could almost hear Tim's eyes roll in their sockets, and he let out an infuriated sigh. "You've got wolf attributes. That doesn't mean you'll turn into one and go howling at a full moon. My, God…"

I understood that as a very firm 'no'.

The spotlights lit the way to a pair of doors made from varnished dark wood and engraved with flowers. I opened them into an oasis of natural hot pools and waterfalls that appeared to be falling through gaps in the cavern's ceiling.

The artificial light in here was minimal, moss had started to blanket the walls, and steam rose from the pools creating a serene atmosphere.

"Are you sure this isn't a day spa?" I asked Tim.

This time he didn't reply, just started collecting towels,

soaps, and a new change of clothes for me. He dumped them on the floor next to the nearest pool and headed for the exit.

"What about my massage?" I called out to him. The slam of the door was my answer.

It didn't bother me that he didn't seem to like me, getting the impression that I wouldn't be making friends with many farmers over the next few days. They didn't seem the most welcoming.

I turned back to the water. I couldn't believe my eyes.

I undressed and carefully stepped into the steamy water, lathering myself in soap and sighing as I washed away my sorrows.

What was happening?

It seemed too good to be true.

I wondered if there was a catch, or if I was still unconscious in Dr White's room. It would make more sense for this to be a dream.

The water worked at unknotting my aching neck, and I let my head fall forward, rolling it from side to side. My feet soaked in the pools, reaching no higher than my thighs.

It felt like heaven.

'*Enjoy the rest of the day before the hard work begins*', Dr White's words echoed through my mind.

I doubted I'd see these pools again any time soon so I made a point to stay there for as long as I could, finding Tim's huffing on the other side of the door amusing until he started to pace.

21

Then I reluctantly decided it was time.

I dressed in the new set of clothes that had been left for me. They were tight-fit and breathable. I lunged out. Snug. They would do nicely.

Tim's fist hitting the door distracted me from the stretching. "You take longer than the girls!" he yelled.

I quickly towel-dried my hair, ran a hand through it, and opened the door to find Tim sitting on a lounger that he'd magicked up from somewhere.

"If you hadn't showered in fourteen years I'm sure you'd take your time, too," I replied.

He shoved me back in the direction of the common room, clearly done with my crap. I decided to keep my mouth shut in fear that he might actually use the gun.

The lift took us back up to the field, and once again I was struck by the beauty of the view. I kept my comments to myself and turned back to look at the silo as we evacuated.

"Incredible," I whispered as the lift door closed behind us, sealing off all evidence that the world underground existed.

Tim led me back to the barn. Two women dressed in the same gray clothes and protective vest as the other farmers guarded the door. The three of them shared a look before the doors opened.

Tim pushed me in and I stumbled, trying my best to stay on my feet.

"Goodbye to you too," I muttered as the doors locked

behind me. I would miss winding Tim up, but I was glad to be rid of his manhandling.

The barn was a decent size, made of nine stalls and one makeshift bathroom. Light poured in through two circular windows at either end of the room, casting shadows onto the concrete floor which was covered with straw, benches, and feet.

The feet belonged to eight hybrids, four girls and four boys, all staring as I made my entrance into the barn.

I did my best to straighten up, run a hand through my still wet hair, and act presentable. "Hi... Everyone..."

I waved a hand awkwardly and internally screamed at myself, "*Why am I waving? Stop it! Dear God, stop it now...*" My hand didn't listen.

"I'm Ares."

A lanky guy with blonde hair and gray eyes which matched my own stood to greet me, unfazed by my appalling entrance. He walked over, reaching for the hand that still hung in the air. I let him take it, feeling thankful for an excuse to stop waving, and instead of shaking the hand, he used it to pull me into a strange hug. Shock immobilized me and I stood there, letting him pat my back and rub his nose into my neck... He inhaled.

I tried not to freak out.

Was this normal?

He took a second large breath.

I was *very* much freaking out.

"Ares." He moved back to a much more comfortable

distance. "Nice to meet you. I'm Hail."

I didn't know what to say, so I stood there with my mouth open, fully aware that everyone had been watching and not finding the encounter unusual in any way.

Didn't anyone on this farm know what personal space was?

"Oh." Hail laughed in a way that almost made him sound like he was hiccuping. "You'll get used to that. It's a wolf thing."

Or was it just an excuse for him to be a creep?

Everyone else started to approach, forming a small line behind Hail. "Welcome to the farm, Bro." He slapped my hand in a weird handshake. "We're gonna have some fun."

He slinked back to his stool and hiked his feet up as a girl filled the vacant spot before me.

"Hi!" She beamed energy in every direction. "I'm Shyla!"

"Hi, Shyla," I replied as she copied Hail's strange actions. I wondered if everyone else in the line was going to do the same.

The answer was yes.

They were all weird.

One by one they took turns *'introducing'* themselves. They told me their names but I struggled to remember them all; it was hard not to be distracted by all of the neck smelling. However, I couldn't help but notice that everybody had similar gray eyes, it was obviously *'a side effect of the metamorphosis'*, I recalled the doctor's words.

Clenching my jaw helped to distract me from my discomfort. I was relieved when it came to the last person in the line as it meant that the nightmare would soon be over, but then I looked at her and all of my previous worries fizzled away.

Her smile created small dimples in her cheeks. Short silver locks framed her face and when she tucked one behind her ear, I couldn't help but want to do it for her.

I couldn't tear my eyes away.

I quickly wiped my hands on my clothes before offering one in her direction. First impressions would count; I didn't want to be remembered as the guy with sweaty palms.

She took the hand. If she noticed the heat radiating from it then she didn't make it obvious, and she pulled me close. Her quiet confidence made me only the more curious. She didn't speak, I tried not to react at the feel of her breath tickling against my neck as she inhaled.

As she pulled away, she studied me. Her eyes burned holes into my skin as she judged me and I wanted nothing more than to melt into the floor.

"Welcome, Ares," she said finally. Her voice was that of a goddess. "I'm Lora, Alpha of the Titanium pack."

"Alpha…" I replied but whatever I was planning to say died in my mouth.

"Yes." She asserted a certain authority in the way she stood and the way she spoke, but her smile was almost playful.

"What-" *Just kill me now.* "What…" I coughed in an attempt to hide the fact that I was struggling for words. "What's an Alpha?"

Her eyes squinted, seeing straight through my act. "You have a lot to learn, Omega." She placed her right hand on my cheek, and I was stuck as to what it meant. I tried not to lean into it. I couldn't help the way it left me short of breath.

But then she walked away.

I remained against the door, watching her go. The moment was over quickly. I missed her already.

"You alright, Bro?"

Hail had snuck up on me as I daydreamed about the Alpha and I flinched away from him.

"Crap, don't do that." My jaw clenched, and I had to fight the urge not to slap him. "Yeah, yeah. I'm fine. It's all just a lot, you know? Waking up in here, the doctor, this..." I gestured to the barn. "And her..." I looked in Lora's direction. She was sitting on a bench with Indigo and a guy I couldn't remember the name of, gazing back in my direction every few seconds.

"Oh yeah." Hail nodded as though he knew exactly what I was talking about. "Don't worry about that weird feeling around her to start with, you'll get used to it."

"She's like a magnet," I said.

"A what?" Hail looked confused.

"A magnet?"

"If you say so." He shrugged, clearly not bothered by the fact that he had no idea what I was talking about. "We call it the Alpha Effect."

"What's that?"

He tried to copy my words, "That magnip feeling that you're talking about, it's the Alpha Effect."

I stayed silent, willing him to elaborate.

"Lora's in charge of the pack. It's her job to lead us, make sure everyone's safe and getting along with each other, and sort out any problems."

"That's a heavy burden to carry."

Hail nodded. "Yeah, well she's been here the longest and it comes naturally to her. But rumor has it, she had to kill people to become the Alpha, so don't piss her off." He laughed.

My body spiked with fear.

Hail didn't seem to realize what he'd said and it only made me more nervous about my situation within the pack.

Lora was a murderer?

"But that's off topic," he continued without noticing my discomfort. "What were we talking about?"

"The Alpha Effect, or something like that."

He nodded enthusiastically, his floppy blonde hair wafting up and down. "So it works both ways, she guides us, and we protect her. The whole pack has this special connection with their Alpha, as you've already experienced. It makes you want to protect her, probably even die for her. It's another wolf thing, supposed to help us bond." He rolled his eyes.

I quickly concluded that Hail was fascinated by death; it seemed to creep into conversation easily with him and it made me uneasy, especially after my encounter with Dr White an hour prior.

"And what is an Omega? I've heard that a few times since I've been here."

"Omega? It's just the name we give to the newest member of the pack, which would now be you."

I looked at the group, trying to remember names and work out who seemed most comfortable. "So who was the Omega before me?"

Hail's face paled slightly. "Oh, that was Zayne."

I frowned. "Where's Zayne now?" I didn't recall anyone with that name. I counted the stalls and the number of people within the barn but the numbers didn't add up.

"He's dead."

"What?" I paused.

Hail nodded slowly. "Yeah, he died yesterday, a real shame."

"I'm so sorry. Do you mind me asking how?"

He shrugged it off, giving the impression that they hadn't been very close. "He failed one of the challenges."

I waited for a few seconds, giving him the chance to finish the joke, but the punchline never came.

"The challenges that the farmers put us through to train us for the war?"

"Yeah."

"He failed, so he died?"

No. That couldn't be right.

The challenges were to help us evolve. The doctor had said

so earlier.

I suddenly felt short of breath. It made sense. Hail's insensitivity towards death had come from experience, he spoke about it as though it were common.

"It's no big deal, it's just what happens here. They're trying to build the strongest team they can. I'm not one to speak ill of the dead, but Zayne was weak. They come and go. You'll get used to it…"

No big deal?

Hail's words faded as panic set in. I sank to the floor, using the wall to lean on. *Breathe in, breathe out.* I tried to calm myself, but my heart was beating too fast.

"Obviously, I don't mean you. *You* won't come and go…"

The challenges that the doctor had been referring to weren't puzzles, or archery, or white-water rafting.

The challenges were deadly.

And we were training for war. Somewhere along the line, I'd overlooked such a vitally important detail.

These challenges were made to push us to the limit, to filter out the weak and kill the ones who couldn't evolve.

It suddenly felt very real.

I was a man training for a war; of which I knew frighteningly little. I had no idea who I would be fighting. I had no idea how long I'd be training before being called to battle.

And that's if I didn't die in training first.

I was a man who couldn't remember anything about

himself, other than the fact that he enjoyed countryside walks and felt tremendous guilt upon causing others harm.

And, in reality, I was only half a man at all. I was a mess of animal genes glued together and stitched up with twine and safety pins, threatening to crumble at any second.

I was a dead man walking.

The memory of Dr White sitting in front of his computer screen once again appeared in my mind, telling me to 'Enjoy the rest of the day before the hard work begins'.

Hard work?

More like "Enjoy the rest of the day before we try to kill you."

HIM

I spent most of my time watching through the various cameras hidden around The Farm. The screens lit up the walls, covering every inch.

Standing in the Observatorium gave me a sort of God complex. I saw all; I controlled all.

No wonder my father had always seemed so privileged, barely paying me any attention throughout my childhood. How had he the time to run The Farm and care for a family at all? Patience, organisation, and practice. Three things I lacked tremendously.

Growing up, my father had always seemed distant, but watching through the cameras now, I realized that Father had been with me through the screens of the Observatorium when he couldn't be there in person.

I had taken classes from the age of six to prepare for a life of leading The Farm, in addition to the standard lessons which the other children in the Infirmary took (English, Mathematics, and Science). Once the others finished their school day, I was led to the Observatorium to further my education.

"Lesson number one," I remembered Father starting. "The animals must follow the rules. If a rule is broken, then the animals must be punished or else the safety of The Farm will be put at risk."

"What will happen?" I had asked.

Father didn't like interruptions, but he allowed this one. "The Farm will descend into chaos. There must be a hierarchy and everyone must be aware of their role. You will lead, next comes the scientists, and then the other farmers. The animals will always be at the bottom. Everyone here has a specific job to do but they all follow my orders, and one day they will follow yours."

And follow they did.

I took a sip from my flask and zoned in on the set of cameras following the new Titanium hybrid. "Sandra, how is the

Titanium Omega settling in?"

Sandra looked up from her computer, her brow damp with sweat. "He is in a state of panic, heart rate reaching one-hundred and sixty beats per minute. Hail revealed the truth about training and the Omega seemed to crumble under the pressure."

A weak one.

Although I had been taught to do everything in my power to help the warriors in training, I did enjoy watching them perish. "Has he mutated again?"

Sandra shook her head and hastily replied, "Not yet."

I made notes on my tablet, watching Ares slide down the wall and wrap up into a ball. A plan was forming in my mind. If the Omega wanted to live then he was going to have to learn to cope with intense pressure and take control of his anger. He needed to earn his place in the program.

I called my assistant forward, ready to commence with plans for the Omega's initiation trial. "Ares," I told the assistant. "He needs scaring. Do your best to make his next couple of days hell. Only then will we see if he deserves a place here."

"It would be my pleasure, Sir," the assistant replied.

I didn't like many of the farmers, but my assistant was an exception. I printed the plans, waited for the assistant to collect them, and sank into my chair with my feet hiked onto the desk. "Well? What the fuck are you waiting for? You've got a busy night ahead."

The assistant read the instructions, nodded once, and

rushed off.

I smiled to myself as I watched a panicked Ares, longing to see him struggle. *"Just wait and see what I've got in store for you,"* I thought. *"You're only going to wish you were dead."*

CHAPTER
THREE

ARES

"You told him?!" I vaguely recalled Lora yelling at Hail through the white noise which fogged my mind.

"This is crazy…"

Lora looked at me, then gave Hail a *'look what you've done'* scowl.

"Snap out of it," she ordered in my direction. Her stormy eyes were all I could see. Her voice was calm. Commanding. "If you can't process this news then you certainly won't survive here."

But that was the question.

Did I even *want* to survive here?

It didn't seem like much of a life. The farmers had experimented on me, put me to sleep for fourteen years, and now they were going to force me into life-threatening challenges made to break me.

Lora could see my doubt. "You can't live in fear. The moment you start doubting yourself is the moment you start making mistakes, and mistakes can cost your life. So get your arse off the floor and stop overthinking."

I nodded, taking a deep breath in and holding it until I felt the tension ease.

She was right.

I couldn't let the pressure get to me, I could figure this out. I could adapt. And if I found that this life wasn't for me? Well, then I could leave. I just had to take everything one step at a time.

My first task was to swallow the anger and find a way to distract myself, I couldn't lose control over my body again. I wouldn't allow myself. "I... I flipped out pretty bad in Dr White's room earlier. I don't know what came over me. I couldn't stop myself."

Lora nodded, her voice less demanding and more understanding. "We've all been there. At least you've experienced what it's like to fully lose control. It'll make it easier for you to mutate and evolve when the time comes."

I nodded, thankful that at least there was one positive to come from a negative situation. "Why do they test us like this?" I asked. "To such extremities? Is it really necessary?"

"The war calls for only the strongest warriors. Once we

35

reach our full potential, the farmers will send us out on missions. We will risk our lives every time we step outside of The Farm's gates." Lora's brows knitted together. "And if we're not strong enough in here, then we certainly won't make it out there."

She stood and headed across the barn to a ladder at the back, before motioning for me to follow. Hail accompanied us to a ledge which I presumed would have once been used to store hay. The overlook had enough space for the three of us, and maybe one more, to sit comfortably.

Lora pointed towards the window. "What do you see?"

I squinted past the iron bars, through the harsh sunlight. "Fields, forest…" The view was impeccable. I felt as though I were at one with nature, cubbied in the depths of the valley.

"Good. Farmland. We are a self-sustained ecosystem. Electricity runs on solar and hydropower. The farmers grow everything that we eat; some of the lands are dedicated to the crops, the chickens, cows, and pigs; the rest is for us to train." She looked back at me now. "What do you think would happen if everyone survived their training, but they weren't strong enough to leave The Farm?"

"They would stay here and help run it?"

"And they would also need feeding. The Farm would become overpopulated, we'd run out of resources and have to ration the food. But we can't afford to be rationing, we need the strength if we're going to be the warriors that the world needs."

"It's survival of the fittest," I offered.

Lora nodded slowly. "I'm afraid so."

"But, I don't understand why they wouldn't just send us out to war anyway? Surely there's safety in numbers."

"Sure," she said. "But this is the twenty-first century. We don't win wars by rounding up the troops and fighting on the battlefield anymore. We complete missions. And say we had a weak link in our team, somebody who couldn't hold their own, they'd be a liability and it could not only cost us the mission but put our lives at risk, too."

"Then leave them behind, every man for himself."

"There's no I in team." Lora smiled, seeming to enjoy the conversation. "Besides, could you imagine what might happen if the enemy captured one of us and realized what we were? They'd use our people against us."

It was a good point. All of the farmer's efforts would be for nothing.

Hail huffed and slumped his back against the wall. He'd lost interest in our conversation minutes ago, and now practiced the skill of dropping straw onto the heads of the hybrids down below. "I'm hungry."

I could understand why Lora seemed to enjoy our conversation so thoroughly if the rest of the pack were as oblivious as Hail.

"You're always hungry," Lora said.

"I could eat," I chipped in. My stomach growled in response.

"I'm sure Marshall will be here soon."

"Who's Marshall?"

"Prick," Hail replied.

"I've met plenty of those since I got here," I joked and Hail snorted.

"Marshall brings our food," Lora explained. I couldn't understand why they hated him so much. I assumed anyone who delivered food would be in my good books. But then I recalled the man who had woken me with the sandwich and an unwanted shower. "The guy with the muscles and scruffy hair?"

They nodded.

"He's a dinner lady?" I scoffed.

Hail's strange laugh echoed through the barn as he enjoyed the joke, throwing his head back against the wall.

There was more to this Marshall guy than I'd been lead to believe.

Lora chuckled as though she'd almost forgotten how to. "It's good to see that you've got a sense of humor. We don't laugh much around here."

I didn't understand why they were laughing but I revelled anyway. If Lora thought that I was funny, then I wasn't going to stand to change her opinion.

She lingered a little longer, as though wanting to say more, but quickly decided against it and descended the stairs. I couldn't help but watch after her as she left. My eyes followed as she crossed the barn, towards a stall I presumed was hers, until she stopped and turned back with her eyes meeting mine briefly. I held her gaze as I tried to figure out why she looked so confused, but then she shrugged it off, smiled, and continued into her stall.

I stared.

She didn't reappear, no matter how much I wished that she would.

Hail stopped laughing eventually and shuffled closer to fill the vacant space that Lora had left. "And that's why she's Alpha and not me," he whispered.

"What?"

"That's why Lora is Alpha. Look at you now, smiling. I made you panic, Lora fixed it like she fixes everything."

"Oh. Yeah…"

"It's the Alpha Effect," he repeated his words from earlier. "She's a miracle worker, I'm telling you."

"Is that the official name for it?" I questioned. "The Alpha Effect?"

Hail shook his head. "No, I made it up. I've been trying to get it to stick for a few weeks but nobody seems to be going for it."

I understood why there would be hesitation, but I liked it.

We sat on the overlook for a while, watching as members of the pack started up a game which involved throwing a tennis ball at the opponent's legs. Hail asked if I wanted to join in, but the game looked a little aggressive and I decided that I'd rather sit this one out, at least until I found my feet.

So instead, I listened to him talk about The Farm and its people. I also concluded that he wasn't all so bright. "The crops are grown on the east side of The Farm." He pointed towards the setting sun. "The chickens are next to the guesthouse and the pigs and cows are to the north, although I don't understand why they need so much room. Why are they even here? We don't eat them. Talk about over-populating."

"Beef and bacon?" I questioned.

He wrinkled his nose up as he suddenly realized, "Yeah, we eat that but I don't know where it's grown."

I tried to keep a straight face. "Oh, never mind."

I watched down on my new acquaintances as they darted about, trying to avoid the tennis ball in the orange blaze of the vanishing sun.

"Are you close to the others?" I asked Hail.

"I guess." He shrugged. "But you learn not to get too attached to people." There was a sadness in his eyes that I couldn't quite place. The emotion swarmed Hail like a virus, sinking through his body until it drowned him.

"So you keep everyone at arm's length?"

"Yeah…" He considered it for a few seconds and it distracted him from whatever memory he had been reliving. The gears turned and then something seemed to click. "Yes! Don't let yourself get too close to anyone, because it hurts when you lose them."

"Got it."

Footsteps approached from beyond the barn, and the pack seemed to go from calm to chaos in a matter of seconds. The game was forgotten as the hybrids began to move stools and shut themselves into their stalls.

Panic.

I sat and watched, wondering what it was all about. The steps halted outside the door and a bell echoed in my ears.

"Time to get moving." Hail scurried down to the barn floor and I hurried to follow him. Something about the look on his face alarmed me.

I clambered down the ladder and crossed quickly to the stall I guessed would be mine as I'd woken in it earlier. I just managed to pull the door shut when the barn door opened and Marshall stepped foot inside.

The last time I'd seen him he had been holding a hose, and as much as I didn't appreciate the rude awakening, I would have willingly taken a splash of cold water over a bullet from the shotgun he now carried. It leaned lazily on his shoulder, swinging as the man walked.

Marshall seemed oblivious to the fact that he was carrying a weapon at all. Maybe it was his ignorance that scared me, or the way that he studied each individual as he stalked past the stalls; a hyena hunting for prey.

His uncut hair was mostly hidden by a baseball cap which may have once been white, some strands of muddy blonde crept out from underneath and stuck to the beads of sweat on his forehead. He walked slowly, letting the sound of his boots on the concrete floor be the only one he allowed within the barn.

I held my breath.

It was Marshall's barn now.

He stopped outside my stall, and I watched the sweat run from his eyebrow to his cheek, and then disappear into the maze of his facial hair. Once I realized that I had nothing else to distract myself with, I slowly but surely met his eyes.

He was already staring at me.

"What are you doing?" he sounded baffled. I remained silent because I would only stumble over my words if I opened my mouth. "Could you be any more *fucking* stupid?"

The aggression made me flinch back, but it didn't help to avoid the spit that left his mouth and landed on my cheek.

I didn't dare wipe it away.

The shotgun fell forwards and hit the wooden door, aiming toward the ceiling above my head, and Marshall didn't so much as blink an eye.

I shook my head quickly, looking at the ground to hide the fear in my eyes. "No." Then I remembered that this was not in fact a farm, but a training facility. "No, Sir!"

The rest of the pack watched as he purposely went out of his way to humiliate me.

"Well?" He waited for some sort of explanation, only I had no idea what he could be referring to. "The cross on the floor!" He spat at me once more. "Stand on it!"

I hadn't even noticed the small engraving into the concrete, but I quickly complied, not wanting to be asked twice. It brought me face to face with him.

He didn't back away as I approached.

"Well done, Ares," Marshall scoffed, his tone less of gratitude and more of sarcasm. His breath stank of three-day-old coffee and the color of his teeth supported my theory. I tried my best not to pull a face at the stench.

I was able to make out a small scar running down his left cheek at this closer proximity. He seemed to notice me looking, and he tilted his head as though to show it off.

"You'd be surprised how many Omega's I've had to put down on their first day," he enjoyed gloating. And then he lowered his voice to speak directly to me, no longer putting on a show for the rest of the barn. "You're a sheep in wolf's clothing, Ares. Prove yourself, or you won't be here this time tomorrow." He winked at me once to seal the deal.

Marshall took a step back and slowly turned his head to the stall on my right. My heart hammered so loud in my chest that I could hear it. A relieved sigh escaped me, glad to be out of the firing line, but his words lingered like rotten eggs because he was *so* right.

I *was* a sheep in wolf's clothing.

This wasn't a place for a guy like me.

I felt my knees shaking from the confrontation, the fear. How could I possibly survive a war?

I considered what would happen if I didn't prove myself as he began to shout at the occupant of the stall next to mine.

"Shyla. Do you, or do you not, remember that you are free to leave at any time?"

I could hear Shyla whimpering through the wall, she tried to clear her throat before replying, "I remember."

"Are you sure about that?" He leaned in slowly, resting his arm against the bars of the stall so that their faces were almost touching.

There was a momentary silence. I gazed at the stall opposite mine and noticed Hail's face was as pale as Lora's hair. He slowly turned to look at me and shook his head. I couldn't work out what it meant, but I knew that it wasn't good.

I looked to Lora then, two doors to the right. She gave me the same shake of the head.

They were telling me to stay still; not to react.

"Yes, Sir," Shyla's reply was so quiet through her tears that I barely heard it. She was afraid, but she kept her voice steady as though she had been preparing for this moment.

"So why did you create a hole under the fence during training earlier?" The anger in his voice pierced through the silence like a knife.

Shyla sobbed, "I- I don't-"

"You put everyone at risk!" He hit the barrel of the gun against the bars. I flinched as the sound rattled through the barn. The sudden change of pace in Marshall's movements nerved me.

He cranked open the door. "Everyone!" Grabbing Shyla by her shirt, he dragged her from her stall and threw her towards the main doors.

She stumbled forwards. "Please, I didn't mean-"

"You made a hole in the fucking fence!" He beat the stall door closed behind her. "How could you not mean to do that?"

I knew that this wasn't going to end well.

"Turn around."

Crap.

This wasn't going to end well *at all*.

My face was now just as strewn as the other hybrids upon realizing what was happening.

He aimed the gun at her back as she turned. My body turned to ice, but it didn't prevent a clammy sweat from breaking out over my skin.

He was going to make an example of her.

This is what would happen if we broke the rules.

I needed to stop it. I tried to think of a way to intervene, but that would surely be breaking the rules too, and I would join her in the public execution.

I looked back to Hail who was still staring at me, his nostrils flaring. He couldn't watch and neither could I.

All I could do was close my eyes and wait for the gun to deafen the room, marking the end of Shyla's life.

So I waited.

I could hear others crying now, too.

The suspense was so thick that I started to choke on it.

Several seconds passed.

I waited until I couldn't wait anymore, and then the gun deafened me, accompanied by the sound of two bodies hitting the concrete. Reluctantly, I opened my eyes.

Shyla panted, reaching out and touching the ground around her; she'd collapsed in fear. I had no idea what was going on.

"We have been closely monitoring you and Torn for some time." Marshall began to explain, pointing towards the stall nearest the entrance. "I admit that it was a very clever plan, but you missed one very important detail. We see *everything*." Marshall leaned over Shyla. "This terrorism will not be tolerated! Torn paid the price for his actions, and you must also face the consequences. Let's see how the puppet fairs without its master." He spat on the floor next to her. She was so scared that she couldn't summon enough strength to rise from the ground.

"And you!" He turned to Lora now. My heart started to race, and suddenly bursting from my stall to fight Marshall back seemed like a very good idea. I could imagine what he would be capable of, and Lora was so tiny in comparison to him. I couldn't let him hurt the Alpha.

The other hybrids shuffled, as though we had all been thinking the same. I reached out to slide my arm through the bar when he spoke again.

"Control your pack," he ordered.

Lora didn't seem phased by his presence. She looked

straight through him as she replied. "Yes, Sir."

"It's embarrassing that they pulled this off right under your nose."

"It won't happen again, Sir." She seemed controlled and confident.

I dropped my hovering arm.

"Make sure it doesn't, or next time you will be joining them."

"There won't be a next time, Sir." Lora's eyes dropped with his use of the plural. Shyla was still in danger. Lora had failed them both.

"Correct answer. And as for you, Shyla." Marshall turned back to the girl who was clearly hyperventilating. "You're free to go."

Shyla stood slowly and regret swarmed her eyes. She shook her head. "No..."

She hadn't planned to leave The Farm alone. Torn was the mastermind behind the whole thing, and he was gone.

"You quite obviously knew what you wanted this afternoon. You've made your bed, now you must lay in it."

The barn doors opened like the gateway to hell, and Shyla was dragged out. She turned back to look at us. She tried to stop, planting her feet firmly into the ground, telling Marshall that she'd changed her mind.

He didn't listen.

He tried to carry her over his shoulder, but something

switched in Shyla.

She was livid.

Her pupils dilated. Her movements became erratic and her entire energy shifted. She leaped away from Marshall, who stumbled and dropped his gun.

I expected to see him rush for it as Shyla attacked, but instead, he reached into his pocket.

Shyla ran towards him with only one intention.

To kill.

I knew exactly what she was feeling. The animal hormones had taken over and she was no longer in control. I had felt the same in Dr White's room.

The tunnel vision; the intense pounding in my head; the knowledge that I could easily take a life in a matter of seconds.

The power.

I saw it all in Shyla's eyes.

She charged at Marshall in a rage but didn't make it. She fell to the ground instantaneously as Marshall tapped a button on the remote that he had pulled from his pocket.

The taser.

It was the farmers' secret weapon.

He sighed slowly, as though it had been such an inconvenience, before slumping Shyla's limp body over his shoulder.

He didn't look back as he left the barn, he simply motioned for the farmers to deliver our food, remove Torn's body from his stall, and then close the doors behind them.

I stared after them.

I tried to come to terms with everything that had just happened, and I continued to stare long after the food was served and the farmers had left.

Everybody ate in silence, traumatized by the night's events. I only picked at my food. I had been so hungry earlier, but somewhere along the line, I'd lost my appetite.

Maybe it was the pool of Torn's blood running through the barn that the guards hadn't cared to clean? A harsh reminder that they were happy to spill blood for the sake of The Farm.

Yes, it could have been the blood putting me off my food.

But something just didn't sit right with me.

If Shyla and Torn were free to go, then why did they try to escape?

Maybe they were too scared to admit it, and thought that escaping would be the easiest option?

Thinking back to my previous conversation with Hail and Lora, and what Lora had said about the weak members holding back the rest of the team, maybe it was a good thing that they were gone?

Shyla couldn't evolve, or else she would have in her moment of need. She was weak.

I felt guilty as soon as the thought crossed my mind, but at the same time, I considered if Shyla could *really* survive life outside of the fence.

Would she live to regret her decisions?

As I finished picking at my food and loading my tray onto the shelf, I looked across at my fellow hybrids.

Some looked more affected by the night's events than others. Hail was already in bed and snoring. Surely he couldn't have fallen asleep that fast?

The short black guy in the stall to his right stared at Torn's blood. I assumed by the somber look on his face that they had been close. I tried to catch his attention, to ensure that he was okay, but he turned and retreated to his bunk when he saw me looking.

One stall to the right again was Lora's. She looked to the ground with regretful eyes until she sensed my stare.

"Are you okay?" she mouthed, not wanting to break the silence.

I nodded slowly.

It was a lie. I was struggling, but adapting to change was never easy for anyone. Getting used to this new way of living was going to take time.

"Are you?" I mouthed.

A sad smile crept over Lora's face as she nodded. *"I will be."* She looked to the door and I wondered if she was thinking about Shyla, considering all of the things she could have done differently. But I couldn't see how any of it was Lora's fault? No matter what Marshall said.

"Goodnight." She smiled before backing into her stall and out

of sight.

I stood there for a little while, wanting her to come back. She never did. Eventually, I turned in for the night too. It was still fairly early, maybe eight o'clock, but everyone seemed to find this a normal time to sleep so I assumed that we would be up at the break of dawn the following morning.

Pulling the quilt up to my neck, I sighed into the springy mattress of my bunk. The wind howled through the gaps in the barn's structure, and although my clothing kept my body warm, my feet and face fell victim to the cold. I considered putting my shoes back on. Instead, I tucked my feet up, snuggled in, and enjoyed the minimalist comfort that the bed provided.

I concentrated on the hoot of an owl in a nearby tree to distract me from the thousand questions spinning around my mind. They were questions for another day.

Finally, I drifted off. My last conscious thought was the worrying predicament that Marshall had access to my stall whilst I slept.

CHAPTER
FOUR

ARES

A cold sweat coated my skin, and a high pitch wail claimed my ears.

Shyla's scream.

I recalled it from the evening before, when Marshall had shocked her unconscious and carried her from the barn.

I doubted that I could ever forget that shrill sound; a banshee in the silence.

The sweat dripped from my brow. I would have wiped it away with my sleeve if my arms hadn't been tied behind my back.

It took me this long to realize.

Darkness enclosed me as I opened my eyes, but it wasn't the kind of darkness to come from a barn. There was no sign of moonlight creeping through the wooden walls, and it was deadly silent. No rustling, and no sound of Hail's snoring.

Dread swarmed my body as I concluded that I was no longer in the barn at all.

The darkness was so dense it seemed to suffocate me. It brought an uncomfortable level of heat as I kicked out, trying to get a feel for the enclosed space.

I had my weaknesses, but it seemed that claustrophobia wasn't one of them. I thanked my lucky stars now as I reached out in every direction, hitting a wall wherever my feet landed.

I grumbled to myself and noticed how muffled the sound appeared. Echoless, as though it had been absorbed by a sponge.

"Hello?" I called out, but the sound once again seemed muted.

After a few minutes, I concluded that wriggling and kicking wouldn't cut it. I needed to get my arms free. They were tightly bound at the wrist by some sort of fabric.

Panic started to grow as the reality of the situation sank in.

This was my first challenge.

I'd been abducted in the middle of the night and left to either escape or die.

I couldn't help but feel like my lungs were struggling to get their fill. It became more apparent as my panic grew.

How long had I been here?

"Hello?!" My voice sounded urgent now.

I kept working at the fabric but no matter how hard I tried, I couldn't break free.

YIELD

The only sound was the beating of my heart, gaining speed as time passed and the air became thinner.

"Hello!" I called out again, getting more and more hysterical each time.

I was going to die alone in a box.

"Don't think like that," I ordered myself, trying to stay positive.

I screamed as loud as I could; half in hopes that somebody would hear me, and fully in fear.

I couldn't escape without help. I wasn't strong enough to break through the fabric which tied my hands together. I needed to mutate for that kind of strength, but then I would lose all control over my body.

I needed to evolve, to gain the strength of the animal state and the control of the human state. Only I didn't know how to.

I felt around for anything that could help; a nail, a rough edge on the wood that could cut through the cloth.

Nothing.

There was no hope.

I wondered where the Titanium pack were. Had they also been put in a sealed box to struggle, or were they outside, waiting for me to emerge?

Were they back at the barn?

Had they even noticed that I'd been abducted at all?

I stopped after twenty minutes or so, closed my eyes, and accepted that my short-lived life was about to come to an end.

By this point, I was gasping for air.

Nobody was coming to save me and I had no way of breaking out.

I gave up.

Laying still, I listened to the sound of complete silence.

It was unusual to hear nothing at all. No birds, no breeze. Even the air seemed quiet. My lungs burned as though they were being squeezed, and I started to lose consciousness.

And that's when I heard the scream again.

Adrenaline pumped through my veins.

"Shyla!" I called out through the silence but there was no reply.

I was oxygen-deprived and it took me too long to realize that it couldn't possibly be Shyla I was hearing. The box was soundproof and airtight.

I was hallucinating.

The lack of oxygen was starting to mess with my mind.

"What a pathetic excuse of a being," I mocked myself. I was glad that I was alone. I didn't want anyone to see me struggle in this way. What would Hail think? What would Lora say?

What would Lora say?

I imagined it would be something along the lines of 'you're giving up before allowing yourself the chance to fulfill your potential'.

And it was true.

I was giving up.

Mainly because I was too scared to give way to the animal inside.

I wasn't cut out for this. Like Shyla and so many others before us, I was weak.

I wasn't warrior material.

I was stuck, and the stars in my vision started to mock me as they intertwined.

I could hear Tim laughing, telling Dr White to wake another hybrid from hibernation, ready to replace me.

Suddenly, I was face to face with Marshall, glee in his eyes as he realized that he would get to put down another animal.

A surge of energy powered through me, charged by the feeling of betrayal and hatred.

I quickly fought against the memory of the night before and avoided any thought about Marshall.

I wouldn't mutate.

Calming myself rid me of the animal hormones. I tried to remember the breeze pricking at my skin and the smell of freshly cut grass.

If I was going to die in this box, then I'd die the same person I was born. I would not die the genetically engineered hybrid the farmers were forcing upon me.

I wouldn't die a ghost of myself.

I wouldn't die a monster.

CHAPTER FIVE

THE TITANIUM PACK:
LORA

I was always the first to wake. As soon as the sun started to creep over the mountain and cast shadows across the barn, I'd find myself staring at the same knot of wood on the ceiling as the morning before. The knot was shrinking and the plank had started to crack. It hadn't been that way three years ago, but time had weathered the wood as it had my soul.

I weighted the world on my shoulders. It dragged me down, heavy; I'd have drowned if I touched water.

And if I didn't make it, who knew what would happen to the Titanium pack? Who would be the next Alpha? Could any of them take the pressure?

The knowledge?

Could any of them keep the truth to themselves?

I struggled at the best of times to keep the secret about the war, but I knew that it would only create unbalance and unwillingness amongst the pack if I told them. The other hybrids couldn't know; not until they'd passed their training.

I swung my legs over the edge of the bed, stretched, and slowly left my stall. It was early, the birds rising alongside me, meaning that I had a couple of hours free to roam the barn before Marshall arrived with breakfast.

I shuddered as I recalled his most recent visit and stopped at the smear of blood across the floor, parting the barn like the Red Sea.

The memory threatened to break through the walls I'd built to keep my emotions at bay.

"Shut them out," I reminded myself. It was better for everyone that way.

But we'd just lost two members of the pack and it was as much on my back as it was theirs. I should have noticed the warning signs.

Torn had been an outsider; a little weird and too skeptical.

And Shyla always needed to get a grip. She was so dramatic. I wondered how she had managed to survive twelve months.

But, as annoying as they both were, they were family. And so, when a single tear fell, I didn't wipe it away as I normally would, I let it roll and mourned my fallen brother and sister.

Only one tear though.

I got to work scrubbing Torn's dried blood from the floor. I needed to take my energy out on something. I could feel it building up inside, stirring beneath the surface, and I knew that the hybrids waking up to this reminder wouldn't make the best of starts to the day. I rolled my sleeves up and filled a bucket of water from the tap, convincing myself that it was just red paint.

But who was I kidding?

The Farm hadn't seen paint in years; redecorating was the least of our worries.

The hairs on the back of my neck stood on end as I started to clean. Something didn't feel right. To start with, I assumed that it was just the lingering memory, but the more I scrubbed, the more apparent the feeling became.

The red stain slowly vanished as I wondered whether my senses were playing tricks on me.

No.

If there was one thing I'd learned in my time, it was to always trust my instincts.

Something was definitely wrong.

I climbed the ladder to the overlook, the sun shining brightly above the forest now. The birds were singing their morning chorus, and there wasn't a cloud in the sky; it seemed as though it was going to be a perfect day.

"Nothing wrong outside," I muttered to myself. And then it

winded me as though somebody had struck my back with a wooden plank. The problem was inside.

I quickly descended the ladder and ran to Ares' stall, fully knowing what to expect but losing my breath anyway upon finding it empty.

I pinched my thumb between my fingers and squeezed down hard. This was not the time to give way to nerves.

We had to go. Now.

"Get up!" I yelled, alarming the rest of the barn. The majority jumped out of bed in panic. "Everybody, up!"

Tye was the first to approach, worry in his eyes. "What's going on?"

"It's Ares." I pointed to the Omega's empty stall. "He's gone."

Noise erupted from the confused and tired bodies as they emerged from their slumber.

"It's his initiation. We need to go." I rushed to grab my shoes and internally screamed at myself.

Why had it taken so long for me to notice? How? It was obvious now that I couldn't pick up his scent. The energy had shifted. But Ares was so new, and I had been so distracted by the events of the night before. I was off my game.

I had let my emotions take over and now Ares would pay the price.

Everyone rushed around the barn. I was about to give a rundown of the plan when I noticed that Hail was still snoring, blissfully unaware of the chaos around him.

"Hey!" I picked a ball of socks from his floor and threw them at his head. "Get up, Ares is missing."

Hail scowled and rolled over, throwing the duvet over his head. "Wake me up when you've found him."

"Absolutely not." I yanked the duvet back and dragged him out of bed. "You're just as much a part of this team. And Ares needs us... All of us."

Hail huffed. "Okay. Okay! I'm up."

I watched him stumble out of his stall and tie his shoes as I climbed onto the bench to gain height over the pack. It wasn't easy being smaller than all of them. "Ares was taken at some point during the night, did anyone see or hear anything?"

The room stayed quiet.

"Then we'll follow our noses. Keep together. Only speak if you think you've found something."

I quickly pushed open the barn doors. Two guards sat outside awaiting our arrival. "Any clues?"

The shorter farmer shook her head. "You know we're not allowed to help."

"It's always worth a try," I sighed as I got a sense of which direction they had taken him.

We left the barn. I lead at the front whilst Hail trailed at the back. Thankfully, everyone followed my rules; nobody spoke in case they missed Ares' cries for help. My stomach knotted. I just hoped that when we found him, he'd be crying and not screaming.

The screams were the worst.

That's when they were in real trouble, and most of the time it was already too late. If they hadn't evolved or mutated, then there was no way of saving them.

But at least if they were screaming, they weren't already dead.

The pack headed towards the lake. It was unusual to see The Farm so motionless, it almost looked deserted. We jogged past the Silo, and towards the Veno barn where the steady tick of the Veno hybrids' breathing became audible.

I could smell the rival pack from several hundred yards away. Although they were also hybrids, they were so, so different. The Veno pack were brutal and careless. They had proved to be unforgiving animals, killing machines, playing by a different set of rules, and I hated them with every inch of my body. Part of me wanted to break into their barn and smother them in their sleep.

But Ares needed our help. We couldn't waste any more time.

I followed his scent past the Veno barn and toward the cow pastures.

"Ah, shit," I murmured, knowing that beyond the pastures came what was known on The Farm as 'The Dark Forest'.

If he was in there then the odds had it that we'd never find him in time. Whatever horrible form of torture that the farmers had in store for him would surely kill him soon.

I prayed that Ares had found a way to hold on. We hiked through the cow pastures. They were empty at this time. The incline started to burn in my thighs but I pushed forward, forcing everyone to pick up the pace.

HAIL

I was slugging it at the back, a little more awake now than I had been thirty minutes ago.

I was starting to feel a little guilty for the way I'd acted, but they would have to understand that nothing got in the way of my sleep.

Not a missing hybrid.

Not even a war.

For in my dreams, I was able to escape the mess. I could finally experience a happiness I'd long forgotten. It was the moments upon waking which hurt the most, like reliving hell all over again as I realized that she was no longer here and that I'd never see her face again.

My stomach growled as we ran, and the thought of sausages awaiting my return to the barn pushed me forwards. The sooner we found Ares, the sooner I could eat. We finally reached the edge of the forest and I huffed in relief, thankful that my legs hadn't fallen off yet.

It had been a long time since I had been to this part of the woods. Memories flashed through my mind, and it made me anxious to the point that my hands started to shake. I clenched them into fists and began to hum a tune that seemed familiar. It stopped me from turning around, but *man*, did I want to turn back and run.

No.

I had to face my demons, for Ares.

Today would not be a repeat of *that* day.

The pack pushed into the darkest part of The Dark Forest. I hated this place; where the sun barely reached the ground and the smell of damp, rotting bark almost made me sick. The earth was covered in a thick moss which sunk underfoot. I imagined that it was alive and if I stood in one place for too long it might swallow me whole. I picked up my pace to fall in line with the rest of the pack. The last thing I wanted was to get lost in these woods.

Like Ares.

The guilt swept over me again.

I should have been more willing to help, but people around here were making a habit of coming into my life just to disappear again and I was starting to become okay with that.

It's just the way things were.

"Keep quiet. We're getting close," Lora announced with a hand in the air. The pack halted in unison for a brief second, before continuing to delve further into the darkness.

I focused on the task at hand in fear of reliving the past, I ignored the screams within my mind for I knew that time was running out.

Ares would not suffer the same fate as Donnah.

"Stop."

Lora's words made me jump.

"It's gone." Confusion clouded Lora's words and I noticed that Ares' scent had vanished completely. "Something's not right. Fan out. Split into pairs so that we can cover more ground. They're trying to confuse us, but they wouldn't leave us clueless."

We obeyed her orders, I was paired with Indigo, and Tye with Beckle, which left Lora with Jayleigh. They headed off in different directions, and I followed Indigo back the way we came to make sure that we hadn't missed anything, and also because I felt a lot safer knowing that I wasn't so deep into the forest.

"There must be something here," Indigo kept repeating. I tried to ignore her as much as I could, but as we continued to walk it became more and more annoying.

I called out to Ares.

Nothing.

Was this second-hand punishment for Torn and Shyla's actions last night? I knew that the farmers enjoyed penalizing the pack for somebody else's mistakes.

We searched for hours.

Ares' scent was starting to fade.

I had completely lost my bearings, unsure if we were still walking in the direction of the cattle field, or back towards the center of the forest. I looked at a large rock that seemed familiar, and once again contemplated sitting on it. It was the perfect height for a stool.

"There must be something here," Indigo repeated again.

"It'll be your dead body if you don't shut up!" I shot at her.

It was no secret that we didn't get along. I figured that Lora paired us together in an attempt to fix our friendship.

Indigo scowled, but she stopped her muttering.

I sighed in relief.

Finally, some peace.

It was very quiet; scary in fact. Even the birds stayed out of this part of the forest. And then I noticed the footsteps breaking through the silence, turning to find Tye and Beckle heading towards us.

"You're in our area." Beckle approached me.

"Oh, I'm sorry, I didn't realize we had areas now. Do you want me to mark it out with string?" I replied.

"Guys, stop." Tye stood between us. "Now is not the time."

"Seems as good a time as any," Beckle challenged.

"Now is *not* the time," Tye repeated. "We may as well work together now that we're here."

"Great," said Beckle. "My legs were tired anyway."

"What's that supposed to mean?" I frowned.

"Well, if we're all going to search the same area then we may as well do it in shifts. You guys start and I'll take a break. If you don't mind?"

"There are no breaks here," I interrupted, wanting nothing more. On second thought, I would have chosen food over a break. I would have even settled for toast, but that was beside the point. I wanted to sit down too, but I continued because I knew the consequences. I was wrong to assume that Beckle would think the same. "If my legs can still carry me then so can yours."

"What does that mean?" Beckle frowned.

"My legs are longer than yours, so they'll ache more."

Beckle was bewildered. He scoffed. "You're nuts, man. I kind of feel sorry for you."

"Hold it in, hold it in," I almost lost it. I felt the hairs on the back of my neck stand and wanted nothing more than to kick the shit out of Beckle. I clenched my fists into balls, nails cutting into the palms of my hands but barely feeling the pain.

Beckle knew that he was getting under my skin and it only pushed him on. "What are you gonna do?" he taunted. "Kick me with those extra long legs?"

That was the last straw. "I'm gonna bury you!" I couldn't contain it. I swung for Beckle and landed a punch square to his nose. It crunched on impact. Indigo started to yell, attempting to hold my arms back, but it only made me all the more eager.

I knew fighting wasn't the answer, and I'd get in trouble for it later, and that it wouldn't help Ares at all...

But I hated Beckle so damn much.

I had been waiting for this opportunity for months, and I wasn't going to sit back and let the moment pass me by. I went in with another punch but missed. Beckle used the beat to his advantage and caught me off-guard as my feet stumbled beneath me, sending an elbow into my cheekbone.

"Bury him," Tye started repeating my words. Something seemed to click into place as he considered them. "Bury. Bur- They've buried him!" he was shouting now. "Hail, stop! We can still save Ares! They've buried him!"

LORA

"He'll be okay," Jayleigh tried to comfort me as we headed east, but I struggled to accept compassion from others. It was belittling. I was in charge, I was supposed to be the strong one. "I know you're too hard on yourself when it comes to these challenges."

I tried to appreciate Jayleigh's attempt at empathy with a deep breath. She was just trying to be nice, she didn't mean to sound malicious. "I have to be. If somebody dies, it's on my back."

Jayleigh searched the trees above as we walked and examined, not picking up on how uncomfortable the situation was making me. This was a good thing though. If she had noticed my annoyance, it would have only highlighted the weakness.

"It's on all of our backs, we're a team. Besides, you're not the one stealing people away in the middle of the night. Or experimenting on kids. How sick is that, by the way? I was eight when they started experimenting on me. Surely that's worse than anything going on outside the fence."

I sighed.

Little did she know.

"I'm not the one experimenting on kids, but I am your Alpha. It's my responsibility to keep you all safe, and three members of our pack have died in the past week. Now another has been added to the pending list so, I think I have a reason to be hard on myself."

"Shyla may not be dead," Jayleigh intervened. "Torn was a psycho, and Zayne would have walked in front of a truck without noticing. You can't save that."

"And what about Ares?"

"He's been thrown in the deep end. Initiation on day one has got to be a killer."

I paused my rummaging for a moment as I waited for

Jayleigh to realize what she'd just said.

Finally, she clicked. "Sorry, just a figure of speech."

I nodded and tried for a smile. "He has to make it. I made myself a promise last night that I wasn't going to let anyone else slip through my fingers. The farmers seem to think that we're easily replaced, but nobody is expendable."

"I just hope your promise isn't short-lived," she sounded doubtful.

But that was the thing, every promise that I made was a gamble. I couldn't even trust the promises I made to myself.

"What's that?" I paused to listen as a commotion broke through the trees.

We shared a look before running towards the sound of yelling. My heart hammered against my chest as I neared the group, and dropped as I realized the noise had nothing to do with finding Ares at all.

"What's going on?!" I burst as I approached the pack, with Beckle covering a bloody nose and Hail sporting a half-closed eye. I wanted to knock their heads together like coconuts in hopes that it might shake some sense into them.

It was like babysitting.

And that's when I realized that my promise had already been broken. At least one of them would die as a result of this fight.

Beckle and Hail stared at me with wide eyes as I tried to think of something to say to wake them up from their stupidity.

Nothing came straight away so I settled for a scowl.

Tye interrupted the scolding with the long-awaited revelation. "The scent ended because we were standing right on top of him!"

My face dropped but a spark of hope returned.

"They've buried him."

Of course.

We had to hurry.

"You two," I separated Hail and Beckle with a hand slammed into each of their chests. They both stumbled backward. "Behave. It's like you're trying to get yourselves killed!"

Hail could sense my anger and backed down immediately. I knew that I could be scary when I had to be.

And then I led the pack back to the area where we'd lost Ares' scent. I had studied everything, from the tops of the trees to the fallen autumn leaves on the ground. Why hadn't it crossed my mind that Ares was there all along? I had been too busy thinking about the farmers' games, searching for clues; I had probably walked over him ten times in the past couple of hours.

"There will be fresh dirt where they've dug, probably covered over in leaves or moss. Try to clear the ground."

The pack followed orders, kicking leaves aside and moving branches.

"Here!" Jayleigh moved a log to reveal a patch of disrupted dirt. In her haste, she started to dig with her bare hands, not considering that something would be buried amongst the rubble.

She elevated her arm after slashing her palm across the hidden shovel, the wound deep enough that it sliced through the flesh.

"Nice one, Jayleigh," Beckle cackled.

Jayleigh didn't bite back or even acknowledge Beckle, and I knew exactly why. Jayleigh, although relatively new in comparison to the other hybrids, was deadly. She was exactly the type of hybrid that The Farm strived for. Sharp. Precise. Fast thinking. She could kill Beckle before he even had time to process what was happening, and she knew it. It was clear that she was toying with him, relishing in his immaturity and arrogance. Her silence was her way of mocking him.

People didn't seem to warm to Jayleigh, but I had a soft spot for her. I envied her self-confidence, although I'd never admit it to anyone.

The team retrieved the shovel and began to work in shifts. It was tedious, and my anticipation expanded with each scoop of dirt. I held my breath as Hail removed the last of it to reveal a large container. "What the hell?" He searched for a way to open the lid. It was square, buried six feet down, and difficult to open.

He pulled at a large rope and I commented, "It can't open whilst you're standing on the lid, Hail."

He nodded, dropped the rope, and passed up the shovel before climbing out of the pit. I waited until he was almost out before adding, "But we do need the rope."

72

I considered it a fair punishment for trying to stay in bed this morning, instead of rushing to help Ares like the rest of the pack.

Hail huffed and jumped back into the pit, handed the rope up to Tye, and once again proceeded to climb. This time he collapsed on the ground next to me as we slowly lifted the lid, scared by what we might find inside.

My heart was still racing. "Please be alive, please be okay," I repeated in my mind. I could still sense him, but the connection was weak. Barely there at all.

"Oh, shit…" Tye's words made my heart leap.

Inside the container were two small boxes, a light on the wall, and a coffin much like the one I had expected to find.

I jumped down, eager to open the coffin and pull Ares to safety. I called to him as I lifted the lid, but there was no reply, and I stopped breathing.

I pulled Ares' limp body from the coffin and whispered. "Not another one."

CHAPTER
SIX

ARES

Lora's face hovered above me, the sun creeping through the trees and illuminating her from behind like some heavenly being.

I was gasping for air and she was standing too close; I didn't mean to head-butt her as I sat up, confused and dazed.

"Ow!" She fell back and held her hand up to cover her eye.

What was going on?

Where was I?

"Ah, crap." It hurt to talk. The shock hit me all at once. The oxygen felt so good, but my lungs felt like a soft fruit. "Lora, I'm so sorry," I wheezed.

I fell back as black dots danced in my vision. Oxygen.

I'd never take breathing for granted again.

I closed my eyes and tried to relax, but the high-pitched ringing in my ears kept me from feeling any peace at all.

Breathe in…

Breathe out…

The air felt clean, yet somewhat painful. I was bruised.

I only reopened my eyes once it felt safe to, and propped myself up onto my left arm whilst trying to ignore the pain.

One guy jumped into the pit and leaned over Lora to check that she was okay. "Looks like it might swell a little. Do you need a hand up?" He offered her his arm.

I watched, astounded. I'd almost died, and yet he chose to check on Lora's eye first.

But it seemed to make sense after considering the Alpha Effect. The Alpha was the heart of the pack and would always come first, no matter the situation.

Lora smiled at him reassuringly. "I'm fine, Tye. Thank you."

"I'm so sorry," I whispered again as Tye backed away.

She turned to me with an expression of disbelief. My heart sank to the bottom of my stomach. "I bring you back from the dead and that's how you repay me?"

"The dead? I- Uh… Dead," I stuttered, more than a little confused. She could resurrect people? "I died?"

Everyone remained silent as a smile crept across her face and she laughed. "Your face is a picture." She snorted between giggles, and it made her laugh even more.

At least somebody found humor in the situation.

A couple of others joined in and laughed at my expense once they realized that she was joking, whilst I stood there grimacing. I wanted to join in, I could feel the tickle, but it hurt too much.

"We need to get you to Dr White." Tye knelt over me, a couple of unorthodox strands of his afro tickled my face as he moved to pick me up. "Put your arm around my neck," he ordered. I reached out slowly, worried that he might drop me. But, although no taller than five foot six, he was deceivingly strong and lifted me without a problem.

I groaned as I stood, not liking the way that my body felt as I moved. I studied the blood that stained my wrists, sliced open from the fabric that I had been trying to escape. "So, did I die, or not?"

Tye chuckled. "You would have died if we hadn't found you when we did. Looks like we got to you just in time. Lora performed a little CPR magic, and here you are, alive and well."

"Alive, yes. Well? Not so much... But thank you." I turned to Lora. "For the CR, or whatever-"

"CPR."

A nervous laugh left my lips. "Yeah, that."

She looked up to the trees as she spoke, examining the branches that shielded us from the outside world. "You're a sloppy kisser," she muttered.

My breathing stopped. "What?"

She'd kissed me and I hadn't been awake to remember it?

"Not that kind of kiss." Tye nudged me, his elbow placed perfectly against my fractured ribs and I yelled out in pain. I couldn't tell if it was an accident or whether he meant it, but based on the fact that he didn't apologize, I went with the latter.

"I'm okay," I wheezed, needing to distract myself from the pain. "Well, thank you. It means a lot to me... to be alive and all."

She looked down at my painted wrists, the cuts now beginning to scab over and heal. "You didn't mutate," she stated. "You'd have been able to break free of the fabric if you had."

"Yeah, that's not exactly my style." I gritted my teeth at the thought.

Lora raised an eyebrow. "Not your style? Ares, you could have died."

"I know. But at least I'd have died human."

Baffled faces met my words.

"Do you understand what's going on here?" Tye asked.

"I understand that my rage results in mutating, and mutating results in a lack of control over my body. I could unintentionally hurt those I care about."

Tye and Lora shared a look.

"We're training for a war, Ares." Lora looked concerned. "You're engineered to inflict pain."

"I know. But that doesn't mean that I'm comfortable with the situation."

The silence returned and I felt awkward under the stares. They were judging me. I understood their confusion, I was more

77

than likely the first hybrid to wish that he hadn't been experimented on; the first hybrid to refuse mutating in fear that welcoming the anger would normalize the malicious thoughts that the animal side induced. I understood why they would think that I'm crazy, but I couldn't get over the fear in Dr White's eyes.

It left a permanent, guilt-ridden scar.

After a moment, Lora decided to change the subject, noticing that the others were starting to whisper.

So much for fitting in.

"Well, it looks like they were trying to force you into mutating or evolving. The plan must have been for you to escape the coffin and open this box." She lifted the lid that had my name on it and pulled out a respirator and an earpiece, holding the smaller item in the palm of her hand for everyone to see.

She moved to the box on the left whilst everyone gazed down with curiosity.

This box read *'Titanium Hybrids'*. She removed the lid and pulled out a note which she recited for us to hear.

"We sincerely hope that you got to Ares in time. If not, then please make your way back to the barn, and his body will be seen to. If he or any other member of the team seeks medical attention, please use the earpiece in Ares' box to get in touch with a farmer."

A scoff came from my left. "Oh, he needs medical attention alright," Tye grunted and shifted his weight under me, trying hard to keep me secure.

"My ribs feel bruised, possibly even fractured." I supported Tye's comment.

Lora picked up the earpiece and switched it on. "Hello?" She flicked it.

A large screech came from the corner of the container, shocking us all. The speaker experienced static for a few seconds.

"Please refrain from tapping the microphone, Lora. I've rather a large headache as is." Dr White's voice flooded the area, bouncing from the metal walls. "I'm so pleased to see that you have reached Ares in time. How can I be of assistance?"

Lora spoke to Dr White as though he were an old friend. "Just keeping you on your toes, old man." She looked around, knowing that Dr White would be watching through a hidden camera. "Ares needs help. He may have a few fractured ribs, and his wrists will need seeing to. And Jayleigh has sliced her hand open, too."

"And it's only ten in the morning." He sighed. "Noted, Lora. Help is on its way for those who need it. Everyone else must return to the barn immediately. Great job, team. Over and out."

The speaker screeched again as Dr White switched off, and Lora placed the earpiece back into the box. "Keep your friends close, and your enemies closer," she whispered to me after reading my puzzled expression. "If you get on their bad side, you'll know about it."

I shuddered.

If today was an example of what the farmers would do

whilst they liked me, I dreaded to think what they'd do if I pissed them off.

I flashed back to last night and grimaced.

"You heard the man," Lora called to the pack. She nodded once at me to question if I was okay. I nodded back and sat in the coffin so that Tye could follow orders.

"I'll see you when you return to the barn." She climbed the rope once Tye was free of it.

Just as they were about to leave, Hail popped his head over the edge. The wind blew in the opposite direction to his ruffled hair, and his eye was forming a small bruise. "Hey, Bro. I just wanted to let you know that I'm glad you're alive."

"Yeah, me too. What happened to you?" I had to ask.

"I'll tell you later."

"Can you tell everyone that I appreciate what they did for me today?"

He nodded. "Of course. Or you could just tell them yourself when you're done getting your bones fixed?"

I laughed. "Yeah, okay."

"Alright." He got to his feet. "See you later, man."

The shuffling of shoes on moss and leaves faded as they walked away, and I felt a strange sense of loss.

I could have died... And I *would* have if not for my peers' help.

I felt indebted to them.

Maybe overcoming the mental trauma was just as much a

part of the test?

I sat in the silence of the woods, finding it strange that no birds sang there. It was creepy. The wind lingered in the trees, I was chilled in their shadow. And suddenly, I felt very alone.

"Jayleigh?" I called. If she was still there then she was standing alarmingly still.

"How are you doing down there, Omega?" the girl with the cut hand called down to me. She seemed shocked that I had remembered her name, or that I even wanted to speak to her at all. I was just as shocked that she'd managed to stay so silent. "You good?"

"Yeah," I lied. "I'm okay, I guess."

She stepped forward so that I could see her and then perched over the edge of the pit, swinging her legs and cradling her hand against her chest.

She was an unusual-looking girl, with a squatty face that almost seemed triangle in shape, and a tiny nose plastered in freckles. Her skin was porcelain, a vast contrast to the orange hair plaited down her back until it reached her hips.

"How did you manage that?" I nodded to her wound.

"Well, finding you required a blood sacrifice and a dancing ritual to the wolf gods, so I, being the heroine that I am, volunteered to sacrifice my hand."

I stared at her. This place was getting more and more strange by the second.

She started to laugh. "I'm joking, don't worry. I cut it on the shovel whilst digging you out…"

"That's more like the answer I'd been expecting. Still a heroic act though."

"You know, I almost forget what the first few days were like. It's strange how fast you get used to it, and the people, too. Maybe it's the pressure that forces us to adapt so quickly? And don't worry about the others, I can understand why you're reluctant to mutate. As with everything, you just need time."

"Thanks." Her words reassured me. Finally, somebody who understood. "So how long have you been here?"

"Two hundred and fifteen days."

"You count them?"

She shrugged. "I like to keep organized, and it helps me to know how many days I've been here. It gives me a sense of control," she said. "God, saying it out loud sounds ridiculous."

"No, it's not at all." If anyone would understand her need for control, it would be me.

"I'm not usually this pessimistic. Actually, my conversations never usually last this long, so maybe I am and I've never noticed." She turned her head to listen as trucks approached. "But I'm not this glum in my head if that reassures you?"

"Yeah, sure." I knew that it would be hard to stay positive in a place with so much death. Hail was proof of that. I could imagine the person he had once been, but the light had faded somewhere along the line. He was tainted red.

The trucks stopped just short of the pit, the engines

replaced by people speaking and walking toward us. I prayed that Marshall wasn't there. I didn't know how I'd have reacted to seeing him, but the thought was enough to send the anger crawling up my spine, tingling like a spider on the skin.

Fortunately, his face wasn't amongst the farmers.

The spider vanished.

Dr White popped his head over the edge of the pit. "Oh, dear God, Ares. You do look worse for wear." He frowned and tilted his head as he studied my wrists and my awkward hunch in an attempt to release the pain in my ribs, and then he nodded once and walked away.

Jayleigh was lead out of sight by somebody else, a medic I presumed, whilst Dr White returned with a stretcher and several farmers to help lift me from the coffin. They handed me a pill to numb the pain which I took with a bottle of water.

Suffocating was dehydrating work.

The pill did in fact numb the pain, along with the rest of my body. It started as an uncomfortable itch which grew into a swelling, and then I felt nothing at all.

I tried to ask if the effects were normal, or if maybe I was having an allergic reaction, but nobody paid me any attention, and it didn't wear off.

I was lifted into the back of a truck on the stretcher, driven to the silo, descended into Dr White's room, and moved onto the bed.

Dr White hovered over me, shining a light into my eyes

when he first mentioned the paralysis. "Don't worry, Ares. You won't be able to move but it is only temporary, I assure you."

I groaned because I couldn't so much as move my mouth.

I wondered if it was a precaution. After what had happened yesterday, I wouldn't blame them. Dr White wore a turtle neck to hide the bruises I'd caused, but every time he moved his head to the right, the purple stain on his skin became visible. My stomach twisted. *I had hurt this man.* I needed to apologize again. The doctor beat me to it.

"I must apologize, but the paralysis is completely necessary to ease your pain," he spoke as he worked. I couldn't see what exactly he was doing, and I couldn't feel a thing. A drip above my head fed me some kind of magical cure. "Luckily for you, titanium frogs are known to heal at extreme rates. They're even able to regrow limbs. I see that your wrists have already started the regeneration process."

"Fantastic," I murmured. It sounded sarcastic through my struggle, but I was overjoyed to hear that I'd be back to normal soon.

"Oh, no. Don't speak, please. Just rest."

The doctor pottered around with a file in his hand, noting down anything that he deemed important with quick scribbles as he studied the monitor above my head.

"Congratulations are in order. You successfully passed your initiation trial. I'm sorry to put you under such intense pressure. I know that it must seem so unnecessary to you…" he babbled as he continued to write. "But it's all part of a bigger picture and one day you'll understand, as your parents did, how necessary all of this is…" his words trailed off and stared at me. It was only then that I noticed his eyes were slightly bloodshot and holding back tears.

I couldn't help but feel that this was very out of character for the chirpy doctor. I wondered what had happened to him overnight.

"You're lucky that you have the Titanium hybrids, they're a good bunch, for the most part. Not many of us are lucky enough to have such companionship these days." The heart-wrenching sadness in his voice left me feeling emotional too. Dr White was the only farmer I could relate to. I didn't like to see him in this state. "Mine was taken from me long ago."

I questioned why he was telling me this.

And why now?

I couldn't even reply.

Or maybe the fact I couldn't reply made him feel as though he could confide in me. He knew that I too missed my family, maybe he needed to talk to somebody who would understand his pain.

He opened his pocket watch, two photos placed within the locket. The first was a photo of a man. Dr White pointed to him as he spoke. "Flynn was the kindest person I'd ever met. My only aim in life is to make him proud." He wiped a finger across the photo and took a second to admire it before turning the locket again to show me the woman on the right. "This is-" he corrected himself, "Was... my twin sister. I lost them both eight years ago to this day."

The steady beep of the monitor accompanied us as we inspected the photos.

I wished I could have said something to comfort him. Patted his shoulder. Used this sharing of information to seep details about my own family.

"They died for the sake of The Farm. They died so that we could continue our work here, *that's* how much they believed in our cause. I can't stress enough how important you and the other hybrids are. Our future relies on you. So I ask once more; follow the program. You may feel uncertain about mutating, but can I assure you that the violence is completely necessary for the greater good. Leverage the power we've given you. Don't let their deaths be in vain."

He stood again and continued to make notes in the folder before leaving it on the desk and excusing himself from the room without another word.

I lay there for a little while, wondering where he'd gone and when he'd return. Eventually, my mind turned back to the doctor's words.

It had become clear that the war had already affected, and taken, so many lives. We needed to win, and the program was a necessary means to get us there.

But I didn't see why I had to be a part of it.

I could leave...

My eyes landed on the folder which remained on the desk. It contained all of my information, including the names of my parents. If they were still alive, I could find them, explain the situation, and hope that they understood my reasons for leaving.

I didn't *have* to play along with the challenges. I didn't *have* to risk my life.

I didn't have to give up my humanity.

HIM

I had only left The Farm once in my life, to travel to a camp in The North where I stayed for a year to master mixed martial arts, weaponry, and war tactics.

I'd learned from the second-best in the country. Of course, the best was Father, but he didn't have the time nor patience to teach me. So I had to make do with the second best; Julia.

Julia wasn't friendly. I had always felt like a burden in her presence. Yet, she owed Father for saving her life on multiple occasions, and this seemed like the perfect way to settle the score.

By this age, I knew how important it was to pay my full attention; so I trained hard. When the time came to return to

YIELD

The Farm, I could outfight the majority of farmers, even though I had yet to reach my teens.

If Father had been impressed then he never showed it.

Mother said that it was just the stress of the job and the war getting to him, but she had started to act differently now, too.

Soon, I began to realize that they had become so used to life without me that they had forgotten how to be parents. I found myself fighting for their attention, doing everything to the best of my ability and yet still feeling as though it was never quite good enough.

The animals always came first.

I tried to ignore the feeling of resentment that still lived within me, years later, as it was my job to train the animals, challenge them, and push them to their limits. But I struggled today.

It was eight years since the incident which killed a quarter of the farmers, including my parents; eight years since my parents chose to give their lives in hopes of saving The Farm, and leaving the burden of the war solely to myself.

Eight years since they made the ultimate decision; choosing the animals over their son.

I screamed out in rage, punching into the bag that I kept in the corner of the bedroom. I liked to imagine that it was an animal, and today the bag was Ares.

"Smart-mouthed little shit!" I punched again, more than annoyed that the Omega had passed his initiation trial, especially as he'd done so without mutating. Ares would have died in that coffin if my plans had been followed precisely, but Dr White always overlooked the challenges to make sure that the animals stood a chance of surviving.

The doctor's face appeared on the punching bag now, and I aimed for the nose, angry that the doctor always managed to get involved.

I ran The Farm, not the doctor.

I recalled all of the times that Dr White had spoken down to me, forgetting his place. Somewhere along the line, the hierarchy had been overlooked, and it was no longer acceptable.

It was time to bend the rules a little.

Father would be turning in his grave, but I knew what had to be done to make things right.

I needed to avenge my parents; I needed the animals to train harder and evolve faster; I needed to play by my own rules.

And play I would.

CHAPTER
SEVEN

ARES

It turned out that Dr White wasn't lying when he said that titanium frogs healed fast. Within five hours, I was back in the barn with ribs as good as new.

I thanked everyone for their assistance in my rescue mission. Some blew it off with a quick 'no thanks needed', whilst others developed a hero complex and embarked on retelling the story.

The pack settled, lounging on the benches, and some waited in line for the shower. It was mid-afternoon and I'd missed lunch whilst recovering in the doctor's room, but a small loaf had been left with a bowl of soup, ready for my return. The soup was cold and distasteful, and an untrustworthy shade of red.

I couldn't help but notice a little tension between certain

individuals as I ate. I assumed it was aimed in my direction for my lack of enthusiasm to mutate, but upon deeper inspection, I realized that Hail and Beckle were the roots of the issue, glaring at one another in hatred.

"How's your hand?" I asked Jayleigh as she sat on the bench next to me.

"Perfect," she said and showed me the evidence. Surely enough, not even a scar remained. "How about you?"

I looked down at my wrists, still amazed at how quickly they'd healed. "Yeah. All good." I smiled. "Listen, did I miss something?" I lowered my voice and nodded my head in Hail's direction. He leaned against the wall, plotting Beckle's demise, and making himself comfortable as though expecting the face-off to continue for a long while. "What's going on?"

"Oh, you'll get used to those two. They don't see eye to eye most of the time. There was a bit of a squabble earlier and they haven't resolved the issue." She sighed.

"I'd better go and see if there's anything I can do to help."

A look of panic flashed across Jayleigh's face.

"What's the matter?" I asked.

She shook her head and looked to the ground. "It's best not to interfere. If something happens between them and the farmers think that you played a part in it, you'll be punished too. Just turn a blind eye and eat your soup."

I cast my eyes to the liquid but didn't eat it.

The whole situation seemed cagey to me. "So what happens

now? Is there a daily routine that you follow?"

"Usually there's a routine. We train first thing in the morning, come back to the barn for lunch, and then we'll have a challenge of sorts in the afternoon. But it always changes on Omega initiation day."

The unamused look on her face suggested that she didn't care much for the changes.

"The initiation challenge is usually anywhere in the Omega's first week. Sometimes the pack is made aware of the challenge, and other times, like today, the pack has no idea. I've never known initiation on day one. You've barely even had time to settle in."

I recalled Marshall's warning and couldn't help but feel targeted by the farmers; they thought I was weak.

"What was your initiation challenge?"

"They hung me upside-down over the edge of a cliff."

I struggled to force the bread down my throat. My mouth had become dry. "What?"

"Yeah, on day three. I wouldn't be here if it wasn't for the pack reaching me in time."

"Is that common then?" I questioned, noting that I had also needed the help of the pack to escape. "The challenges are pretty much impossible to complete on your own."

"Yeah, I guess. Unless you evolve."

I spoke as I processed the information. "The pack is urgent to save the Omega so it builds a sense of community, and going through such traumatic ordeals together is bound to bring us all closer. So, I guess initiation is just as much about helping the Omega fit in as it is about weeding out those who won't survive training," I suggested before trying one more spoonful of soup and giving up. "Do you want the rest?"

"Hell yeah." She reached for the bowl. "I don't know what they've put in it, but your brain is working overtime and I want a bit of that."

I smiled as I finished the bread. "Organisation is your thing, overthinking is mine."

"Intelligence but no common sense," she replied with a smirk.

"Whoah! That's no way to treat somebody who just gave you food."

"You're clever, but your survival instincts stink. Your first lesson; never turn down a meal. You won't be offering food in a few days, I promise you." She grabbed the bowl anyway.

"If I survive a few days," I thought, left her with the bowl, and headed in Lora's direction. She was the only one I hadn't yet thanked, mainly because she had been in the shower half the time that I had been back, and maybe because, as much as I hated to admit it, I was too nervous to approach her.

I knocked on the stall door as she towel-dried her hair, and then crossed my arms over my chest to hide the fact that my hands were shaking.

She looked up, surprised to have a visitor. "Oh, Ares. Hi."

She started to pull a wooden comb through her waves. "How are you feeling?"

I nodded once. "Fine, yeah... Good," the words disappeared as I watched her. "So, um... I just wanted to thank you for earlier."

"Oh. Not at all!" She seemed shocked. "It's what we do here, we've all got each other's backs."

"Even those two?" I joked as I gestured to Hail and Beckle.

"They've got everybody's back except each other's. Come in."

"I, uh..." I paused for a second before opening the door and closing it behind me. "Sure." I slid the lock back into place.

"Take a seat," she offered, motioning to the bed. "I actually wanted to talk to you about last night." Lora started as she separated her hair into three sections, and began to plait it to her shoulder. "Marshall doesn't usually do that."

"He doesn't usually try to intimidate us?" I questioned, "Or shoot us?"

She flinched when I mentioned the shooting. It was the first time I had seen any sort of vulnerability within her. "The shooting... Yeah." She nodded. "Marshall's a little mad. He always has been, but he's never done that before."

"I'll be on my best behavior around Mad Marshall then. He's certainly not your typical dinner lady."

She nodded in approval to the nickname. "Yeah, he's not one to be trusted. His ways are certainly unorthodox, but don't let it distract you from the end goal."

"I'm not intimidated by him or his need for violence," I lied. The truth is that I was scared of him, but that wasn't the reason for my reluctance when it came to mutating.

Lora crossed the room and sat on the bed next to me. "I want to understand."

"That makes the two of us." I scooted over to put some space between us. "I wish I could help, but I don't even know where to start."

The intensity of her gaze had me stuck. "You said that you're not comfortable with inflicting pain. Is that because of what happened yesterday? With Dr White?"

The memory flashed before my eyes. "You should have seen the look on his face, Lora. I wanted to stop, but I couldn't," I said. "I don't want to be this way. I don't want to live in fear of myself."

"Fear is a trick of the mind."

"You're telling me that I can train myself out of it?"

She shrugged. "I've seen others train themselves out of fears. I don't see why you would be any different."

"But, I don't want to," I realized. I couldn't become a warrior if it meant giving in to the animal alter-ego. "He looked at me as though I were a monster, and I felt like a monster. That's not who I am nor who I want to be."

Her eyes softened. "Then we do have a problem."

We both sighed.

It was hopeless.

"I'm never going to fit in here." I looked back towards the main living space, the majority of hybrids playing the same game as the night before.

She smiled reassuringly. "You won't believe it, but I used to feel the same."

She was right, I didn't believe it. "But you're the Alpha. How could you not fit in?"

"I earned my title. It was a few years ago and let's just say that my first few days were a little different to yours. I always felt weak compared to the other Alpha candidates, but it turned out that my difference was my greatest weapon."

"You think that you're weak?" I almost laughed.

"Everybody's evaluation of weakness and failure differs depending on what they consider success. What you might see as a flaw within yourself, I might see as the potential for greatness." She rested a hand on my shoulder.

"Wha- Really... Potential? Me?"

Nice one, Ares. Real smooth.

"I think that you worry so much about hurting others, that you've forgotten about those out there who want to hurt you. But you stand up for what you believe in, with no worry of how unpopular it might make you or how much danger you could be putting yourself in. I admire that."

My heart swelled and my words failed. I stood suddenly, pulling my arm away from her as the nerves sent me running.

"Thank you," I turned when I neared the door, as far away as I could get without leaving completely, "I'll leave you to it, thank you- Thanks again."

Lora didn't follow, she watched after me as I awkwardly hurried away.

"Ares." She called out, slowing my exit as I unbolted the door. "For what it's worth, I think that we need somebody like you in the team."

I stopped.

I didn't turn, I just let her words sink in and smiled to myself. I wished that I could have replied without mixing up my words, or looked at her without my eyes giving away just how much her acceptance meant to me.

Out of the darkness, a spark of hope had formed, and I grasped at it with both hands in worry that if I didn't give it my full attention, it would quickly slip away. I clung to it as I closed the door behind me and crossed the barn towards Hail, completely forgetting about Jayleigh's advice to steer clear of the situation that had arisen between the rivals.

Hail was still staring at Beckle, and he didn't look up as I approached.

"What's the beef?" I asked, the giddiness fogging my mind.

Hail frowned, but still didn't look away. "It was tomato, not beef."

I didn't catch on for a moment, still too distracted by Lora and how fantastic she was, but eventually it clicked that he was talking about the soup. I laughed quietly, unsure of whether he was joking or not. "What's going on?"

"Beckle's a prick."

"That's the reason you're staring at each other?"

Hail shook his head slowly. "No," he huffed. "I may have accidentally punched him."

Reality hit.

"What?" Suddenly everything crashed. The bubble of happiness popped. The spark of hope that I'd been grasping dimmed and slowly faded out. It was a rude awakening.

When Jayleigh said that the pair had a squabble, I'd assumed that it was a mere argument. I had forgotten about the bruise on Hail's face which had now healed and vanished.

I didn't know much about The Farm or its rules, but I knew this wouldn't sit well. "Why would you do that? You know how-"

"I know better than anyone what could happen!" he snapped. Hail tore his eyes away from Beckle for one moment to look at me. Pain painted his face. Regret filled his eyes. "I tried to control myself, but he was asking for it! Everything just happened so fast." He looked down at his hands, nervously picking at his nails. "I shouldn't even be talking to you about it. It's probably best if I don't speak to anyone for the rest of the day." He looked directly to a spot on the ceiling above the door. I recalled Marshall mentioning cameras. They were watching us, probably listening too.

"Why?"

"If the farmers think you're part of it…" he trailed off and I knew that he was replaying what happened to Shyla and Torn in his mind.

My heart sank at the thought of something like that happening to Hail. "Don't worry, I'm not going to let them do anything to you."

"You don't get it. We don't have a choice, Ares!" His voice grew louder with stress and he had to pause to contain the sound. "If they want it to happen, it'll happen. If you try to stop it then they'll kill you too."

It broke my heart to hear him say it. He was certain that he was going to die.

I wanted to comfort him in some way, to suggest that maybe the farmers would let it go. But, as though right on queue, the bell rang and pure dread circulated my body. I could only imagine how Hail was feeling.

We looked at each other, and fear clouded his eyes.

"It was nice knowing you," he whispered.

CHAPTER EIGHT

ARES

I hurried to my stall and shut the door. As soon as the locks slammed closed, Tim walked in with a group of farmers dressed in matching gray overalls and guns in their hands.

Tim glared at me, obviously still annoyed by our conversation yesterday. "Don't say a word to me," he snapped as he walked by.

I wanted to but I bit it back. The pack already considered me odd for not wanting to mutate, and winding up the farmers wouldn't help my situation when it came to fitting in. If I wanted to fit in…

Leaving sounded more appealing by the second.

He stopped when he reached the furthest stall in the barn. "Time for training," he announced.

It put me at ease to know that they weren't planning on repeating last night's events just yet. But looking over towards Hail, I could see that he was still expecting something to happen and fearing the worst.

The stalls opened again once a farmer assigned themselves a hybrid. Of course, a gun was pointed at my back as we left the barn. I imagined one of them using this opportunity to shoot Hail as he walked.

As we made our way out, I looked back at the short woman pointing the gun at me. Her green eyes scowled.

"Hey," I whispered just loud enough for her to hear. I motioned at the machine in her hand. "Could you put that down? It makes me nervous."

She looked at me from the corner of her eye. "Putting it down would make *me* nervous."

I sighed. Why did the farmers always assume we were out to hurt them?

We were the prisoners and subjects of experimentation. A little respect wouldn't hurt.

I looked back to the lady as she pulled her cap down further over her eyes. I wondered if it were to shield herself from the sunless sky or to avoid eye contact with me. I guessed the latter. "What's your name?"

She jabbed the barrel of the gun into my waist. "I'm not supposed to be talking to you." She pulled the cap down further still, and I wondered if she could see anything at all.

"You look like a Katie," I suggested. "Do you mind if I call you Katie?"

She didn't reply but I clung to the fact that she didn't say no.

"Where are we going?"

She sighed, answering this time only in hope that it might shut me up. "The Silo."

"Why? Oh, are we going back to the underground pool? It was nice in there."

She shook her head. "Your kind don't usually ask this many questions."

"My kind? You mean fellow humans who have been experimented on?" I almost laughed.

"Omega, eyes forward!" Tim's voice cut through the air from the back of the line.

I turned to face the silo as we approached, but my eyes drifted aimlessly across to the lake and scenery behind. Maybe it was the sound of the small waves rippling to the rubbly surface which drew my attention.

It was so easy to imagine that the lake could once have been a tourist attraction, one that people flocked to on a sunny day; filled with boats, families sitting on picnic blankets, and kids playing out on the rocks.

"It's so beautiful," I whispered.

"It is," Katie agreed without thinking. And then I felt her slowly lower the gun.

I drew a deep breath in relief. "Thank you…"

We walked the rest of the journey in silence. The lift could only take six people at a time and the wait for its return was a little awkward. We stayed in line, nobody speaking, before entering the lift single file. The journey was brief and cramped, accompanied by strange music.

It was a relief to see the doors open into the common room. After descending the stairs we joined the group on the oval sofa.

"Why are we here?" I asked Hail.

His face was so pale I worried he might throw up. Beads of sweat clung to his forehead. His eyes still held that same fear.

The deer in headlights kind of fear.

He looked towards the guards every so often, as if expecting them to have formed a firing squad in the ten seconds since he'd last looked.

"Hey," I tried to reassure him. "The more suspicious you look, the more attention you'll draw to yourself."

He nodded once.

"Try and think of something else," I suggested. "What do you usually do in training?"

"Depends on what they have planned for us." His eyes continued to dart around, but he made an effort to distract himself. He turned towards the tunnels which branched off from the common room. "Down there is the gym." He pointed. "And that one is the library."

"A library?"

That seemed odd.

I was under the impression that the farmers didn't want us to learn anything about the outside world. They selected which memories we were allowed to keep, but we could use a library to research anything we liked?

"Yeah, I guess it's more of a classroom. It just has a few books on first aid and a couple of history books. So, it's really not a library at all."

My heart sank. I longed for a knowledge of the world I lived in; a thirst I feared that I'd never quench.

The lift opened for a final time and I watched as Lora and Tim descended the stairs. I stared a little too long and she caught me looking, but it didn't seem to bother her. She simply smiled and continued towards the gym whilst the rest of us scurried into line behind her.

There was something homely about the cave, even though it was cold and harshly lit. Maybe it was the fact that it was so well hidden; nobody would expect to find it under The Farm. I certainly didn't.

Forget the war, we could start a new life down here, away from the violence.

I could see that Hail was also feeling a lot safer after leaving the farmers and their guns in the common room, guarding our exit.

The gym was a lot bigger than Dr White's room, filled with sorts of apparatus that I'd never seen before. Mirrors coated the walls and blue safety mats covered the floor. The center was occupied by a boxing ring, which Tim used as a stage.

"Not today. Not today," I prayed. I couldn't face fighting with another hybrid. I wasn't sure if I wanted to stay on The Farm, but combat training would definitely have sped up and swayed that decision.

"Today we'll be building up your core strength," Tim instructed.

A relieved sigh escaped me.

"Your strength and stamina play a key role in combat. Lack either and you may as well throw in the towel before even starting…"

He led us in some warm-up stretches which everybody seemed to recognize, and I fumbled about as I tried to copy what they were doing.

"You're all at different stages of your training. Group One, you'll be on the weights to start." He pointed towards the left side of the gym. Lora, Tye, and Beckle walked in that direction. "Group Two, you'll be coming with me." My face quite obviously portrayed how clueless I felt, as he added, "Omega, you're Group Two."

I nodded and fell into line behind Hail. We marched past Group One, towards the far end of the gym where a trap door engraved the ceiling. Tim used his height to his advantage and yanked on the door. It swung down and I leaped back into a stack of apparatus when something fell out of it.

"Bro, it's just a rope. Don't panic." Hail nudged me.

But I did panic. It was a natural instinct.

The rope resembled a snake as it fell and I wouldn't have put it past Tim to test us while we trained.

I didn't trust him one bit.

"Omega, you're first," he called me forward with glee. My legs moved but my mind screamed to run away.

"You want me to climb this?" I asked. Following the rope up with my eyes, it must have been at least 25 meters long, disappearing into the sky above.

"No, I want you to eat it," Tim replied bluntly.

I was taken aback by the human boulder's attempt at sarcasm. "I'm not sure which I'd rather."

"Just climb, Ares!" he cut me off. His bull-like nostrils flared and I knew that he'd be more than happy to wrap the rope around my neck if I didn't follow his orders.

"Okay." I held my hands in surrender before I placed them on the rope and pulled, making sure that it was stable.

"Don't panic, don't panic, everyone's watching, don't panic…" I moved my right hand higher on the rope and pulled again. "Here goes nothing."

I hefted myself up, my legs scrambling beneath me.

Thankfully, whatever they were feeding us during hibernation meant that every member of the Titanium pack had muscle. Using mine properly for the first time since waking made me feel a little stiff, but fortunately, my arms carried my weight with little problem.

I moved my hands, and then my feet, and then repeated. I tried not to think about what I was doing, or question how I would make it to the top without falling; concentrating solely on the task at hand.

And then I was through the trap door and entering the caved tunnel that would lead to my escape.

"Go on Ares! You can do it!" Hail shouted up to me, his voice echoing against the walls of the cave.

Once my feet were in, I used them against the rock to steady myself and walk up the tunnel in hopes that it would take the pressure from my arms. It worked until my foot stumbled. I heard Hail gasp from below and he shouted up to me, "I'll catch you if you fall!"

"Thanks," I tried to reply but my voice was held back in fear; shaky, just like my arms.

I started to spin, grunting as I struggled. It was making me dizzy.

It became difficult to catch my breath, and I was transported back to the coffin, buried six feet under. My heart hammered against my chest and sweat dripped down my face.

"I'm going to die."

I relived the fear, kicking against the sides of the coffin. No escape.

The same doom swallowed me now.

Only this time, my fate rested solely in my own hands.

YIELD

There was nothing that the pack could do to save me.

All I saw was darkness. It was closing in on me, suffocating. I gasped for air but it was salty from the rock surrounding me. My tongue felt dry as I tried to spit the taste away.

Focus.

Closing my eyes, I tried to calm myself. I took several deep breaths, listened to the sound of the birds overhead, and noticed how the damp air felt on my skin.

Picking out things to focus on distracted me from the noise in my mind and once I relaxed a little, it was clear to see that this was just another obstacle I had to overcome.

The fear was all in my head, just as Lora had said.

I tried to remind myself that I was physically capable. All I needed to do was push on and ignore the searing burn in my muscles.

I moved my arms and legs in unison, powering up the rope.

Appearing fragile wasn't an option.

If Tim sensed my weakness he would surely single me out and make a scene. I just wanted to do my bit and survive. If the rest of the pack could complete these tasks, then why couldn't I?

I neared the top whilst my mind was preoccupied, then hefted myself over the ledge of the hole and peered down to the hybrids, giving them a quick thumbs up. They whooped in response and I fell back into the grass, looking up at the sky and gulping the fresh air as I waited for them to follow.

My breathing started to calm a little as I relaxed into the

safety of the solid ground. My body ached as though it had been hit by a truck and blisters formed in the palms of my hands.

But mentally, it felt good.

I studied my already healing skin as somebody's hand reached from the hole in the ground and a head popped into view.

"Bro! That was sick." Hail beamed at me as though he hadn't just followed me up the rope of doom. He was barely out of breath. "I've never seen an Omega climb so fast."

I was still struggling for air as I replied. "Really? It felt like I was climbing forever."

He shook his head as he clambered over the ledge and sat on the grass next to me. "Nah, you sped up there like..." he struggled to think of something that moved quickly. "Really fast."

I laughed and fell back on the grass again. It was so much easier laying down.

"Mind if I join?" He lay next to me before I could answer. "I'd enjoy a quick nap before we move on to the next task." He motioned to something over my shoulder and I almost didn't look.

Next task?

I wasn't sure if I could take any more.

Of course, curiosity won out.

I groaned as my eyes fell on the life jackets. Group Two joined us in turn. It seemed that climbing the rope was a common task and something that shouldn't be feared. The other hybrids were completely unfazed. Jayleigh held her thumbs up, with a big smile painted across her face. She stood next to the lake, knowing what was about to follow.

Maybe if I pretended to faint they'd let me sit this one out? I buried my head between my legs and wrapped my arms around them.

Maybe if I just ignored the lake it would disappear?

Group One appeared as I tried and failed to prepare myself.

Tim was last to climb the rope. I was impressed that a human of his size could climb it with such ease, and I hid the newfound respect that I felt towards him. He reached the top and noted something down on the digital tablet hung around his neck.

"Ares," he said. "An Omega record."

He seemed less than impressed, almost as though he'd been hoping I would fail. A sly smile crossed his face as he finished typing on the tablet and turned towards the lake.

"Here is your next task." He held his hand out as though he were revealing a prize of some kind. "The lake…known by many, hated by all." Certain members of the group groaned. "Swim to the island wearing the weighted life jackets, ring the bell, swim back. It's that simple."

My heart dropped.

It wasn't simple at all.

The island was further than I was comfortable with and the

autumn water would be cold. Plus, we didn't have a spare change of clothes and I doubted we'd have towels to dry off afterward.

"Wearing this?" I cut Tim off before he could continue.

His face didn't hide his irritation. "Those suits are engineered to keep you safe under the most difficult of environments. They keep you warm when it's cold, and vice versa. They also keep you dry when it's wet. But by all means, if you'd rather go skinny dipping, be my guest."

Skinny dipping? *Hell* no.

It was obvious to see that Tim was trying to make me feel uncomfortable in front of my peers. I had gotten under his skin over the past two days, and he wasn't going to let it go lightly.

"I will if you will?" I suggested, fully expecting him to lose it. I crossed a line. I danced over it and then used it as a limbo pole, taunting him and relishing in every second.

A giggle came from my left, I was just as surprised as Tim to find that it came from Lora. He looked at her as though she'd just slapped him.

"Let me remind you of what is at stake here!" Tim's face creased in on itself and a vein popped out of his temple as he yelled. "We are at war and you are the only hope that we have. There is no time to question the things that we do. There is no time to joke around. You are warriors! It's time you start behaving like it and stop this immaturity!"

That last part was directed at me. He kicked one of the life jackets in my direction and I scurried to avoid it.

The silence that followed was intense. I no longer felt like dancing, I had partied too hard and now the sickness was starting to kick in.

"A change of plans," Tim finally finished. "Swim to the island, swim back and then do it all over again. Everyone is to ring the bell twice. Ares, you will wear a second belt on your jacket. And the Veno pack will automatically win the challenge."

Nobody said a word this time.

I wanted to.

What, or who, was a Veno?

"Go!" Tim yelled, catching me off guard. Everyone charged forward to put on a jacket and start their swim. I broke into a run too, a little late as I fumbled to put on a jacket and add an extra belt to it. I hit the water at full speed.

The lake was steep. It sucked me into its depths and I wasn't sure if I even knew how to swim, yet my body seemed to react once I was deep enough. I struggled into a not-so-speedy front crawl, fighting against the jacket and trailing far behind the other hybrids. My hands felt the wrath of the icy water. I was too scared to dunk my face in.

So, Tim had been telling the truth about our clothes. They somewhat resembled wetsuits in the water, insulating, but not protecting me from the weight of the jacket.

I soon realized that the jackets weren't made to hold us afloat. Whatever gave them the name *life* jackets had been removed and replaced with the weighted belts which threatened to drag me down to the lake's bed.

It was a death jacket.

I shouldn't have expected anything less from the farmers.

I was halfway there when I heard the first ring of the bell, signalling that somebody had reached the island. I knew that I was in trouble, I was so far behind and struggling to stay afloat, my arms weakening as the jacket threatened to pull me under.

I splashed about, drinking the regret with each gulp of water which burned my lungs as I choked on it; and I wondered if this was hell.

Had I ever really woken from hibernation? Or had I died? My wandering spirit winded up here to be tormented for eternity?

Eventually, I reached the island in the middle of the lake, long after the rest of the team had made their way back to land. My knees hit the rocks as the lake became shallow and I scurried to stand up and ring the bell.

I felt out of control. Running after swimming was a strange sensation, especially as the jacket was so much heavier out of the water, and I was almost pleased to dive back into the arctic sea. I could see that the stronger members of the pack were already reaching shore where Tim stood watch, sipping from a flask which he kept fastened to his belt loop. His eyes were on me. I knew that he would enjoy this; watching me suffer and let the rest of the team down.

"Come on, Ares!" he yelled as I approached the shore, too

long after the others. "This isn't a leisurely dip in the pool. Not good enough!"

I held my breath, partially to stop myself from any foolish replies, and partially because I had to, or else I would have inhaled more water.

The second trip was every inch as painful as the first, and then some.

It was too much for my body to handle in one day. My muscles throbbed as I moved, reaching a point of exhaustion. I couldn't continue any further. I stopped swimming for a second in hopes that it would ease the pain, but treading water only contributed to it.

I struggled on, unable to understand how putting us under such immense pressure in a short period of time could be beneficial.

We needed time to recover.

I couldn't take it.

Would my parents have wanted me to suffer in this way? Had they really known what they were signing me up for?

The idea of leaving The Farm was becoming more and more tempting. Because this was to be my life now, every day the same as today. But I had a choice. I didn't have to go through with this. I didn't have to risk my life.

At this moment, as the rest of the team were finishing their final lap, I decided that I should leave The Farm. I'd ask to go, as I'd been told that I was allowed to do at any time. I could put all of this nonsense behind me. No more intimidation. No more life-threatening challenges.

No Tim or Marshall.

No warrior *crap*.

I wasn't built for this kind of life. I'd ask Dr White for the names of my parents from my folder and then I'd leave.

Freedom.

The longing made me weak.

My thoughts were disrupted as my body suddenly began to shut down. Exhaustion had kicked in. I took in a large breath before slowly sinking into the depths of despair and darkness.

My hopes of leaving The Farm died.

Sinking lower and lower, I willed the density of the water to take the weight from my jacket.

I opened my eyes to the new world below the lake's surface and it took me too long to notice something that would have seemed obvious to me if I hadn't been so fatigued.

The water.

I summoned the energy to push myself to the surface once more, filling my lungs with oxygen, and then stopped fighting gravity as it pulled me down to the bed where the weight of the jacket was no longer a problem, then used my arms to propel me forward.

As I drew closer to the island, I rose to the surface, hearing the worried yells of Jayleigh and Hail who must have assumed that I had drowned. They voiced their confusion and relief as I appeared, reached the bell and rang for a final time.

My tactic proved to be a success as I journeyed back, willing myself to hold my breath the entire way so as not to lose momentum. Everyone watched as I reached the shoreline. Nobody cheered, obviously too tired and annoyed after I'd made the challenge twice as difficult as it should have been, and forfeited the prize.

They hated me.

Tye and Beckle were already glaring.

Even more of a reason to leave.

I eventually reached land and crawled my way up the rubbly shore, feeling as though my body might crumble. My stomach was queasy. I tried to stand but my legs couldn't take it. I fell forwards, vomiting at Tim's feet.

"That's more like it," he muttered, obviously a lot happier with this failure of a performance than he'd been with my success on the rope of doom. He grabbed the back of my head and pushed it towards the mess I'd just made on the floor. "Know your place, Omega."

At this, I threw up again. I was *so* leaving.

"Can I speak to you for a second?" I pulled Lora aside from her discussion with Indigo. She didn't reply but she smiled at her friend and briskly walked away, looking everywhere but in my direction.

She was obviously annoyed by how I'd acted this afternoon. I'd let my newfound love for annoying Tim get in the way of the pack's success. I'd been selfish.

Is that how Lora viewed me? Was I self-centred?

I started to sweat at the thought of it. I wanted so badly to make a good impression on her, even though I planned on leaving The Farm.

Lora climbed the ladder at the far end of the barn and perched on the overlook. I followed and sat at the opposite end of the window.

"Well done for today." She nodded in approval, finished eating her apple and threw the core down to the bin with little effort. It bounced in.

The expected lecture and list of everything I'd done wrong never came. I was a little taken aback. I wasn't prepared for this, I was prepared for a scolding. The words got stuck as I looked at her and noticed how perfectly her skin absorbed the golden sun. "I... uh."

"Ares, speechless?" She raised an eyebrow. "You certainly had enough to say to Tim earlier."

I nodded and suddenly my feet took my full interest. "Yeah, I'm sorry about that."

"It's no problem. I found it quite amusing, actually. Most of the hybrids fall into line and do as they're told. Nobody questions or tests the farmers like you do. It's refreshing."

Relief.

She didn't hate me.

"Get back on subject, Ares." I had to force my mind away from thoughts of her. "Actually…" I bit back the nerves. "That's why I want to talk to you. I absolutely don't fit in here, and I know that I'm not right for this. I'll only end up doing more harm than good. Today was proof of that. And so… I think…" It was more difficult to say the words than I had anticipated. Lora looked at me expectantly, and I realized that my reluctance was less about leaving The Farm, and more about leaving her. I felt as though I were letting her down. "I think I'm going to leave The Farm."

I watched as the color drained from Lora's face; no longer golden but as pale as the moon.

"I can't make that decision for you." She slowly crept closer so that only I could hear what she said. "But I'd recommend that you try to stick it out for one more day. You kind of get used to the craziness, and the people, too."

"But that's the thing, I don't think that I'd survive here another day. I had a panic attack on the rope of doom, and I was so close to drowning in the lake." I shook my head as I relived the pain.

That being said, I did want to stay on The Farm. I *really* did. It's where she was.

"You're doing it again," I scolded myself.

But, I was convinced that it wasn't just because of Lora. This was the life that my parents had chosen for me and being

118

here made me feel closer to them. Knowing that they wanted me to be here was actually all that I knew about them.

I felt overwhelmed with guilt.

What would happen if I left The Farm and found my parents alive, but they turned me away because I had gone against their plans? It wouldn't be the first time they'd turned me away; what would stop them from doing it again?

And if they weren't alive, I could be going against their dying wishes.

"Do you think that you'll survive out there?" Lora interrupted my thought process.

I shrugged. "I don't know. As long as I stay away from the action I'll be fine, right? I can lay low. My main worry is that the farmers will kill me for wanting to leave."

Lora frowned. "What do you mean? Why would they…"

"You said yesterday that we couldn't risk the enemy getting ahold of one of our own. So why would the farmers let us walk free?"

She sat in silence for a while, studying me. I held her gaze and her frown eased a little.

Was she expecting that I'd change the subject, or forget what we had been talking about after so long?

I wasn't that stupid.

Actually, I was willing to bet that I was the most intelligent of the group.

But about thirty seconds in, I got lost in the gray of her eyes and the smell of lilies engulfed me. It became hard to ignore. It seduced me, beckoning me forward. I wanted to lean in.

But that wasn't a sensible idea at all.

We were sitting so close now.

I wondered if she was thinking the same, and for a moment I let my mind run away with the idea.

Of how it would feel to press my lips against hers.

Run my hands through her hair and hold her close.

Just for a moment, the world could fizzle away.

And I was starting to forget what we had been talking about. The trance broke when she finally spoke again. "You're smart, Ares."

I laughed, suddenly reminded of the serious nature of our conversation. How ironic she had chosen this moment to call me smart when I had been thinking the most foolish thing in the world. Even if I stayed, for her the feelings would never be mutual. I was no match for the Alpha. I could never be good enough for her.

I took a moment to appreciate her admiration before I came to my senses. "You're avoiding the question." I cocked an eyebrow as I called her out.

She rolled her eyes and leaned her head against the wall. "Wipe that smirk off your face." She smiled for the first time since the conversation started. "I'll tell you, but not whilst you're looking at me like that."

"Like what? This is just my face." I tried to play it off.

"Like you know that you've outsmarted me."

I took a deep breath but it did nothing to hide the smile on my lips. "I'm sorry, but I can't."

She laughed quietly and continued to hold eye contact as she planned what to tell me. "You want the truth?"

I was baffled and it clearly showed on my face. "Always." Why would I want anything *but* the truth in this situation?

"I don't know."

"What do you mean, you don't know?"

I assumed that she was wondering if she could trust me, but the following silence revealed that her answer was her truth.

I was stunned. "But you're the Alpha. I thought that you were the girl with all of the answers."

"Then you thought wrong. I'm the girl who keeps everyone working as a team. I'm not a farmer, they only tell me what they want me to know, the same as you guys. But I have a theory," she said.

"Oh, pray tell?"

"This is a science experiment, so it'd be unethical to hold us here against our will."

I was more than a little disappointed with her theory. Nothing about The Farm so far had been ethical. "It's also a training facility," I reminded her. "Do you really think they'd let me walk?"

"I like to think that they would. People have left in the past," she said.

I wasn't convinced. The farmers didn't seem like nice people, and after seeing the way that Marshall had treated Shyla last night, I presumed that he'd actually enjoy getting rid of anybody who opted out. He was the leader's slaughterman.

"There's too much risk." I shook my head as I recalled the way that Shyla had mutated. If she did so outside the fence, then the enemy would take notice.

"So why do you want to leave if you think they'll try to kill you first?"

I took no time in replying. "They've tried to kill me more than once today already. Why not add another tick to the tally?" It was a sad joke and I didn't laugh. "At least I'd have a chance of surviving if they let me leave, whereas I'd surely die here. I just don't want to be the source of pain. It's not who I am."

Lora pursed her lips and we watched through the window as a flock of birds flew south for the winter. I wished that I could be as free as they were. No responsibility. No rules to abide by. I wondered if Lora felt the same.

"Would you ever walk?" I asked.

She shook her head in a firm 'no'. She didn't have to consider it. "An Alpha's love for their pack is eternal. I could never leave them."

I believed her. I could feel the pride and worry radiating from her, and I broke into a sweat as I panicked over the idea of leaving Lora. She was bound to the pack by an invisible force, whether she liked it or not.

It was all she had ever known. Her only goal was to guide the pack to victory.

"What, for argument's sake, if you weren't an Alpha?"

Lora shook her head and paused, as though this was a new thought to her, and then the air left her in a winded gasp. Being an Alpha meant that she would always put the pack and their needs first, she probably had never even considered having another option.

Something in her expression changed, as though imagining this life was a weight off her shoulders. Her eyes softened as she fell into the image of a stressless world.

"I would want to leave." She confirmed after a few seconds of weighing her options. "I would try to get far away from it all. In an ideal world, I'd find a cottage on the coast somewhere; tend to the flowers in the garden whilst I listen to the sound of the waves crashing in. I'd like to learn to paint. And I'd sing along to any old music I could find without the worry of anyone judging me." A sad smile crossed her lips. "God, it's been so long since I've heard real music, not the stuff that they play in the common room, music with lyrics..." she rambled. "Oh! And I'd want a dog, and maybe one day find somebody to share my home with..." Her eyes filmed over as she built the dream, and a frown appeared as what started as a sweet sentiment transformed into a nightmare. "I'd choose freedom."

It was the perfect image of a world she could never have, for as long as Lora was Alpha, she could never leave. She had to put everyone else before herself.

I suddenly felt guilty for putting the idea there.

She spoke so quietly, her voice frail. "Yeah, I'd risk it all to have that…"

Our eyes met but neither of us spoke.

We'd reached a common ground, both wanting to escape, to run from responsibilities, but neither of us was willing to tell anyone else about it.

She looked away and I assumed that it was to hide the tear that crept down her cheek which she wiped away as though she were moving her hair.

"Lora…" I started but I had no idea where I wanted the sentence to go.

I wanted to comfort her. Physically. It's what she needed. But I recalled how I had reacted to her fingers on my arm, and I knew that I couldn't control the nerves enough to do the same for her.

"We'll find you that cottage by the sea," I whispered. She looked at me, not staring as she had earlier, but this time *really* seeing me. The Farm and the pressure of the war had changed her, as it would change us all, and I questioned if she had actually been telling the truth about her early days. "One day, when the war is over," I added.

Our moment was pure but short-lived. At the mention of war, she rebuilt her walls, windows and all, and cast me out once more. "I fear that the war will never be over in our lifetime," her voice remained sad, yet it no longer sounded frail. "And if you do choose to leave you won't be able to avoid it. It's not that simple, you know?" Lora shook her head as she spoke and then paused in dread, realizing what she had just given away with wide eyes.

Any other hybrid wouldn't have noticed, it would have gone straight over their heads.

But not me.

"Why isn't it that simple?" I held my breath. "What aren't you telling us, Lora?"

She seemed hesitant and my heart started to race for a different reason.

"I can't say." She squinted her eyes closed and I could see that she was internally screaming at herself. "Please just trust me on this one?"

I nudged her with my elbow. "Can't, or won't? Oh, come on, you can't leave me hanging like that. I promise that I won't tell anyone." I crossed my heart.

She paused and scowled. "You did this on purpose."

"What?" I was taken aback by her sudden accusation.

"Trying to lower my guard and then squeeze information from me when I'm at my most vulnerable. You wanted me to slip up."

"Woah." I held my hands in surrender. "I don't know what you've been through, Lora. I'm guessing it's a lot for you to assume the worst in me straight off the bat, but that wasn't my intention. I promise that you can trust me."

She gave me a look which promised that she didn't trust anyone at all as she considered whether or not to enlighten me with the information that she had been withholding from the pack for so many years. "I'm sorry, I guess I'm just a little rattled."

She wiped the hair away from her face and took a deep breath.

"So…" I pushed. "You know that I won't drop it until you tell me."

She didn't want to share her secret. She'd already shared more with me this afternoon than she'd intended, but she caved. Maybe it was pity. "If you stay for one more day then I'll tell you."

"You drive a hard bargain, Alpha," I muttered as I considered my options. This was classified information, and I needed to know it.

To stay for one more day and risk my life to the anger-inducing challenges? Or to go; unprepared, alone, at the risk of never finding my parents, or being resented by them if I did? All the while trying to avoid a war that apparently wasn't as simple as it seemed.

And that's if the farmers didn't kill me first.

I closed my eyes and hit my head back against the wall.

As much as I hated myself for my decision, I concluded that I would have to be stupid to leave now. I'd survived one day on The Farm, I knew the deal. But I didn't have a clue what would await me if I decided to leave.

I just had to grit my teeth and cope with the challenges a little longer. I'd managed to do it today. Without mutating. Without hurting anyone.

"One day," I confirmed. "On the condition that you tell me what you know. Right now."

She considered before replying, "Okay."

Her tone seemed less agreeable.

I could sense the nerves radiating from her as she spoke. She gripped her thumb with her fingers and squeezed, before leaning in to whisper into my ear. Her eyes darted around to make sure that nobody was listening and when she spoke, I barely heard her myself. "The enemy…"

Her voice wavered.

Whatever she knew scared her.

The reluctance. The pressure.

She didn't want to tell the rest of the pack because she knew that it would scare them too.

Nobody would want to train for a war that they couldn't win.

But at the same time, I questioned what could be so bad about the enemy to make her act this way? Enough for her to fear the thought of me leaving The Farm at all. Enough for her to fear even *telling* me about them.

Did I really want to know?

"The enemy…" I prompted, and the longer she let it hang

in the air, the more nervous I became.

My heart was pounding.

The anticipation and nerves made a claim over my lungs, affecting me almost as much as the next three words.

It suddenly made sense.

Marshall's craziness.

Tim's irritation.

Dr White's emotion.

She closed her eyes and squeezed her thumb tighter as she replied.

"They're not human."

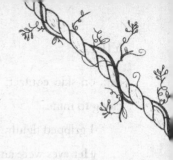

CHAPTER
NINE

ARES

It's strange how three small words could change the way I perceived the world.

It all came crashing down at once.

Lands crumbled away; seas turning red and thick as blood; animals twisting and turning into shadows of creatures I no longer recognised until I didn't know what to imagine of the world at all...

It was the stuff of nightmares.

There was no longer a line between the possible and the things I had once regarded as make-believe.

If man was no longer in control, then I begged to question: what *was*?

Lora held my hand in an act of comfort. Any other time I would have been worried about my sweaty palms and the rush of skin-on-skin contact, but I barely even noticed it as her fingers clung to mine.

I gripped tightly.

Her eyes were an image of relief. Finally, she could share the burden with somebody else. The secret's shadow was a little less dense now that she was able to talk to me about it.

I needed to know everything that she knew. I had assumed that the war was more World War Three, a fight between men. An apocalypse had never even crossed my mind. "What do you mean? Not human?" I asked, but my voice sounded more of a squeak than audible words.

"Not here." Lora shook her head.

"Then where?" I asked.

Lora had been right; I couldn't leave yet. I needed to know more about the situation before I could even consider walking away from the safety of The Farm.

I almost laughed at myself.

So now The Farm is safe?

A cough interrupted our conversation and we both turned quickly to find Tye standing on the ladder.

"What's going on up here then?" he asked, his knuckles turning white as he studied how close we were sitting.

Out of shock and worry that he'd overheard our conversation, we quickly stood. Lora dropped my hand and rushed toward Tye. She kept her voice low, and all previous signs of fear for the enemy had been swept away as though they had never been there at all. "What did you hear, Tye?" she demanded.

He didn't reply straight away. He took some time to glare at me and I quickly learned that I wasn't the only one around here who had growing feelings for Lora.

"Enough," he snapped, climbing the remainder of the ladder and onto the overlook with us.

He was aggravated. I sighed in relief. That meant he hadn't heard about the revelation, only our last few words. I understood how that could provoke jealousy if taken out of context.

Apart from using him as a human crutch earlier today, I hadn't yet spoken to Tye. I'd tried to reach out to him the night prior, as he'd stared at Torn's blood, but he had ignored me. He wasn't the most friendly.

"Holding hands, arranging a rendezvous. What the hell, Lora? If this is some kind of sick joke then I'm missing the punchline."

Oh, he was *so* in love with Lora. It was obvious to now; the way that he followed her around and his constant need to impress her. He was definitely the overprotective type and it rang warning bells in my mind.

"And Ares, of all people? You've known him for all of five minutes. He's not warrior material!" Lora let him rant. "I just don't understand. He's weak. I know it, and you know it. He'll be dead come this time tomorrow."

I looked to Lora, the glare in her eyes insisted that she would throw me off this farm herself if I told him the truth. I just wanted to be rid of the situation so that we could get back to the more pressing matters at hand.

I just didn't know how Lora would clean this one up without telling Tye what we had really been discussing.

"It's exactly what it looks like." She stepped between the two of us.

The air left his lungs in a winded gasp. Tye shook his head. His jaw twitched as he fought back the anger. "I beg you not to continue with this, Lora. What will the farmers do to him if they don't agree? What will they do to *you*? You can't be with him, you're our Alpha."

I unintentionally rolled my eyes. "So, what? She doesn't deserve happiness?"

"Stay out of it!" they both snapped in my direction and I held my hands up in surrender.

I'm obviously missing something here.

I was more involved in the situation than Tye, yet he seemed to have the upper hand in the conversation. I decided to do as they said; keep my mouth shut, and listen.

Tye shook his head in disgust and tried to sway Lora from a different angle. "You know what happened to Donnah for falling in love, right?"

Who's Donnah?

"Of course I remember," she said.

"What happened to Donnah?" I asked, forgetting that I was supposed to be keeping quiet.

Tye turned to me with daggers in his eyes. "What the hell is wrong with you, Ares? All of your questions? Your constant need to break every rule in the book? It's like you're trying to get yourself killed. You're not normal, man."

I agreed with him. I wasn't normal.

At that moment, the bell announced the arrival of dinner and we stared at each other without saying another word. The conversation was far from over, yet I feared that Marshall and his gun would dampen the barn any minute.

"Later," Lora whispered to Tye.

Without another word, we quickly descended the ladder and made our way to the stalls.

Tye waited for me at the bottom and pinned me against the wood with his arm. He was short, but *damn* was he strong. "If I ever see you talking to Lora again, I'll squash you like a bug. I won't let you drag her through the dirt." He leaned his elbow into my shoulder, emphasizing the squashing. "You get me?"

I nodded.

I got him, but his threat wasn't going to change anything.

I didn't know why Lora would let him believe that we were anything more than friends. She must have known that Tye would react this way, and I was sure that my time here would become even more challenging with Tye's target now painted on my back.

He let me go. I watched him walk back to his stall with a confidence that I could never pull off. He was proud of himself.

133

He'd put me in my place and felt that I was no longer a threat to him.

That was the thing about being a part wolf, I realized; we were very territorial. Did Lora feel territorial over me? Is that why she wanted me to stay?

I closed the door behind me, watching Tye's glare from the stall directly across from mine, and this time I remembered to stand on the cross as the sliding doors opened.

Surely enough, Mad Marshall entered the barn with his gun hiked over his shoulder. He seemed rather upbeat today, walking with a swing in his step which made him look even more psychotic.

Hail had started to break into a sweat, obviously still expecting to be punished for his scrap with Beckle this morning. He had that look in his eyes again and I prayed Marshall would walk straight past him.

Beckle stood with his arms crossed, perfectly at ease.

Mad Marshall dragged the barrel of the gun across the bars of our stalls and it made a sound that rattled my brain. The rest of the hybrids reacted in the same way as I did, holding their hands over their ears and calling out in pain.

Marshall smirked, stopping only when he got to my door. "Tim tells me you've been breaking the rules, Omega." He leaned the gun on top of my door, using it as a tripod, and aiming it in my direction.

I probably should have been scared, but I seemed to have

reached the point where an early death didn't seem like such a bad option anymore.

Staying on The Farm would probably kill me, and leaving was only just as dangerous (if not more so). I had unintentionally made an enemy out of Tye, and I was sure his friends also hated me for my stupidity at the lake earlier. And, to top it all off, Tim would forever try to make my life hell for my immaturity.

I needed to do better, but I feared that it was already too late. I'd already made so many mistakes; ones that I couldn't take back. They'd haunt me for the rest of my days on The Farm.

So, once again, I considered if taunting Marshall was a better idea. He could end the misery as quickly as he'd ended Torn's life the night previous.

"How should I know what the rules are, if you never tell us?" I replied. "You never tell us anything."

I felt the eyes of the other hybrids on me as they wondered what I could possibly be thinking. Answering back to Tim was one thing, but Mad Marshall? It was basically a death wish. I counted on it.

At least it would distract him from Hail and Beckle.

Marshall dropped the gun and squared up to me. We were a similar height, but he was built a lot broader. There was no question who would win the fight if it ever came down to it.

Marshall seemed amused by my reaction, his yellowing teeth making an appearance as he chuckled. Apparently, he enjoyed my sudden burst of courage.

"Watch yourself, Omega." He held his hand towards his head, pointing two fingers at his skull like an imaginary gun, and then he turned it in my direction. "Bang," he whispered.

He slowly backed away.

Then he picked up his real gun, spun on his heels, and left the barn.

The pack let out a collective sigh of relief.

"He's nuts," I muttered.

I told Dr White the same thing the next day.

Following breakfast each morning, we were allowed a short counseling session with the doctor. He asked me how I was getting along with the *'staff'*, and so I reeled off every problem I had to him.

"I'd like to speak to the manager," I joked.

"We're not permitted to tell you who runs The Farm, Ares."

I nodded. "I assumed as much. You like to hide all of the important things from us."

This spiked the doctor's attention. "Such as?"

Crap.

"Nothing in particular…" I said. "I just have so many questions and nobody is willing to answer them." I wasn't sure if the farmers had been able to hear my conversation with Lora last night. She'd done her best to stay quiet, so I played along as though the doctor wasn't aware of it.

"I've noticed that you are a lot more curious than the rest."

"I feel like I don't fit in because of it. They just accept that this is their fate, but if I'm going to war, I want to know the context, I need to know how the war started, and why we're engineered in this way. I need to know why the violence is necessary."

He paused. "I will try to answer your questions as far as I'm permitted to so long as it will help you relax into your position on The Farm."

A flood of relief washed over me. This was the best news I'd heard since... ever.

"When did the war start?"

"2033." The doctor wrote in my folder as we spoke.

"What started the war?"

He chose his words carefully. "There is no certain answer to that question, Ares. Usually, you cannot pinpoint an exact moment throughout history which marks the start of a war. There are only a series of events that lead to it. In this instance, I would call it overpopulation."

"So, this group started killing because they thought that there were too many people on the planet?"

"No. Yes. It's a difficult question to answer under the conditions I'm forced to abide."

It was enough for me. Dr White gave nothing away, yet Lora's secret patched up the missing information. Whoever, or whatever, they were; they were intent on wiping out humanity. That much had become clear.

"You told me a couple of days ago that we were losing the

war. So why are we still fighting? I know there must be more to the story, things you're not telling me."

Dr White closed his eyes. He wasn't used to hybrids behaving this way. He realized his mistake. "I cannot tell you, Ares."

I nodded. "I understand. How many of us are left? Judging from the stress levels of the farmers I've met, I assume that the stakes must be pretty high?"

"In this country, we have four known allies. They're safe zones, like The Farm." He sighed and rubbed his hand over his face. "I shouldn't have told you that."

I smiled. Enough of the war. I had more questions for the doctor. "So, who first decided that experimenting on kids was okay?"

He slammed his pen down, pursing his lips and squinting his eyes at me through his glasses.

"I like you Ares, and I do have high hopes for you. Although you're not the strongest or the fittest, your mind is promising. It draws you apart from the rest of the group and it makes you dangerous. You remind me a lot of my younger self." He studied me. "You'd be intelligent to keep this information quiet. If I'm to share with you, I need to know that you won't take it any further. Not even your Alpha may know."

I nodded. I'd take any intel, no matter the conditions. "Of course."

"The only reason I'm telling you is to help you fit in, I'm not favoring you in any way."

I nodded again in understanding and he sighed once more, studying me; trying to see if he could trust me.

He glanced up to the ceiling, shaking his head, and then took off his glasses and placed them on the table between us. "We found that the process isn't as successful on adults. The metamorphosis is most successful whilst the human is still growing, meaning that the new abilities are amplified to their utmost potential. As the war went on, we could offer safety to those who needed it, children, especially. Your parents accepted the conditions that you would be kept safe until you were able to fend for yourself, and in return, we'd give you the tools and training needed to fight the war."

"Did my parents know that you'd be experimenting on me?"

There was a dead silence. "Yes."

"Did they know you'd be trying to kill us in the process?"

Dr White shook his head. "We don't try to kill you, Ares. We always hope that the experiment will be successful, but the weaker hybrids wouldn't make it on the other side of the fence, and if the enemy got ahold of a hybrid... God only knows what would happen. For the safety of us all, filtering out the weaker hybrids is vital."

I didn't miss a beat. "So, if I wanted to leave The Farm, would you let me?"

Dr White gritted his teeth, realizing that he'd walked straight into another trap, and scowled. He clicked the top of his pen twice before replying. "Un-permitted."

The lack of an answer was answer enough, and I took a moment to mourn Shyla and the previous hybrids who had asked to leave, only to find themselves face to barrel with a farmer's gun. Most likely Marshall's. I had almost found myself in that same situation. I would have, too, if not for Lora.

"I feel a lot better after this conversation, thanks, Doc." I lied.

What could I possibly do now?

After some more note-taking, he put his pen on the desk and joined his hands. "I've always worried that telling hybrids the truth would scare or overwhelm them."

"I felt scared and overwhelmed waking up here with no sense of history or connection. We're still people at the end of the day. Now I have context, I can see why the work that you're doing here is so important. I have more of a reason to try, other than just being told to. I'm connected on a personal level."

If Lora hadn't slipped me some useful information last night, none of this would have made any difference. But knowing that the enemy wasn't human made this conversation much more insightful.

"So you will consider mutating in the challenges?"

I smiled.

Of *course*, this had all been a ruse on his behalf to convince me into playing along with their challenges, even if I had squeezed more out of him than he had been willing to let go.

140

"Yes," I lied once more.

But the truth was, I would hold off for as long as I possibly could. Just because the beings outside of the fence weren't human, it didn't change my worry about unintentionally hurting others.

I stood. "We're on the same team, Doc," I added. "It's time that The Farm understands that, and stops treating us like animals."

Dr White nodded slowly and flipped through the pages in my folder. I was on my way to the door when the doctor spoke two names that I would forever hold in my heart. "Joe and Samantha Smith."

My parents.

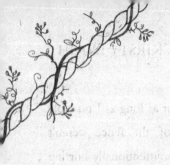

CHAPTER
TEN

ARES

The stink of testosterone became stronger with each step closer to the common room. The source of the smell was Tye, who sat next to Lora. Go figure...

He gave me the sort of look that said *'I know something you don't know'*, and my rage spiked at the thought of it.

Knowledge was quickly becoming an obsession. I didn't care how dangerous a situation could become, so long as I learned something in return. I didn't even consider the risk of walking towards Tye whilst he sat next to Lora. It was only when panic rose through Lora's eyes that I realized it would create an unwanted conflict, so I tried to distract myself with the first thing that came to mind.

The fish tank to my left.

I made myself appear interested in the fish, but I used the reflection in the glass to spy on Tye and Lora. From what I could gather, Tye had considered my retreat a victory. He kept his eyes on the back of my head, but he smiled as Lora whispered to him.

Lora looked beauti-

Pull yourself together, Ares.

Fed up.

Lora looked fed up.

Were they talking about me? About what happened last night? Lora had told Tye that the conversation wasn't over; were they finishing it now without my prying ears?

"Which is your favorite?" A voice appeared over my shoulder. I was so focused on their conversation that I hadn't noticed Jayleigh approach.

"Crap, don't creep up on me like that!" I tried to hide how startled I felt.

"You're a hybrid. Your hearing is supposed to be impeccable. I shouldn't be able to creep up on you at all," she noted and then paused. "Well?"

"Well, what?"

She nodded in the direction of the tank. "The fish. Which is your favorite?"

Oh...

"Um." I pointed to the first fish I saw. "The orange one."

"Benny?" she sounded baffled. "Really? Interesting..."

I shrugged. "How so?"

She looked back to the tank before realizing that I hadn't been looking at the fish at all. She stared at the glass and then turned to face Tye and Lora.

"Don't!" I turned her around quickly by her shoulders. She smirked and nudged my bicep with her fist. "Ow…"

"You've got a thing for Lora!" She seemed so excited that if I'd poked her with a pin she might have popped.

"No-" I shook my head quickly. "No. There's no *thing*. Not any more than any other hybrid. Just the Alpha Effect." I tried to pass it off, but I was just lying to the both of us.

"Oh, you have been spending *way* too much time with Hail." She looked at me, and then back to Lora in the reflection of the tank. "You are one smart cookie."

"I don't know what you're talking about."

"You're blushing. God, you're such a cutie." She squeezed my cheek and I slapped it away, looking around to make sure nobody was watching. "Don't worry. Your secret is safe with me." She winked.

"Please don't…" I shook my head. "Can we switch subjects?"

"Sure. How much would you give to punch Tye right now?"

"Please stop."

This was not good; Tye thought something was going on between Lora and me; Jayleigh knew that I had feelings for Lora; and to top it all off, the farmers were potentially planning my painful death because I was 'distracting' Lora from her duties.

"I'm just messing with you." She giggled.

"I know…" But that didn't mean I liked it. I desperately tried to change the subject. "So, which is your favorite?"

She pointed to the large gray fish with blue spots. "Dotty."

"Dotty? Really?" I mimicked her earlier reaction.

"Dotty would batter Benny in a fight."

I raised an eyebrow and laughed. "Oh, I didn't know that we were picking favorites based on how well they would do in a fight. Can I change my answer?"

"I'm afraid that I can only accept your first and final answer. You're stuck with Benny now."

"Fantastic."

Our conversation ended as a woman entered the common room, tablet in hand and a stern look on her face. She could have been Tim's sister or cousin, sharing his mountain-like build, similar skin tone, and bored-to-hell facial expression.

"Fall in!" she ordered, and we followed her single file to the gym.

After the same warm-up as the day before, we took a leisurely climb of the rope of doom to reach the surface. The rope was just as difficult as the previous day but I kept reminding myself that I'd done it before, and so I could do it again.

Everyone else followed, gathering in a huddle near the lake.

"Field trip." Tim's sister read from a tablet fastened to her wrist as though it held some sort of top-secret information, shielding it from us with her spare hand. "We're trying something

145

new. Usually, we'd never let you train at the same time as the Veno pack, but today you're going head to head."

Nerves fluttered through me. I had so many questions about the Veno pack but I hadn't yet been given the opportunity to ask anyone. Lora had avoided me all morning, probably in worry that I'd ask more questions, or that Tye would create a fuss if he saw us together. I could feel his glare every now and then, and I wondered if he had a hidden ability to use laser beams through his eyes; it sure felt as though his gaze was burning holes into the back of my skull.

I felt relieved when the coach's speech came to an end. "You will hike to the top of Four and await further instruction. Time starts now."

I stood and waited for somebody else to head off first, not understanding what 'Four' was. I fell to the back of the pack and walked in time with Hail.

"Care to help out an old friend?" I asked.

"I don't like that you call yourself my friend. Didn't you learn a thing on your first day?"

I rolled my eyes. "Do you mind explaining what's going on?"

"We're walking to the top of Mount Four." He pointed around to the various mountains in the area, counting them all. "Then we'll have a head-to-head challenge with the Veno pack."

"And, what about the Veno pack? They're like us?"

Hail laughed. A few heads turned our way to see what the

commotion was about, and I wondered exactly the same thing. "No, the Veno pack are nothing like us."

"But they're hybrids, right?"

"They were experimented on, just like us. They live in a barn, just like us. That's about where the similarities stop."

Jayleigh had fallen back to walk with us after hearing the laughter. "They have different... qualities," she finished. "Whereas our instinct is to come up with a plan, consider things, only mutate when necessary, the Venos... Yeah, they're pretty much the opposite. They're always ready for conflict, not afraid of anything. They seem to get off on the idea of killing people. You can see it in their eyes."

"Their eyes? So you've been in the same room as them before?"

She shook her head. "Sometimes, instead of training, the farmers will show us videos of the Veno pack's victory from the day before. We're asked to analyze what they did right and what we did wrong."

"In the library," Hail added. "That's where they show us the videos."

Jayleigh looked dumbfounded, obviously unaware of my previous library conversation with Hail. "I think I can speak for the rest of the Titaniums when I say that the idea of training with the Venos is a bad one."

I could imagine why.

"What do we get if we win?" I questioned, wondering if it

would be worth the fight.

By the sound of his voice, Hail's saliva glands were tingling just at the thought. "Nice food."

"And thirty minutes in the rock pools," Jayleigh added. "It's such a treat. It feels like heaven after using the cold shower in the barn for so long. But, we always seem to win the tasks that involve using brainpower, the Venos tend to win the physical challenges. Taking into consideration that we're currently climbing a mountain, we're not going to be winning anything today, so don't get too excited."

The road began a steady incline which wouldn't relax until we reached the top of Mount Four. I followed it with my eyes as it meandered around the natural dimples of the land, passing an old brick house that crumbled on the side most exposed to the weather. The tiled roof caved and the windows had cracked over time. I wondered who had lived there previously; whether the past owners of the building now worked on The Farm, and whether they'd mind me camping out in there whilst the rest of the Titaniums continued our mission.

I was struggling not to pant, unfit in comparison to the other hybrids.

"Breathe, Ares." Jayleigh nudged my ribs. "You've only been here two days, it's okay to struggle in the first few weeks."

I gasped, trying to relieve the shock. She was stronger than she looked. I should have expected it; all hybrids were. "I doubt I'm going to make it a few weeks."

Hail and Jayleigh shared a look as the words left my mouth. "You won't if you keep thinking like that."

I shook my head, on a serious note now. "Come on, guys. I'm not warrior material." I quoted Tye's words from last night. "I know it, and you all know it. I'm just a sheep in wolf's clothing."

Jayleigh shrugged. "I've never heard of a warrior who refuses to mutate," she started. "But maybe you can make it work."

"Don't just tell me what I want to hear."

Hail looked back at the scenery as we spoke, I joined him, noting how small the lake looked as we climbed further and further away. The two barns looked as though they could have been neighbors.

Jayleigh tried to explain herself. "Like the Veno pack are known for their attack, we Titaniums are known for our intelligence."

I looked to Hail who was still gazing off into the distance as I pondered. "Right…"

"Maybe the warrior frame of mind doesn't come naturally to you, but you do seem to have more intelligence to make up for it. Even if you're lacking common sense."

I shot her a look.

"Speaking back to the farmers is not something that anyone with common sense would do." She held her hands in surrender as she justified her answer, and I shrugged it off. "As I was saying. If you can find a way to harness both sides equally you'd be a force to be reckoned with." She could see the doubt written across my face, but her theory reminded me of Dr White's words. "Of course, some pack members differ from the others, Hail isn't the brightest button in the box-"

"Hey!"

"But he's the only hybrid who has managed to evolve."

There was a pause.

I thought I'd misheard to start with.

"What?"

Evolving was so openly talked about, so encouraged, I'd assumed it was more common.

"He's the *only* one?" I felt shocked and confused and somehow, a little betrayed. I felt as though I had been lied to. "What was it like?"

Hail's eyes clouded, warning me not to push any further. "I don't want to talk about it."

He seemed angry at the thought of evolving, and I couldn't understand why. Evolving was the highest state, it's what we all strived for. Hell, even I'd evolve if it meant I got to keep control whilst accessing the mutant powers. "But why? If it can help-"

"Leave it, Ares." I heard the warning in his voice this time too, almost like a low growl as he spoke. Jayleigh rested a hand on my arm, holding me back.

"It could w-"

"It didn't help Donnah, and it won't help you!" he snapped

and I stumbled back in fear that he might hit me or worse.

He didn't, thankfully, do either.

Instead, he picked up his pace and marched to the front of the pack, putting as much space between the two of us as possible. I didn't run after him. He needed time to cool off, and besides, I couldn't have moved any faster than my current pace if I'd tried.

An awkward silence lingered between me and Jayleigh, occupied by my heavy breathing.

I should have listened when she warned me not to push any further.

I assumed that she was thinking the same as we trailed at the back of the pack. She didn't support the way that I'd acted, yet she continued to walk beside me, despite my behaviour.

"I'm missing something here," I noted. "Who is Donnah and why does Hail get upset every time her name is mentioned?"

Jayleigh seemed to hold her breath for a while before replying, darting her eyes between Hail and Beckle. It was obviously something that the pack was trying hard to forget.

"Donnah... God, where do I begin?" She shook her head and lingered in the silence. For a while, I thought that she was going to drop the subject. I focused on perfecting my breathing techniques instead of wondering if I'd ever get an answer to the pack's best-kept secret.

"Were you close?" I asked eventually.

My persistence broke through and Jayleigh let out a long

sigh. "No, I've never really been close to anyone here."

"So you'd be the best person for me to ask."

She hated that it was true.

"Donnah was very caring, very sweet," she spoke quietly so nobody else could hear, holding back to put more space between us and the rest of the pack. "I always presumed she wouldn't make it. She seemed so timid, fragile almost. Both Hail and Beckle fell head over heels for her, and over time she became very close to Hail. They used to spend every evening watching the sunset on the overlook, they'd train together, and eat lunch together. As time went on, Beckle became more and more jealous, and one day he found them kissing. Beckle, being the oh-so entitled person he is, didn't take the news well and a fight broke out."

She stopped as the memory became too much.

"The farmers found out, and I'm sure you can guess who was first on the scene?"

"Marshall..." I muttered. I didn't think that it was possible for me to hate him more than I already did, but I was about to be proved wrong.

"The farmers usually don't care for relationships, they take away our ability to reproduce so there's no real threat, so long as it doesn't upset the flow of The Farm," she continued.

I interrupted. "But the fight did?"

"Of course."

I questioned if I really wanted to know what happened next.

My heart said no, but my mind kept playing through different possibilities and theories. If I didn't ask, I'd risk once again putting my foot in my mouth around Hail. I had already upset him once and I didn't want to do it again.

"So, what happened?"

Jayleigh shook her head. "Your curiosity is going to be the death of you," she joked, but the sadness that drowned her submerged the punchline too. "Are you sure you want to know?"

"No, I don't, but I feel like I *need* to. I can't say anything else that might upset Hail."

My reply was met with nodding.

"I'd better give you the details then."

I knew that I was asking a lot and it pained me to make her relive it, but there was nobody else to ask.

"Marshall told her that only one of them could stay, and it was up to her to choose. She was handed Marshall's taser and told to pick one. But, Donnah being Donnah... She couldn't do it. She only had feelings for Hail, but she didn't want Beckle's blood on her hands. She couldn't live with the fact that her happiness had cost somebody else's life.

"Beckle should have been the bigger man and stepped down. He claimed to love her; if he loved her more than he loved his own ego then they all could have lived. But he only made things more difficult for her. He didn't want to die and he was practically begging in the end. Nothing he could have said would have helped Donnah in that situation... Nobody should have to make a choice like that."

I felt an odd sort of connection to Donnah, probably because, like me, she opted against the violence. I imagined myself in her position and knew exactly what I would have done.

"She chose to remove herself from the situation..." I finished.

Jayleigh nodded slowly.

"What happened to her?"

"She was taken away. The next day Hail and Beckle woke in the forest with a note in their hands. The farmers took mercy on Donnah for sacrificing herself and wanted to give her a second chance, but it was up to Hail and Beckle to save her.

"They had five minutes to find her. Hail could hear the screaming and it pushed him enough to evolve. He truly loved her, you know? Her death completely broke him."

It had. I recalled Hail's warning.

"Don't let yourself get too close to anyone, because it hurts when you lose them."

He was still in mourning, and he was so scared of losing anyone else that he'd shielded himself away, unable to see that friendship was the only way he could begin to heal.

"I almost wish that he'd been just ten seconds later so that he didn't have to watch, but he saw the whole thing and I think he still has nightmares about it; reliving the memory every night, hearing her calling out his name as he found her," she trailed off. "Just a few seconds too late... All he could do was watch as the trapdoor swung open and she dropped with a noose around her neck."

The rest of the walk was quiet.

I could hear murmurs of conversation from the group ahead, but I was stunned into silence. Had the temperature dropped at this higher altitude? I shivered through the layer of sweat I'd built up.

It pained me to think of what Hail was going through. He let himself get close to one person and she was taken from him in the cruelest of ways. He couldn't escape it. It was a living nightmare. He blamed Beckle for starting the fight, and Beckle hated Hail for making a move on Donnah.

The whole situation made me feel sick.

I looked towards Lora and Tye, walking together, and wondered why Lora would have Tye believe that we were in a relationship if *this* is what it could cost? I needed to remove myself from the situation before the farmers did it for me.

I put my concentration back into the hike. One foot in front of the other and repeat. It's all I could do.

Not soon enough, Lora shouted, "We're here!"

The feeling of relief almost collapsed me.

We gathered around a large boulder, taking a seat on anything that looked remotely comfortable. I chose a dry patch of grass overlooking the world outside. This was the first time I'd seen the fence enclosing us within The Farm's boundaries. Even at this distance, I could tell that it stood three times taller than the average man.

There was no need for it to be that tall.

There was no way we could climb it, and I doubted even an evolved hybrid would be able to get past it.

I recalled Marshall accusing Shyla of digging underneath it, and how angry he'd become. And then slow horror sent the hairs on the back of my neck standing. His anger was a result of his fear, and the fence was less about keeping us within The Farm's boundaries, and more to keep *something else out*.

I felt unsettled. Was it the sight of the fence? Donnah's story? Tye's occasional hateful glares? The fact that the Veno pack were near? Low sugar levels?

My hands shook as I reached for a bottle of water from the basket that had been awaiting our arrival. I felt that it was a little unethical to make us walk this far without water at hand. But, on second thought, nothing was ethical about The Farm at all.

The basket also included sandwiches, which we ate quickly, knowing that the Venos could appear at any second. I finished my last few mouthfuls as the rest of the group started to look for any indication of what would follow.

I was keeping an eye out for the opposing team when I noticed a red flag a small way down the mountain, via a different path to the one we'd taken to get there.

"Guys." I pointed towards it, nestled at the meeting point of Mount Four and what I could only presume was Mount Five, where a small river flushed away water collected from the streams and formed a waterfall which dispersed to the forest, fifty meters or so below. "I think I've found something."

Lora rushed forward to see what I was talking about. "Great eye, Ares." She smiled at me and rushed off in the direction of the flag, quickly followed by the rest of the pack. I stared after her.

"Good job, Omega." Indigo patted my shoulder as she passed. I tried my best to cover the shock. She had never made an effort to speak to me at all.

Tye shoved me and ruined my one moment of acceptance. "Nerd."

"Prick," I muttered to myself as I found my place at the back of the pack once more.

The walk to the flag was nerve-racking, stepping down from one cragged rock to another, and made only more daunting by the heavy drop to the left of the path. One wrong move would be fatal; if not deadly.

I felt queasy at the thought of losing my balance, so I distracted myself and made sure to focus only on the path, and not the cliff.

The lower we descended, the more at ease I felt. I managed to make it without slipping and I considered that in itself a small victory, releasing the twinge in my shoulders as we crossed the wooden bridge over the river and towards the checkpoint.

Lora found a note attached to the flag and she read through

it quickly. Her face slowly drained of color. I knew that the following task was not going to be pleasant.

That's when I noticed the ropes on the floor.

"It's a race. The first team to the bottom wins." She confirmed as she held up a bucket of tangled ropes. "Looks like we're abseiling."

"I guess that means that the Veno pack are hot on our tails then," I suggested, as they weren't already on the ground.

"Concentrate on the task and we'll get through it quicker. If we're distracted by the threat of the Veno pack then we will lose time," Lora ordered.

We nodded in understanding and quickly got to work.

I was sure that I'd never been abseiling before, it didn't come naturally to me but everyone else seemed well-practiced. The equipment was passed around and Jayleigh did her best to teach me the ropes as she set them up. We were all responsible for our own safety, so if I tied anything wrong then it would be my own fault. I copied with extreme concentration as she attached her clips.

As I finished, I stole a glance in Lora's direction. She peered over the edge of the cliff, expressionless, and pinched her thumbs. She turned around and noticed me watching, her smile reappearing and seeming almost sheepish. Something told me that she was every bit as nervous as I was.

"Okay?" she asked, her voice appearing confident. She had everyone else fooled, but not me; not now. I'd seen her at her most vulnerable and I recognised that look in her eyes.

I nodded once as I buckled myself in and concluded that I was ready to start. Jayleigh was teaching me how to feed the rope when we heard yelling and shouting from Mount Five.

The Veno pack.

My heart started to race. Every part of me wanted to steal a glance at the opposing pack, to see if the horror stories were true, but I had to stay focused on the challenge. The rest of team Titanium had started the descent down the cliff, and I was left at the top trying to remember Jayleigh's instructions. The ropes were attached. I was clipped in. But I was frozen. I turned to look at the Veno pack, knowing that the fear of the unknown was holding me back, wondering if maybe the image in my head was worse than the reality.

Or maybe not.

The first thing I noticed was the speed and assurance with which they moved, and a confidence that nerved me. They'd already noticed us and were approaching with precision, not blinking an eye to the height or danger of it.

Not blinking much at all, in fact.

Something about the way they moved reminded me of a snake. Movements were smooth and controlled, but their eyes darted around, taking everything in. Different sounds caused a jolting tilt of the head in said direction.

They approached nearer as I leaned myself back over the edge of the cliff, accompanied by the faint ticking of their breath. I didn't know what scared me more; continuing down the cliff face and risking the fall to my death, or being left to the mercy of the Veno pack?

The Alpha of the Veno pack stopped suddenly as he met my eyes. He was tall, not quite as tall as Hail, but certainly a lot taller than me. A noise erupted from within him which resembled both a hiss and caw. His raven hair framed his cheekbones, parted in the middle, and he had a wired energy which seemed to send me into a panicked frenzy.

What struck me most was the craziness in his yellowing eyes.

The ruthlessness.

The hair on the back of my neck raised as I realized that I was in danger. *Real* danger.

My mind screamed for me to move as the Alpha charged forward.

"Crap!" I panicked, fumbling my hands with the ropes. "Cr... Oh, Crap!"

The rest of the Titanium pack were nearing the bottom of the cliff now, I could hear them shouting. They urged me to hurry because we all knew what would happen if the Veno pack got to me before I reached the bottom.

I looked towards the ever-nearing Venos, and then the bottom of the cliff and realized that it was too late.

I'd never make it to the ground before they reached me.

"Intelligence but no common sense," I muttered as I made a

split-second decision. One that could be considered both genius and suicidal.

I quickly unclipped my harness and stepped out of the ropes. Under this intense pressure, there was no way I could have concentrated on feeding the rope through my shaking hands and safely descended my way down the cliff without clumsily dropping myself. Even if I had managed to concentrate, I'm sure the Veno pack would have found a way to cut me off. I wouldn't have been surprised if they had deformed teeth able to chew through the rope, leaving me to fall fifty feet to my death.

The Titanium pack watched as I abandoned my ropes and unclipped myself. They were yelling now; the ones who actually cared about keeping me alive, anyway.

I would have bet my dinner that Tye was rooting for the Veno pack.

I just hoped this worked.

I used the adrenaline pumping through my veins to my advantage, pushing me into a sprint, heading upstream to a point where it was steady enough to jump in.

I tried not to think. There was too much at risk.

The water was cold and fast-moving. As it pushed me closer to the edge, my eyes fell to the Veno pack who now stood over the bridge. They were deadly still. Their wicked gazes pierced my soul as the water picked up speed and threw me over the cliff, hitting heavily against my back. It pushed me down.

I took a deep breath and squeezed my eyes shut.

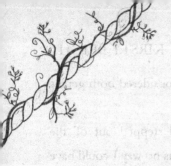

CHAPTER
ELEVEN

ARES

The water pushed me deep into the plunge pool, churning me up and spitting me out on the riverbank further downstream.

My whole body ached. Holding onto the corpse of a fallen tree proved to be a task as the current so desperately tried to carry me away.

Lora and Hail hovered over me with concern, each offering me a hand out of the water.

"That was the single most stupid thing I've ever seen." I couldn't tell if Lora was mad or relieved as she hoisted me out of the river.

"Bro, that was insane!" Hail released my hand to slap it forward and backward in his favorite handshake. I let my hand flop everywhere, not really sure of what he expected from me. It hurt to hold it in the air for too long.

I fell to the grass, turning onto my back and letting my arms fly out to the sides.

"Remind me to never do that again," I choked.

The Titanium pack circled me, some questioning if I needed a doctor. My answer was yes, but I knew that I would be fine enough in a couple of hours.

"We won," I said. Everyone paused their conversations to look at me. "We made it to the ground first."

"I'd rather basic food and a barn shower if somebody leaping down a waterfall is the price we have to pay to win." Lora shook her head in disapproval.

I couldn't see what her problem was. "I would have died. The Veno pack were too close."

"What happened to don't turn back?" Lora questioned. "You hesitated because you watched them approach. If you'd just concentrated on the task as I'd asked then you would have been fine."

Okay, she was mad.

"Would I?" I got up now, not liking that everyone still towered over me. It made me feel small. "Or would I have struggled because I had no idea what I was doing, and ended up falling to my death anyway? Or, I could have been reeled back up by the Veno pack. And God knows what they'd have done to me."

I had risked my life to win us this challenge and rectify yesterday's mistakes, and this was how Lora decided to treat me? She's the one that wanted me to stay, even after I'd told her that I felt like a burden.

This was exactly the reason I had wanted to leave.

The look in Lora's eyes alerted me that she didn't take well to others biting back. Nobody ever challenged the Alpha. She gazed around, knowing that everyone was watching our disagreement and waiting.

"You shouldn't have been in that situation in the first place," Tye piped up as he stepped forward. "First you disobey Lora's orders, and then you argue with her? Complete disrespect!"

"That's enough, Tye," Lora shut him down.

"I don't want to argue. I'm just fighting to see another day, and hopefully do right by you all in the process," I admitted. "I know that my reluctance to merge and my curiosity has created some discomfort, but I promise that I have never set out to intentionally sabotage the challenges. I'm trying to do better."

"You want to do better? Maybe try growing a pair," Tye bit.

I sighed.

Lora stopped him from saying anything more. "It's done now. You did what you thought was right at that moment, even if it's not what was asked of you. We'll all move on from this, enjoy the win, and forget it ever happened. Just don't ignore my commands again." She pointed at me. "And I need to talk to you privately, Tye." She led him off for a scolding.

"Fine by me," I muttered, raising a hand to my twinging neck.

Lora may not have liked my defiance, but I knew full well that I'd made the right decision. I was alive, and I'd hopefully gained a little more respect from the rest of the Titaniums for doing what had to be done in the heat of the moment.

Because that's what it all came down to.

The odds of surviving my training were slim; the odds of leaving The Farm were even more so. If I was going to stay, then I needed to start thinking about my place within the group. I couldn't continue to upset the farmers if it put the pack in jeopardy, and I needed the hybrids' approval or else we'd never be a functioning team.

I looked back to the waterfall, noticing that the Veno pack remained at the edge, hovering over us like birds of prey zoning in on their kill. Why hadn't they made the descent down the cliff? They had the ropes to climb.

Or, maybe intimidation was their game?

I tried not to let it get to me.

We waited for Tim and the woman who'd directed us earlier to make their way over. I took a small peek over my shoulder every now and then to make sure that the Veno pack were still where I'd left them. Every time prepared for the worst.

"Not at all what we expected." Tim was typing something onto his tablet as he approached. "That was a fair jump, Ares. And yet, you seem fine. Nine lives…"

"I had to secure the win," I replied.

Tim tilted his head from side to side and I knew what he was about to say before he even opened his mouth. "You didn't really follow the rules... I do have grounds to disqualify you."

"No! That's not fair. The rules stated that the first team to the ground wins, and we're down here whilst the Veno pack are still up there!" I pointed as I pleaded my case. "I didn't risk my life to lose."

I was already angry from Lora's reaction and Tye's interference, I didn't need Tim adding fuel to the fire.

Tim sighed. "You showed resilience, I will praise you for that." He turned to his companion, they watched over something on the tablet and I figured that the farmers had recorded the challenge on hidden cameras. They chatted for a while in hushed tones, seeming to forget about our advanced hearing.

"We can't give them the win."

"They got to the ground first." The woman argued. "Technically they didn't break any rules. Next time the instructions need to be a little more specific if you want to avoid loopholes. Ares didn't use the equipment provided, but he did as the card asked. You can't punish him for using his initiative."

I was glad that at least one person had my back.

The argument went back and forward for a little while longer before Tim grunted. "I hate you sometimes, Sally." They turned back to face us and Tim reluctantly announced, "The win goes to the Titanium pack."

Everybody celebrated. Hail turned to me to repeat his handshake whilst Jayleigh patted my back. Lora nodded once in my direction but her smile faded as she continued to stare. There was something behind her eyes. For a second I assumed it was hatred, but that didn't make sense. I turned away and tried to ignore it, to get Lora out of my mind.

I couldn't.

Turning back, I found that she had continued to congratulate the pack, but every few seconds her eyes targeted me.

My stomach twisted.

The last thing I wanted to do was upset Lora. I needed to settle things with her once we returned to the barn. This was fixable.

I hoped...

It had to be.

Still, redemption tasted sweet, and although I knew that I had a lot to prove before I'd be fully accepted, I felt that this was a step in the right direction.

We started the venture down the mountain with Tim leading the way whilst Sally stayed behind with the Veno pack to lead them back to their barn.

Jayleigh and Hail walked beside me. It seemed that Hail had either forgotten or forgiven me for what happened on the climb up the mountain. I wanted to apologize and explain myself, but he already knew my reasons. The best thing I could do was drop it because bringing it back up would only dampen our victory. If he ever wanted to talk about it then I'd be there to listen.

And so, nobody spoke.

We were all a little exhausted and the walk seemed never-ending, but just before the sun started to set behind the forest, we reached the silo. Golden light cast down on it like the gates to heaven. We piled into the lift in small groups before gathering on the oval sofa in the common room. The coffee table had been replaced with a dining table, fitting the sofa perfectly and creating a large booth. It was like being at a fancy restaurant.

The smell of food hit me straight away. Thankfully, Mad Marshall wasn't serving today. A woman I'd never met emerged from the lift with a trolly. She was possibly the oldest farmer I'd met, with cropped gray hair and wrinkles dragging at her under-eyes, and she smiled a lot which felt odd.

The farmers never smiled.

Maybe it was because she knew that the food that she presented was fit for royalty.

Beef cooked medium-rare, loaded with vegetables and slathered in garlic and herbs; gravy and a variety of condiments were placed in the center of the table for us to help ourselves to. For a second, I was fooled into believing the image that the farmers were selling.

A glimpse of normality.

A restaurant setting, with amazing food and friends. They wanted us to believe that this could be possible once the war was won. It was motivation.

And I almost bought it, maybe I would have if I hadn't felt so damn awkward under Lora's stare, obviously still annoyed that I'd gone against her wishes, but refusing to bring it up for the sake of the pack. And of course, Tye joined in because he could see Lora looking at me and it was making him jealous. I avoided eye contact with them both for the entirety of the meal. To top it off, Beckle still had it in for Hail, rilled up after their fight yesterday. Hail didn't even seem to notice with his eyes only on the food.

My God, the food... It made it all worth it.

Nobody spoke, even once we'd finished eating.

I felt very content as I leaned back, resting my head on the cushion of the sofa and closing my eyes. I could have slept there and then if Jayleigh hadn't dragged me to the cave pools. We entered through the wooden doors and a salty breeze welcomed us. As soon as the doors closed, everyone began to strip off.

"Woah!" I shielded my eyes but it was too late. "I'll never be able to un-see that." I winced.

Jayleigh laughed at me. "What's wrong?"

"I was happy not knowing what everyone looked like under their clothes, thank you. It feels so wrong."

She laughed. "Why? If you think about it, wearing clothes is more unnatural than walking around naked."

She had a point but it didn't help me feel any more comfortable about the situation, so I hid behind a plant as I

169

undressed and everyone else got into the water, keeping my eyes on the ground.

Once I was sure that nobody was looking, I carried the plant in its pot towards the pool, quickly climbing in and perching on a rock so that I was submerged to my shoulders.

The water was warm, soothing my aching muscles. My body had already started to heal. I washed my hair, brushed my teeth, shaved, and then relaxed into the serenity of the underground oasis, watching the timer above the door tick away and wishing that it would stop. I wasn't ready for this small glimpse of paradise to be over quite yet. It was the calmest that I had felt since waking on The Farm.

Once dry and dressed, we made our way back into the common room where the farmers waited for us on the staircase.

I was ready to get back to the barn. I longed to close the door and climb into the comfort of my bed for a good night's sleep.

We were led from the silo, single file, each with a farmer at our side. I snuck a look to my right. "Oh, Katie! Hi."

She let out a long held breath. "My name isn't Katie," she replied with a somber face. Unlike yesterday, I sensed a nervous energy around her. Every now and then her eyes shifted direction. Her pace was swift.

"Well, until you tell me your real name I will continue to call you Katie. Don't think that you're special though, I have nicknames for other people too. There's Tim's Sister," I referred to Sally, "Mad Marshall, and I just met the Alpha of the Veno pack, I reckon he looks like a Dickward."

She cocked an eyebrow, a little more at ease after my rambling, but not fully. "Really?"

I shrugged. "Do you have a better suggestion?"

She considered for a moment before coming up short. "If you have any sense at all, you'll be sure to stay away from Dickward and the rest of the Veno pack." She spoke through gritted teeth.

"Is that who gave you…" I pointed to the scar over her eye.

"No." She shut me off without any hint of an explanation.

I tried to move the conversation on. "So, how was your day?"

"Fine."

"Ah… Good, good. Mine was horrendous, thank you for asking." She looked at me with such confusion, I guessed that she had never made small talk with a hybrid before. "Have you always been here, on The Farm?"

The silence continued for so long that I expected she had gone back to ignoring me.

"I know what you're doing," she replied abruptly but kept her voice hushed.

I paused. "What do you mean? I'm just trying to be nice."

"I shouldn't be talking to you at all. You're hoping I'll slip up, that I'll feed you some information that I shouldn't."

"No, that's not what this is at all. I- Wait…" It was only

then I realised we'd turned down a different path than the one we'd usually take towards the barn. I had been on autopilot, following the crowd and not paying enough attention to my surroundings. "Where are we going?"

She shook her head, making it clear that she wasn't going to answer any more of my questions.

Ahead, I could see Lora looking around, also confused and wondering where we could possibly be going.

We followed the path for five minutes further, to an area of The Farm that I'd never been to before. We stopped in the middle of an abnormally level field. It was dark now, but small beam lights had been dug into the ground, forming a perfect circle.

Within the ring of lights was a pit, about eight feet in depth. We swarmed around it, but somebody from the back of the line continued to move forward as we stopped in place. My stomach churned as soon as I saw the cap.

Marshall.

My mind spun in alarm.

Of course, it had been too much to ask for a nice night without his presence.

But why would he bring us all the way out here when he could just humiliate us in our stalls?

He was off the grid, hoping that the people running The Farm wouldn't find out, away from the cameras and watching eyes. Was it for me?

Was it because of the challenge earlier?

I had disobeyed the rules to save my life, and now that same decision would be the cause of my death.

Katie's nerves made sense now, but they were nothing in comparison to mine. She knew what Marshall had in mind, and she knew that she was leading me to my death. Could she hear my heart hammering against my chest? Her gun was aimed in my direction, getting ready to shoot if I refused to go willingly.

I braced myself.

"Why can't you just follow the rules?" Marshall stalked around us, his voice calm. I would have preferred any other version of the farmer because every time he used this tone, somebody always ended up getting hurt.

This is when he was at his most psychotic, ready to switch at any moment.

It was the voice of a madman.

We were all thinking the same thing. Eyes flitted in my direction because I was vast becoming known as the rule breaker. But the only thing that I was breaking now was a sweat.

"Haven't I already made it clear," he questioned, "that breaking the rules has consequences?"

He had.

I never listened.

He took his cap off and ran a hand through his greasy hair. I just hoped that Katie would be the one to pull the trigger and not this slime ball. I didn't want to die at the hands of Marshall. I didn't want to give him the satisfaction.

He returned the cap to its rightful place on his head and stepped forward. "Fighting will not be tolerated on The Farm."

I gritted my teeth and clenched my fists, waiting for Katie's push to send me flying into the pit-

Wait.

Fighting?

I didn't-

"No!" I yelled out, and the beef dinner threatened to reshow itself as Hail and Beckle flew into the pit, a cloud of dust welcoming them into the small arena.

Marshall towered over the pair with satisfaction. Beckle was straight to his feet, glaring up at Marshall with hatred in his eyes, whilst Hail coughed into the dirt and looked as though he'd already given up.

"Killing that poor girl didn't kill the rivalry between you, it seems." Marshall wasn't one for sensitivity, he took pride in his gloating. "It's time to settle this once and for all. Only one of you will be leaving that pit alive, and if you refuse to fight then you'll both be left to rot."

Hail turned back to look at me through bloodshot eyes. His cheeks burned red and his eyes began to tear. My heart broke for him. He didn't want this, he never asked for any of it. As I stared at the broken man, I concluded that there were certain instances, such as this, where violence was the only option.

There was no other way out, and this was his opportunity

for closure; his chance to put everything behind him. Once Beckle was out of the picture he'd finally be able to forgive himself for what happened to Donnah. Beckle was a constant reminder of what happened, and so long as he was around, Hail would never be able to move on.

He had to fight, he had no other choice if he wanted to live, much like my situation on The Farm. The only way out was to participate in the farmers' twisted challenges.

Marshall was a starving man, rubbing his hands together and looking as though he were about to tuck into a long-awaited meal. His clap signalled the start of the fight and seemed to slow down time.

The pair stared at each other, not quite believing what was happening.

I didn't know Beckle well, but I knew that destroying his pride and ego would be the easiest way to break him. He carried the characteristics around like an invisible force, nobody could see them, but I could sense them wherever he walked.

"What the fuck are you waiting for!?" Marshall yelled out into the night. He was ready for the bloodshed. He thrived on it.

Hail was still kneeling on the ground when Beckle turned on him. "You piece of shit! Look what you've done now." He started to run his mouth as expected and kicked Hail's stomach in the process. I held in my gasp. "You can't defend yourself, you can't even stand up. Pathetic." He kicked out again. "You call yourself a warrior, but I call you stupid."

Hail grumbled, spat bile onto the ground beneath him, and then quietly muttered something through the pain.

What was he doing?

Was he just going to roll over and give up?

"Get up, Hail!" I yelled, but he refused to listen.

"You could have saved her!" Beckle shouted. This was the first time I'd seen any sort of emotion from him. Usually, his face resembled that of a rock. The frown and resentment didn't look too great on him either. "If you really loved her then you would have."

Hail didn't react, although I imagined that Beckle's words hit like a punch to the gut.

I wasn't the only one shouting as Hail curled into a ball on the floor. Part of me wanted to jump in and defend him because he didn't look like he was planning on defending himself, but what help would I have been? I didn't know the first thing about fighting. Besides, Marshall and Katie wouldn't have let me. I couldn't break any more rules today.

The dirt clung to the blood on Hail's face and clothes as though it were already trying to claim him.

Maybe he had accepted that this was his fate.

Or, maybe he just wanted to be reunited with Donnah.

I was going to do everything in my power to delay it. "Hail, you have to get up!"

Beckle continued to beat him down, shouting about Donnah, but after a while, something in Hail's posture changed.

Relief swelled within me as I clocked on to Hail's game-plan.

Beckle didn't notice. "You didn't deserve her love! What would she think if she saw you now?" He continued to use his words as an attack on Hail's heart, only he didn't realize that Hail was feeding on them, growing, and becoming stronger. "She fell for a wimp."

Hail slowly climbed to his knees with a broken lip and purple eye. His movements were slow but he managed to block an incoming attack from Beckle as he spoke. "There were two of us there that morning. What were you doing whilst I was out trying to save her?" He tried to control the anger for just a moment longer before rising from the dust and towering over Beckle with fury in his eyes. "Where were you?"

Beckle replied with an attempted swipe at Hail's face.

"What were you doing? Because you didn't even call out to her." His voice cracked, and I figured that there was more to this story than he'd ever let on.

"I was looking for her... like you were."

"You're lying!" Hail roared out and threw his rage into his fist, landing it on Beckle's right cheekbone. I became nervous for Beckle as I watched the light in his eyes fade, and his pride and ego abandoned him in his moment of need. He was left standing alone. "You sat and hid like a child!"

Beckle held a hand over his bruised eye with a shocked expression on his face. "You knew... all this time?"

Hail yelled into the night, sharing the truth that he had been hiding for so long. "I saw you hiding behind the bush, crying to yourself. You gave up before starting. You didn't even try! And you have the cheek to tell me that I should have done more!?" He was starting to lose control. "You failed her."

"I froze! Okay?" Beckle retreated until his back hit the wall of the pit. "I was so scared. I don't even remember what happened."

"And you call me useless? You call me a wimp?" Hail threw his anger into his fist but Beckle ducked. The crunch of Hail's knuckles hitting the solid wall left me shuddering. He yelled out in pain and it flipped a switch somewhere inside of him. He threw his head backward and screamed into the night. When he turned around, I barely recognized the expression on his face.

I feared for Beckle now.

A mutated Hail wasn't friendly. The animal controlled him and even I was scared. Beckle did his best to block the attack but Hail was too strong; too consumed; too far gone. The pit quickly became a blood bath as Hail attacked.

We stopped yelling; too traumatized to make any sound at all.

I watched in silence and felt defeated.

Somewhere down the line, Beckle mutated too, and I prayed that it might level out the playing field. But it was already too late. Hail had exhausted him and I couldn't help but compare Beckle to the morning I'd spent in the grave.

Every ounce of energy he exerted was wasted. He spent too

much time trying to fight back when he should have been blocking the incoming punches. It tired him out faster and Hail was only getting stronger.

The human state could understand that. The animal state didn't understand anything except rage, and so Beckle continued to fight back until he couldn't fight any longer.

It became painful to watch.

Hail's actions were beyond recognizable. We tried to reason with him, to calm him down, but it only fuelled him on.

Lora pleaded with Marshall to call off the fight.

"You've proved your point. Beckle isn't able to fight back anymore. It isn't fair! At least let me help them-"

Marshall swatted Lora's comments away with his hand. He was enjoying this too much.

I winced and turned away as Hail bent Beckle's arm back at an ungodly angle. It popped. Beckle screamed out in agony as Hail laughed.

I hadn't known Hail for long, but I knew that this wasn't him.

This was torture.

"Hail stop!" I tried again.

The moment would be scared into my memory and I knew that it would haunt Hail, too. He'd regret his actions come morning. There would be no closure if he continued in this form of revenge.

But, there was only one person who could get him back

from the state of mind that he was in now, and she was dead.

"Think about Donnah!" I panicked. "She wouldn't want it to end like this."

I needed to try anything and everything I could to bring him back from his animal state.

He didn't listen.

He started to press his thumbs into the sockets of Beckle's eyes until he eventually registered my words, and his head snapped back to look at me.

I thought that he was going to leap out of the pit and start on me next, but somewhere in his mind, my words started to sink in. The anger started to fade and the savage expression changed.

It was working.

"Think of Donnah," I repeated.

"Donnah," he replied as though in a trance. His dilated pupils shrank slightly.

"That's it." I held my hands out in front of me as though calming a wild dog.

He paused.

Then his gray eyes started to glow. I thought that the light was playing tricks on me to start with, or maybe I was going a little crazy.

But I wasn't imagining it.

Everything went silent; even the owls held their breath.

He fell still, appearing composed and controlled. The hairs

on the back of my neck stood on end as I took him in. Something about Hail in this moment was both intimidating and magnificent, radiating static energy which left me feeling extremely unsettled.

He was still staring at me, and I didn't dare break eye contact. My skin glazed over with ice. Relief came as he nodded once in thanks and turned away to stalk his audience until his eyes fell upon Marshall who grinned like a child on Christmas Day.

"He has evolved!" Marshall clapped his hands quickly in excitement.

Katie and the other farmers aimed their guns in Hail's direction. Nobody knew what to expect; what Hail would do next. But, if Marshall felt any sort of fear, he didn't show it. He was simply awestruck, unable to see the danger that he had put himself in.

Hail stared Marshall down, and it was only when a pained gasp came from beneath Hail's feet that his eyes fell to Beckle, who was barely recognizable at this point due to the swelling around his eyes, the splits in his skin, and his limbs protruding at unusual angles. And, Hail suddenly registered what he had done.

A small tear escaped his glowing white eyes. "I'm so sorry, Brother." He knelt, placing a hand gently against Beckle's bruised face, and whispered into his ear. "I hope that you will forgive me."

Beckle whimpered and struggled to speak through the

bruising. "Just get it over with."

He didn't want to suffer any longer.

I gasped as Hail quickly complied, snapping Beckle's neck in one swift motion.

We stood around the pit in silence as Hail hoisted himself out of the hole. He leaped over us, leaving a small crater in the ground where he landed. And then he ran off, faster than I'd ever seen anything move in my life.

HIM

I watched the night's events over on the cameras in the Observatory, delighted by Hail's shift into the evolved state, but not thrilled by how it had come to pass, or the chaos that followed.

I yelled orders to the farmers through their tablets, sending some to escort the Titanium pack back to the barn, and others to hunt the evolved hybrid before he escaped.

If Hail had made it passed the fence then there would have been an enormous amount of trouble. The Farm was a sitting duck and the enemy was close, although I hadn't realized quite how close until tonight.

The commotion must have enticed them in. They were

waiting now, aware of The Farm and what existed inside the fence. Just one mistake could have been catastrophic.

As a result, time was becoming an issue and the warriors weren't ready. I was left with only one option...

The doctor wouldn't like it, but he would have to understand that it was no longer about what was best for the animals. If the enemy broke through The Farm's perimeters then everybody would die.

This was about survival.

The Titanium pack had the resources they needed to evolve. Much to my disappointment, Ares had become a valuable asset to them and so long as he stayed alive, the pack had everything they needed to progress.

I kicked off my boots and rested my head back against the chair. It was all becoming too much. I needed a moment to compose myself before putting a plan together for the coming weeks.

I knew that I needed help. This was too much pressure for one person alone, but I couldn't trust anybody other than myself.

I took a sip from the flask.

Too much pressure. All too much.

I pulled open the top drawer and eyed Father's pills. They helped for a short while, even though they'd been sitting abandoned for almost a decade. I'd been taking them for a few months whenever the world seemed to crash down around me.

They calmed the chaos in my mind.

YIELD

They took the weight off my shoulders.

I popped one into my mouth and washed it down.

And then I got to work.

I just hoped that I was doing the right thing. If not, then the human race would truly come to an end.

CHAPTER
TWELVE

ARES

We found Hail sitting underneath a large oak in the dark forest. Lora knew exactly where to look because it's where Hail would feel closest to Donnah, and it was a sad sight to be seen.

The platform which once held Donnah still swung open above his head, but at least the farmers had removed the rope.

Hail sat still, hugging his legs to his chest. He had returned to the Hail I knew, no longer in his evolved state. The oak's branches dipped in as though cocooning the troubled hybrid.

No birds sang.

Everything was still.

We tried to talk to him but he didn't so much as blink, never mind acknowledge us. He'd spent the night there alone, and it appeared as though he hadn't slept at all.

That made two of us.

After Hail ran for the woods, we had been guided back to the barn, all of us shocked into silence. Marshall had run after Hail, along with numerous other farmers, climbing into trucks to hunt down the escapee.

Most of the pack stayed up for several hours; worrying about Hail; expecting his return. We talked about where he might go and what he might do. Would he try to escape? Or would he make his way back to the barn?

The majority retired to bed halfway through the night, but instead, I climbed to the overlook in hopes of seeing something, *anything*, that would reassure me of Hail's safety.

Too many questions circled my mind.

Would the farmers kill him for running off? What would happen if Hail tried to escape?

Lora joined me on the overlook, leaning her head against the glass. We didn't speak. We appreciated each other's company and nothing more. Lora eventually fell asleep with her forehead pressed against the window and I tucked my blanket around her, in hopes it might provide some comfort.

I was starting to drift into a restless sleep when sunlight first appeared. The shuffling of feet on gravel brought my consciousness back, and the doors slid open with no instruction so we knew that it was up to us to find Hail.

We followed Lora to Donnah's tree. I took Hail's right side

whilst Lora took the left, hefting him onto his feet and walking him slowly back to the barn.

Hail was in shock, as were we all.

Dr White awaited our return alongside a couple of farmers in white coats. They carried a stretcher and took Hail briskly away.

Our routine counseling sessions continued after breakfast and I sat in front of Dr White unable to speak.

"I've never seen you this quiet, Ares. Why don't you start by talking about your jump from the waterfall yesterday? How do you feel?"

I shook my head. Had that really been just yesterday? I took a minute to think about my feelings and attempt to put them into words.

"I feel cheated."

The doctor frowned. "Why do you say that?" The chair squeaked as he leaned back and crossed his left leg over his right knee, pursing his hands on top of each other.

"The rules." I sighed. "We were told that the first team to the bottom would win. Yet, jumping down the waterfall instead of using the ropes was classed as breaking the rules. We almost lost the challenge because of it." I was too tired for this… "Who made these stupid rules anyway? And why weren't they read to us on day one? How are we supposed to follow rules if we don't know what they are? It's pathetic."

"It bothers you that you don't know who runs The Farm,

does it not?"

"Of course. I like to know things, and not knowing who is doing this to us is aggravating."

"What would you say to the leader of The Farm if you could talk to them?"

I considered this for a moment. There were so many things that I would say, yet at this moment everything just faded away. I was tired, and I was traumatized.

I looked at Dr White and wondered if it was him pulling the strings. He had a close relationship with all of the hybrids. He knew everything there was to know about The Farm, and from all the farmers I'd met, he was the one to care most about the outcome of the challenges.

"I would tell them that I understand the pressure they're under," I started, "but I would ask them to consider treating us like human beings, and not like animals. We are capable of feeling emotions; of trusting, grieving, resentment, and betrayal. How can we trust a leader who hides away from us? How can we fight a war if we don't know who or *what* we're fighting for?"

Dr white sighed. "Very valid points. We try to treat you as humanely as possible. But we also have to consider our own safety."

"I do understand that, but I don't understand the hatred and disgust that some of the farmers feel towards us. We're just like them, except we've been experimented on. Take Marshall for example…"

Where do I even begin?

A thousand words came to mind all of a sudden and I didn't know which was most appropriate.

"You don't like Marshall?" he prompted.

I almost laughed. "I've never hated anybody more. I think I prefer Dickward to Marshall."

Dr White cocked an eyebrow in question. "Dickward?"

"The Alpha of the Veno pack," I tried to explain.

"Ah, you mean Steven."

Now I did laugh. I don't know what I'd expected; something stronger; less casual. "Steven? He doesn't seem quite so intimidating with that name."

Dr White started to scribble into his notebook.

"So, why don't you like Marshall?" He got back on track.

"He's insane!" the words spilled from me. I couldn't believe that this was an honest question. "He tries to belittle us in any way possible. He'll do anything to intimidate us. Quite frankly, he hasn't actually given me any reason *to* like him."

"And what about the fight last night. How do you feel about that?"

I shook my head and tried to piece together exactly what was going on inside. "It scared me, seeing my friend turn into something I didn't recognize." The image of Hail pounding his fists into Beckle's swollen face flashed behind my eyes. "But everything made sense once he evolved. *That* is why we're here. If the whole pack managed to reach that state of being, we'd be a

189

force to be reckoned with."

Dr White seemed to deflate as a result of his relief. "That is what we are trying to achieve here, Ares. I know that our methods may seem harsh, but it gets the results that we need. Every challenge is carefully planned to evoke a certain reaction from the hybrid."

"So, last night was to push Hail to evolve again? You didn't think that Beckle could have won?"

Dr White shook his head. "I'm not sure that I follow... The fight last night wasn't a challenge, Ares."

I frowned. "But Marshall... He took us out to the field and forced them to fight to the death."

A look of bewilderment passed over Dr White's face and vanished as quickly as it came. "I see," is all he said.

"You weren't aware?"

The doctor pursed his lips. "We would never kill without reason. That is not how The Farm is supposed to function. We're supposed to give everyone a fair chance."

"Then it looks like you and bossman need to have a nice long talk with your good friend Marshall. He's mad, I'm telling you."

Dr White's nostrils flared in a quiet rage. "Thank you for bringing this to my attention." He nodded to me and hastily began to pack a pile of papers into his briefcase. "I will be keeping a closer eye on the farmers from now on. If anything happens which you deem obscure, Ares, please let me know."

"Sure."

I left feeling just as confused as I had upon entering.

I returned to the group in the common room and it wasn't long before Tim appeared to escort us into the library. This was the first time I'd ever ventured into the right-wing of the underground world. The tunnel was narrow and dark, dimly lit in comparison to the rest of the cave and I was more than a little excited to see what the room behind the door contained.

I was underwhelmed.

Hail was right when he said that it held no more than a couple books and a few tables. It did in fact look more like a classroom.

One lonely bookshelf occupied the back wall. Of the book titles I could read from this distance, they were about health and safety, survival in the wild, and a few on global warming.

I grunted. There was no mention of the inhuman species that haunted the planet.

"Take a seat." Tim welcomed us in.

"How is Hail doing?" Lora asked as she took her place at the front of the room.

Tim nodded. "He's absolutely fine. We're just monitoring his levels, making sure that he stays hydrated, the basics. We like to make sure that we absorb as much data from an evolved hybrid as possible."

"You're not hurting him, are you?" I questioned. "He's been through enough over the past twenty- four hours."

"No." Tim, for the first time, actually smiled at me. I wondered if Dr White had already spoken to the farmers about my suggestion. "He's not in any pain. He's resting."

I took my place next to Jayleigh at the back of the room. She patted the chair, inviting me to sit, and whispered, "You've got a great view of Lora from here."

I rolled my eyes.

Tim started by congratulating us on yesterday's victory, once again stressing the importance of keeping to the rules, but then actually singling me out and praising my resourcefulness. I wondered if somebody had slipped something into his flask? He was unusually nice today.

"Over the next few days, you will be learning basic survival skills; how to build a camp, start a fire, make water safe to drink, the list goes on. This is very important stuff so pay close attention, and don't fall asleep." He started to unpack foraged items from his bag, setting them down on the fireproof mat on the table before him. I watched with interest as he demonstrated how to use rocks and sticks to start a fire, making a mental note to use dry grass to ignite the flame.

Then he gave us a chance to try it for ourselves. I made my way to the demonstration zone and copied his actions. I quickly succeeded and returned to my seat, accompanied by the standard "*Nerd*" comment from Tye which starting to expect.

"You're twenty-four. Grow up," I replied as I walked past him.

192

The lesson ended with an introduction to knot tying. It was more complicated than I'd initially expected but as with most things, it became easier with practice.

Tim called the session to a close as we returned the ropes to the basket. "Now, remember what you've learned here today. You may need these skills sooner than you think."

Something about the way he said it caused alarm bells to ring in my mind, but I didn't have too much time to overthink it before he continued, "Make your way back to the barn. Three new hybrids will join you today."

Three?

A thrill of emotions zapped me.

Nerves. Excitement. Fear.

I felt more than a little relieved that the title of Omega would be passed along and I'd no longer be viewed as the least experienced member of the pack. Something about that thought comforted me as we marched back to the barn for lunch.

But, what if they progressed faster than I did?

What if they found their feet within the pack easier than I did?

The air was crisp but cold, the sharp breeze tickled the back of my neck as I walked next to Katie. I didn't want to speak to her today, she still looked wary after last night's events and I didn't want to relive the trauma, so I took in the view instead and tried to ignore my worries about the new hybrids.

The forest behind the lake was no longer the same vibrant

orange that it had been four days ago. The leaves were turning yellow and brown now, shedding into the water below. The tide washed some of the leaves ashore and once dry, they blew across the path and crunched underfoot.

"What month is it?" I asked Katie, forgetting that I'd promised myself not to talk to her today.

"October thirteenth," she replied quietly.

I left the conversation there, appreciating the bird call which filled the silence as we reached the barn and took a seat on the benches to await the arrival of our newest pack members. It felt odd to me, knowing that four days ago the hybrids had been awaiting *my* arrival in a similar fashion.

Jayleigh slipped onto the bench next to me with her broth in hand. "I'll bet you my vegetables that it's going to be two boys, one girl."

I frowned. "Why?"

"They're replacing Torn, Shyla and Beckle. It just makes sense," she said.

What I'd really meant to ask is why she would bet me her vegetables when the last time I'd offered food away she had questioned my common sense, but I didn't dare correct her. "Our numbers are dwindling, it'll be nice to have a full barn."

She nodded. "Back up to nine. I can't believe that we've lost three people in four days."

"I can," I said through a sigh, for as long as Marshall was going rogue, nobody was safe. "What's the routine when the

194

Omegas get here?"

"Fall into line and introduce yourself, that's it. Oh, and try not to freak them out as Hail did with you."

I nodded. It sounded simple enough.

Footsteps approached and the new pack members entered with overwhelmed expressions.

Jayleigh grunted quietly as she realised that she'd lost her bet, and handed her bowl to me as I counted two girls and one guy.

"You can keep your vegetables." I pushed the bowl back with a laugh and joined the back of the queue.

The first girl was short, with eyes the shape of almonds and a big smile which tried to mask the nerves. "I'm Teri." Her voice was recognisable over all other sounds due to its mouse-like quality.

"I'm Ares. It's nice to meet you." I tried not to feel awkward as I registered her scent, burying my nose into her neck. I kept the introduction brief and welcoming, knowing how unnatural this situation seemed.

The next girl was Zee. She was several inches taller than me, with broad shoulders and hair that chopped off just below the ears.

I introduced myself in the same welcoming manner, and she showed no sense of nerves or worry as she waited expectantly for me to lean in.

She wouldn't have a problem adjusting to life here. She

didn't seem phased by any of it.

The last in line was Diego. He had a jawline sharp enough to kill and an accent which I couldn't quite place. Calm and collected. He was almost too cool; it was starting to make *me* feel nervous. I aimed to copy his mannerism as I welcomed him and retook my seat next to Jayleigh to finish my food.

"Hold this whilst I swoon over the new guy." Jayleigh motioned to her bowl as she patted the sweat from her forehead with her sleeve. "What a hunk."

"I bet you said the same thing when I walked through the door." I sipped my broth casually.

A splutter came from beside me as Jayleigh choked on her food, thumping her fist to her chest.

Eyes turned on us as I patted her back, working to dislodge the vegetable. When it didn't budge, I resorted to wrapping my hands around her chest, thrusting against her back until a half-chewed piece of carrot came flying out and landed at Diego's feet.

Jayleigh held her hand up, assuring me that she was okay as she continued to cough, more than aware that Diego was looking between me and her, and the regurgitated vegetable on the ground.

"Death by carrot," I joked to the group as I retook my seat, trying to break the silence. "Who would have guessed I'd be the one saving *your* life today?"

"Death by bad joke," she corrected as the group continued

their small conversations and she returned to her spot on the bench. "And you can't save my life if you're the one to put me in danger in the first place."

"Hey, it's not my fault that you didn't chew your food." I held my hands in the air.

"And it's not my fault that you just compared yourself to Diego," she countered. Then, after taking a moment to compose herself, she continued, "I'm sorry, I didn't plan for that to sound harsh, but it was. Wasn't it?"

"I'll live." I laughed and Jayleigh smiled. "Don't worry."

"Every part of me wanted to say yes, you are one hell of a hunk, my friend." She settled a hand on my shoulder. "But it's just not true. You're too pretty for my liking. You're cute, like an excited little puppy. But this guy…" She nodded toward Diego with lustrous eyes. He was still watching us and listening in. "This guy is a beast."

Diego smirked and turned away to revel in Jayleigh's admiration. And that's when the so-called 'Beast' caught sight of Lora from across the barn. His eyes fixated on her for several moments without blinking.

I couldn't help but compare a puppy to a beast.

It made my blood boil. Part of me wanted to go over to Diego and set some ground rules. He could have *anyone* else, Jayleigh was practically throwing herself at him, so long as he left Lora alone.

"Dear God, I'm starting to sound like Tye."

I tried to distract myself by watching the rest of the group interact. Only then was it that I noticed that even the girls were staring too.

It was the Alpha Effect.

They were just experiencing that initial attraction, the invisible force which bound the group together.

Relief washed me. It would fade over the next few hours and only resurface in a moment of need... Unless they were like me, and that feeling never faded; keeping them awake at night and distracting them throughout the day.

The Omegas sat on the benches opposite us and picked at their broth. "So, what's the deal?" Zee seemed keen to figure out what she was doing here. "Do we always sleep in a barn, or what?"

Everyone nodded.

"This is home," I muttered.

"That's fucked," she replied.

I was startled at her choice of words. Not many of us swore in casual conversation, but I shrugged it off because she was right; it was kind of fucked.

"What about these challenges?" Diego joined in on question time. "What do they involve?"

"It changes every day." Lora took the reins on this one, knowing that it was difficult to answer without scaring the Omegas. "Each challenge tests one or more of the key attributes; resilience, stamina, strength, or unity. Being able to master these attributes will bring the pack closer and help us to evolve, making us the ultimate weapon."

"Right, for the war," Diego finished. "And what about the war? How much do we know about that?"

Lora shot a warning glance in my direction as I opened my mouth. "Not a lot, they seem to hand out information on a must-know basis. So, until we're ready to leave The Farm, they probably won't give anything away."

Lora looked relieved as I finished answering. She was still mad at me for what happened at the waterfall yesterday, but she was trying her best to hide it. Everyone continued the conversation, but Lora's gaze remained. Her pupils dilated and I was submerged by their pressure. I needed it to stop. My heart raced. My sweaty palms made a return.

I winked at her, my nerves taking over. It was the first thing I could think of doing to shift the energy. Surprisingly, it paid off as she tried to hide the smile playing on her lips and turned away quickly to make sure that nobody saw the Alpha mask drop.

"Ew," Jayleigh interrupted, neither of us had been aware that she was watching. "Did you just wink at her?" She made gagging noises in the back of her throat. "See, now this is a perfect example of why you're cute but not hunk material."

"Ah, shut up and choke on a carrot." I rolled my eyes.

"Get a room," she replied.

Tye was shifting glances now, listening in on the conversation and suddenly aware that I hadn't listened to a word of his warning. I looked back in his direction, acting unfazed. I knew that I couldn't fight him, but just like Tim, I enjoyed winding him up too much. I smiled in his direction as though I had no idea what I'd done wrong.

I was two and a half bowls of broth deep by the time the doors opened and the silhouette of a tall man slowly approached.

A wary silence filled the barn, nobody really knowing what to expect from Hail as he entered.

Was he okay?

Was he still angry?

Was he going to snap somebody else's neck?

Surely going through an ordeal such as that would change him in some way. I doubted anybody could go through it and not be mentally or emotionally affected, unless they were completely heartless, maybe? My mind floated back to Dickward. He wouldn't have even flinched if he were in Hail's place. The thought of being stuck in the pit with the Veno Alpha had me feeling all kinds of hopeless.

We stared as the doors closed behind Hail. He looked normal; neither crazy eyes nor superhero eyes were present.

I didn't know what to say or how to react. Being the closest person to him, I felt that I should have been the one to welcome him back, but I didn't know what to say.

"Congratulations…?"

No, that wouldn't sit right.

I considered apologising, trying a touch of sympathy, but a

little too much might have made him upset or angry, and I didn't want him to mutate again.

I looked at Lora. As the Alpha, she should be the one to welcome him back, but she didn't. She had been friends with Beckle and I guessed that it was too difficult for her. Or, like me, she simply didn't know what to say.

And so, we stood there in silence for so long it almost became unbearable.

Finally, somebody spoke.

It wasn't me, and it wasn't Lora.

It was one of the new Omegas. Zee was oblivious. "Who's this? And why are you all acting as if someone died?"

Hail broke into tears.

I approached him now, not wanting him to feel alone, and lead him away from the wary eyes of the pack and into his stall. He sat on his bed whilst I paced, hoping that the pack would leave us alone until he got himself under control. "Everyone hates me," he whispered.

I shook my head. "Of course they don't hate you." Although it probably looked that way from where he was standing. "I think we're all just a little sleep-deprived. We stayed up all night worrying about you."

And we're all a little scared of you.

"I'm so sorry," he sobbed quietly.

"It's not your fault. You were just doing what you had to in order to survive. If anyone is to blame, it's Marshall."

YIELD

Hail was still as he relived the night's events. I could see the trauma sketched into his face. "But I didn't just do what I had to, did I?" His eyes fixated on the blank wall in front of him as though the emptiness comforted him somewhat. "I tortured him. I murdered him with my bare hands, and some *sick* part of me actually enjoyed it…"

CHAPTER THIRTEEN

ARES

The crisp autumn air gave way to an icy breeze in the days that followed. The few leaves which remained on the trees battled gallantly against the storm which made our training near impossible. But Tim and Sally liked to remind us that the war wouldn't stop for bad weather, and therefore neither could we. And so, we trained hard.

Unlike the leaves, we didn't fall. We prevailed in the storm. Or at least, the other Titanium hybrids did.

I tried my best to keep up.

My unwillingness to mutate was proving to be a hindrance to my progression. Only, the more I watched my friends lose control of their minds and bodies in an attempt to evolve, the more unwilling I became. The farmers pushed, and I always managed to find a loophole in their plans. But I waited for the day when they would finally outsmart me. It was coming, and I'd have no choice but to give in to my animalistic alter ego.

It was a difficult balance. I didn't want to weigh the pack down, but I couldn't lose control. I couldn't relive what happened to me in Dr White's room. I often dreamt that it was Lora, or Hail, or Jayleigh standing before me as I mutated, and I internally screamed against my body as I hurt them.

I couldn't stop myself.

But I could prevent it in reality, even if it meant slowing the pack down within challenges. Omega 3 (as I liked to call the three newbies) had yet to taste the delicacies of winning, and that could arguably have been my fault.

Tye continued to sabotage me in any way possible. Lora continued with her intense glare. Hail remained at war within himself.

The only person I could truly rely on was Jayleigh, although she scared me more and more each day. She proved to be everything that I wasn't; skilled, powerful, self-assured. I wished I could be more like her. I wished that I cared about everything a little less and could follow orders without questioning them. However, I found that seemed to come easier with sleep deprivation.

Our sleep was cut short in favor of additional training, some nights we'd barely manage four hours.

Before breakfast, we were made to run miles with weight on

our shoulders; sometimes bags of sand, sometimes barrels of water, and occasionally other hybrids. If we didn't make it back in the allocated time then we wouldn't eat.

At some point down the line, I started to consider food and sleep a luxury.

The challenges themselves were brutal, testing both our mental and physical strength. Giving in to the pain was not an option. I survived on pure adrenaline, trying to avoid the exhaustion that so desperately wanted to consume me.

The only bright side was that we hadn't seen Dickward or the other Venos since the waterfall challenge. But every day we would critique the past day's performances, both Titanium and Veno, picking out weaknesses in our plan and execution so that we could learn from our mistakes.

Watching the rival group made me feel like something was crawling about underneath my skin and scratching at my spine. I knew that they were no danger to me on the screen, but I couldn't shift the dread-filled memories which occupied my mind every time I saw their Alpha.

The Veno pack successfully completed every challenge, charging in with no sense of a plan and yet still managing to pull it off. We decided one day to adopt their tactics, but it only ended in chaos.

"How can it work for them but not for us?!" I asked Tim during one of our daily revision sessions. The exhaustion was making me frustrated.

"The Veno pack has a different hybrid basis. Whilst both packs are almost twenty-five percent wolf, the key gene which makes it possible for us to successfully modify your genome with so many other species is different. We call this the hybrid gene. Your hybrid gene comes from the titanium frog, and the Venos' come from the veno snake," Tim replied.

Tye let out a loud yawn from the front of the class. Obviously, his attention span was too small for this conversation.

Tim continued regardless, "It's these animals that decipher the pack's characteristics. The veno snake is known for its quick attack when put under immense pressure. That is why the method works so well for them, and not so much for you."

"So what about the Titanium frog?" I asked. "What are our strengths?"

Tim sighed. "It's not for me to tell you what your strengths are, Ares. You should be able to work that out for yourselves." He shut down the conversation.

It was true, yet I still struggled to see any correlation in the team's strengths. Over the past week, we had discovered that Diego was able to lift a log almost three times his body weight. I knew for certain that I couldn't do that; not that I'd tried, but I didn't want to risk the back injury.

We also realized that Tye could hear further afield than the rest of the pack. I made a mental note to lower my voice whenever he was around.

"We all have different individual strengths and weaknesses,

and I can't find a common strength that we all share. Most of us have nothing in common at all."

"You're thinking too far into it. Your hybrid basis is not made of only two animals. Some of you have up to twenty different variations. If one of you is super strong, it's just a good match in the cards that you were dealt." Tim had been much more optimistic lately, I wondered what could have changed to make him so chirpy because it was certainly nothing that we had done. "You'll work it out soon enough."

It seemed to be a reoccurring theme with the farmers. They seemed to enjoy dropping hints for us mice to chew on. I started to think that maybe we were coming to the end of our training. It would explain why Tim was suddenly so much happier; he knew that he'd be getting rid of us soon.

But my gut was telling me otherwise, that this was all building to something more.

My gut feeling was right.

Soon the challenges stopped, replaced by target practice, combat, and more skill-based training in the library. We spent a lot of time perfecting our rope skills, building shelter, and learning how to make use of our surroundings. The more we learned, the more anxious I became.

One day, a man dressed in green entered the library as we took our seats. He perked my attention due to the color of his clothes. All of the other farmers wore gray, what made this guy so special? At the back of the room, he pulled up a chair, hiked one booted foot onto his knee and leaned back, making himself at home. When he saw me frowning, he gave me a small salute and began typing something onto his tablet.

"Huh," I muttered to myself, and he studied me almost as often as I studied him throughout the entirety of the lesson.

The man didn't speak. Ever.

He seemed to pop up here and there, following us around our daily routine, but never ventured into the barn. It gave us time to speculate on who he was and what he was doing.

He quickly became known amongst the pack as Greenman, thanks to the rapid nickname generator that was my brain. It wasn't the most inventive of names but I blamed that on exhaustion.

Greenman never missed a combat session. In fact, he was so eager that every time we entered the gym, he would already be seated and waiting. I found his gaze off-putting, especially because he spent so much time gazing in my direction whilst Lora threw me around like a fish out of water.

Every day she would choose me as her partner, and every day I would wonder why.

I wasn't an even match for the Alpha.

Sally and Tim would demonstrate a set of moves (of what appeared to be mixed martial arts) and we were given time to practice afterward. Although I absorbed everything they taught us like a sponge, reciting the moves didn't come naturally to me.

Maybe it was because of *her*.

That intense glare followed me everywhere. Every time I questioned Lora about it, she would refuse that it existed at all. Was it anger? Was it something more?

There was a darkness in her eyes. It ran deep, bottomless. I drowned whenever I lingered too long.

We were stuck in this equilibrium; a roundabout that never stopped spinning. It made me giddy and sick, but the confusion didn't affect how I felt for her at all.

She huffed as she flipped me over her shoulder. "I thought you were supposed to be a fast learner?"

"Ignore how close she is." I had to remind myself every couple of seconds.

"Why would you think that? I never said I was a fast learner," I countered, but it was barely audible with my face pressed into the blue gym mat and her knee nudging into my neck. She was practically holding my hand as she pinned my arm behind my back.

"Mr Intelligent, how far is that brain going to get you if you can't hold your own in a fight?" Her words were placed somewhere between playful and aggressive, I seemed to get that a lot recently and I had no idea what it meant.

We'd barely spoken about anything more than our training since our little disagreement at the waterfall a few weeks ago. She shut down every other conversation with little hesitation, yet she still chose me as her gym partner. She was a mystery to me. I mentally added her to the list of puzzles that needed solving.

YIELD

"I yield." I tried to pat out, but she held me there a little longer.

"This isn't a game, Ares." Her voice was barely a whisper as it tickled against my ear. "You know what we're up against, you know the consequences of not taking these lessons seriously. And if you're still refusing to mutate then you need to learn to fight or you'll never make it out there."

She let me go and I sat up, rubbing the back of my neck where her knee had pinned me down.

"Do I, though?" I asked. "Do I know what we're up against?" Or better yet, "Do *you* know what we're up against?" Her face was blank, she gave away nothing. "Because I can't help but notice that we're learning to fight with knives in the middle of the apocalypse. No gun in sight. Why are we learning hand-to-hand combat? Do you know?"

"*Shh.*" She hushed me with a hand over my mouth. She glanced around to make sure that nobody had overheard my outburst. If anyone, it would have been Tye, but he was busy forcing Zee into a triangle choke and there was no way he'd have heard anything over Zee's swearing.

Greenman was watching us from across the room, but thankfully his human ears couldn't pick up a conversation from this distance. I tried to ignore him as he watched with anticipation, never seeming to blink.

Once Lora was happy, she turned back to face me. We were standing so close; our chests rising and falling, inches apart as we tried to catch our breath. Her gray eyes became hypnotic. Without thinking, I lightly tickled the palm of her hand with my tongue as she started to pull away. Her eyes widened and a small gasp escaped her lips before she could stop it.

She seemed neither mad nor pleased. "What the hell was that?" she questioned.

"Reflex," I whispered.

"No, you can't do this." She swallowed hard and shook her head. "We need to talk later, but please, no more of this."

She pulled her hand away and took a few steps backward, tightening her hair in its band. She was trying to hide the fact that she was shaking.

It was a stupid thing to have done, any person in their right state of mind could see that. I might have just ruined any sort of progression that we had made in the past few weeks, however little it was.

"Reflex..." she muttered to herself in disbelief before ordering, "Again!"

Any sign of insecurity had been wiped away and she was back to the Alpha stature. I knew she planned on making me pay for the distraction.

She lunged in for another attack and after a few seconds of spinning, I found myself with my face pressed into the mat once more.

Hail and Jayleigh sat with me that evening on the overlook, watching as the sun gave way to the moon. Winter was fast approaching and the days were becoming shorter; it was dark by the time our evening meal was served.

"I don't like it," I said as we waited. "Don't you feel it too?"

Jayleigh shrugged and replied, "After two hundred and thirty-five days, I've learned to stop thinking too much into it. You should too or else it'll just make you paranoid."

"I feel hungry," Hail chimed. "Is that what we're talking about?"

I shared a look with Jayleigh, both of us trying not to laugh.

"I'm hungry too," I agreed. "But I was referring to how the challenges have stopped, we've been learning to fight, and Omega 3 didn't even have an induction challenge."

"I didn't notice." Hail shrugged. He hadn't been his usual self since the fight with Beckle. I'd not been called *Bro* in almost three weeks and it was starting to worry me.

"I just want to know why everything is changing."

"Surely it's a good thing?" Jayleigh said. "Nobody has died in a long time. The Omegas are actually getting a chance to settle in before they're forced to…" She looked at Hail and chose her next words carefully, worried that he might shatter into a million pieces. "Do something they don't want to do."

"Do you reckon they're holding back because I told Dr White about Marshall going off the rails?"

They considered this for a while and then Jayleigh shook her head, sounding a lot like Tim. "The war stops for nobody. The farmers wouldn't stop for the sake of one man going a little crazy, they'd just deal with him. You're right, there's definitely something else going on, but you're only going to drive yourself mad if you keep thinking about it."

I felt defeated.

"But I need to know. It actually makes me angry not knowing."

Hail shuffled backward. "If you're going to mutate, don't do it around me."

I rolled my eyes. "I'm frustrated, but I'm not going to mutate. It's a different kind of anger."

Lora's head popped over the ladder then, her voice making us jump. There was no warning or apology as she interrupted. "Can I speak to Ares for a moment?"

Hail and Jayleigh both looked at me with the same quizzical expression. I pretended not to see it. "Of course."

Hail made way for Lora on the overlook and traded places with her on the ladder. Jayleigh followed, giving me a wiggle of the eyebrows as she disappeared from view.

"I'm sorry about earlier. I don't know what I was thinking," I started.

"No, that's not why I asked to speak to you. We're just going to forget *that* ever happened."

I nodded once in understanding. Forgetting it happened meant there would be no scolding, no lecture. I saw this as a win.

"Then it's about our previous conversation?"

She nodded and peered down towards the rest of the group to see if anyone was listening in. Everyone seemed preoccupied. Hail and Jayleigh chatted amongst themselves and leaned against the ladder to stop Tye from following Lora up to the overlook.

"What do you know?" I asked her. I felt like rubbing my hands together with anticipation until I remembered that Marshall had done the same thing right before tossing Hail and Beckle into the pit.

"Promise not to tell anyone else? It could cause havoc if the wrong people find out."

"Then why are you sharing it with me?" I questioned. My heart raced a little faster.

She paused for a moment, studying my eyes and seeming to doubt her answer. "Call me stupid, but I seem to trust you."

I was taken aback. She hated me, so why would she share anything of value?

"Of course you can trust me, why wouldn't…" I let my words die as I remembered all of the reasons I'd given her *not* to trust me.

Going against her advice. Forfeiting challenges. Speaking out of place. Breaking rules. Not learning from past mistakes.

"Why *do* you trust me?" I laughed after a moment of consideration.

"I don't know." She shrugged. It had been a long time since I'd sat so close to her, I'd missed our casual conversations, the way she had to tilt her head back to look at me, and the smell of lilies. "You're a pain in the arse, but most of the time, you're right..."

"I'm right?"

"Wipe that smirk from your face." Her dimples made a rare appearance. "I didn't say always... I think that I trust you because you have a mind of your own. You test me. But I do hate you for it at the same time. It makes my life all the more complicated."

"So when I went against your orders at the waterfall..."

"You were too cocky about it and that damn right pissed me off. But I should have trusted your judgment. You're not stupid."

I basked in the glory for as long as I could, giving her my best smile. "Yeah, I'm sorry about that. And for the record, I didn't do it to spite you. I generally thought that it was my best option to get out of the mess I'd created. Of course, if I had just listened to you in the first place everything would have been dandy. So, I'm sorry."

"Thanks."

"Anyway, as much as I'm loving this sharing of heart, we're going off-topic and we don't have much time."

She nodded as she suddenly remembered the real reason she had come to speak to me and lowered her voice to a volume that even I struggled to hear. "We're not training with guns because bullets can't hurt them."

My eyebrows raised on their own accord. Of course, I had already worked that out for myself. "So how do you kill them?"

She shrugged. "I don't know. Knives, I'd presume. Otherwise, the target practice would be a waste of time."

"Oh… Yeah, of course." I'd almost forgotten how the nerves affected my speech whenever she was near. "So- So what are they, if not human?" I asked the million-dollar question.

She shook her head slowly. "I don't know that either, but they're intent on wiping out humanity. The Farm is the only safe-zone within the midlands. I've heard that there are other safe-zones out there, but they are just camps, not training facilities like this one."

"What else do you know?" I pushed my luck.

"I know that you're going to die if you don't start concentrating in combat," she answered abruptly. "I chose you as my partner because I wanted to make sure that you had a good teacher," she paused, "but I think that you get distracted by me."

"I- uh… I don't know what you mean."

She cocked an eyebrow and tugged at a loose wave of my hair. "Your heart reaches a thousand beats per minute any time I touch you."

She knows.

"You know that I'd die long before my heart ever reached a thousand beats per minute, right?" I rambled to try and distract myself from hyperventilating. "I'd struggle anywhere past two hundred beats per minute-"

"You need to find a way to distract yourself from this." She gestured to my heart. Her voice dropped in pitch and she spoke slowly. "We are here to fight, Ares." Something about the way she said the words was as though she were trying to convince not only me but herself, too. "We are warriors, and love in war can only result in weakness."

A cold sweat glazed over my body before I could whisper, "Not necessarily."

My love for Lora had grown like vines of poison ivy; intricate and beautiful, yet painful to touch. I had kept my distance because I didn't want to overstep any boundaries. But now it appeared that the ivy was beginning to blossom, and I questioned if maybe I had been wrong? Maybe it wasn't poison ivy at all?

Could it be that she didn't hate *me*, but the feelings that I provoked? It seemed mad that I was even considering it, yet it explained why she kept her distance. Especially if she believed that there truly could be no love in war.

The whole idea was just laughable. I wasn't a good fit for her; too unruly, too disruptive, and too reluctant. I wouldn't make it through training and we both knew it.

"It could also result in power. To give you something to fight for other than yourself," I suggested.

She gave me a look which suggested that I shouldn't test her, and I wondered whether she might cave.

"Would you risk your life to save me, even though I'm better trained and more likely to survive?" She slowly reached for my wrist, twisting my arm so that her fingers could find my pulse

217

and closed her eyes. My palms started to sweat.

"You're the Alpha. Of course I would. We all would." I played it off. I suddenly registered what she had said earlier. "Can you hear my heartbeat?"

She laughed. "No, but I'm aware of it, like an invisible presence, or a sixth sense. And earlier I could feel your pulse going haywire when I had your arm pinned behind your back. I figured it couldn't be from the fight because you'd barely defended yourself enough for it to affect your heart rate."

"I don't fight girls," I joked as I tried to play off the panic.

"Oh, how gentlemanly of you." She rolled her eyes and dropped my wrist. "So if something out there," she gestured out of the window, "tries to attack you, are you going to turn around and tell her that you don't fight girls? She'd kill you in a second. We are all equal, Ares. If you want to impress me, fight back. I expect to be the one pinned to the mat in training tomorrow."

I couldn't help but feel that she was flirting with the idea, and it only confused me more. She told me that we couldn't be together, yet her actions were suggesting otherwise.

"I don't understand you."

I hadn't meant to say the words aloud. They lingered in the air around us.

She paused and looked out of the window. "Well, maybe I don't want to be understood."

I considered for a while, wondering if this was the reason she seemed so contradicted all of the time. But there was

218

something else. It wasn't as simple as *not wanting*. I'd seen the look in her eyes, the internal battle she seemed to fight whenever I was near. "Maybe you're too scared of what people think to let them see the real you?"

"The real me?" She shook her head and laughed quietly as though it amused her.

"The girl who dreams of cottages by the ocean," I said. "A far cry from the battle-ready Alpha you appear to be around the others."

The laughter stopped suddenly and she turned back to face me. It was simply an observation, yet it seemed to get under her skin.

She rallied, "Maybe you like to annoy everyone because somewhere, deep down, you don't really want to fit in? You don't want to be here, you want to be out there, with your family."

I hadn't really thought much about my family at all since the night that she told me her secret about the enemy. I no longer wanted to leave. Originally, I'd thought that it was because I was too scared to enter a foreign world and find my parents, but now I was starting to realize that I was too scared of losing the strange comfort that I had found with Lora, however sparse our interactions had been recently.

I continued the game that she played, hoping that I'd get it right this time. "*Maybe* you don't let people get close to you because you're too scared that you'll lose them?"

"Now you're getting me confused with Hail," she scoffed

and turned away to hide the expression on her face. She thought for a while before turning back. "*Maybe* you ask so many questions because you're lost? You think that you need to know everything in order to find yourself. But you don't. You'll never find yourself in external answers. Everything you need to know is in here." She pointed to my chest.

I caught her hand in mine, refusing to let her look away this time. "And *maybe*, Alpha, you're too scared to let anybody love you because you think that you don't deserve it, that your sole purpose is to lead the pack and nothing more? It's been drilled into you for so long that you've forgotten that you are *so* much more. Life is full of horror and death, why not allow yourself this one happiness?"

I expected her to draw her hand back, to shut me out, but she didn't. She allowed me to hold onto her as she replied, "Because love is a distraction. And every time I get distracted, somebody else pays the price…"

She dropped her mask just long enough to reveal the suffering, and I realized she had learned this the hard way. I recalled all that I'd heard about Donnah; Tye's warning to Lora on the evening he'd found us on the overlook together. The day that I'd risked my life as I took the plunge over the waterfall (the day I'd first witnessed Lora's scowl), and how angry she had been, not because I'd gone against her orders, but because she'd realized that she had feelings for me and that my death scared her. And *that* realization scared her even more.

Hail had killed Beckle that night, and she'd been so distracted by her feelings that she hadn't noticed we were turning down the wrong path until it was too late. She couldn't have done anything to stop it anyways, but I came to the conclusion that Lora felt responsible for every death that the pack encountered. The farmers wanted her to feel that way. She would always find a way to make it her own fault.

The intense glare was back and I finally felt as though I could understand what it meant.

"Whilst the war remains, we can never be more than this," she whispered and squeezed my hand tight, afraid to let me go. "I have a responsibility to the pack, to the farmers, and to the few surviving humans outside the fence. I cannot let my feelings get in the way."

She was right.

Of course she was right.

Every day I was becoming more and more aware that I was a very selfish person. Lora was the polar opposite. She knew that the whole of humanity could suffer the consequences if we lost sight of the war in favor of each other.

My heart fluttered as my mind repeated her words. "Your feelings? So you admit it?"

"I chose you in training because I needed to make sure that you paid attention," she sounded desperate. "I want you to survive, Ares. Hell, I *need* you to survive. Or who else will share my little house by the sea?"

Suddenly, something lodged itself in the back of my throat, and tears threatened to surface. "You mean it?"

"It's a promise." She squeezed my hand gently.

My smile was small, but this was everything I needed to hear. "I'm sure Tye would be overjoyed. To move in- The house...." I tried to lighten the mood with a joke but my mouth and mind didn't tally. "But on a serious note, I know that I have to do better. I meant what I said earlier about love in war making us stronger. I don't have it in me to fight for myself, but... I'd fight for you."

Lora couldn't hide the smile, bright and beautiful, and not for the first time I imagined how it would feel to press my lips against hers. I was sure that Lora was thinking the same thing as her eyes studied my face, both of us leaning in. The sweet smell of lilies enticed me closer. Her eyes fluttered closed.

We were caught in the moment, a passing of time where our minds were numb to the morals and pressure of the war. For one blissful second, we were just us. Two beings expressing their feelings for the first time. Intimate.

We paused, faces so close I could feel the warmth of her breath against my mouth.

"You're contradicting yourself again," I sighed against her.

"You talk too much, Ares."

Her chest fell with rapid breaths and I slowly brought my hand to her cheek. Her skin was soft under my touch as I traced the line of her jaw.

"Tell me this is a bad idea," I whispered. "Maybe I'll start to believe it if I hear you say it."

"It's a terrible idea," she said, but her heart wasn't in it.

Terrible, terrible idea…

The farmers would have my head for this.

Regret circled at the back of my throat, resulting in a quiet groan. Lora seemed fixated, but she managed to regain control of the situation when laughter from the other hybrids erupted throughout the barn.

The war had to come first.

She sighed heavily and opened her eyes. They revealed a hunger I'd never seen in her before. I smiled, although my body swarmed with need. A need for Lora.

She felt it too, and as though she were trying to distract herself, she retracted and said, "Just try to concentrate on what really matters."

"Is that an order?"

"Yes."

I was still short of breath. "But… What if it's you, Alpha? What if *you're* the *only* thing that matters?"

Lora scowled. "Stop calling me Alpha."

"What?" I smiled. "Why?"

Her silence was the only answer I needed.

There was more distance between us now but I kept hold of her hand. I only noticed how small it was as I cocooned it in mine. I wanted to take all of her into my arms, but that couldn't happen for a long, long time.

If ever.

But it was the motivation that I needed to continue. It was no longer about playing along with the farmers' challenges in hopes that I didn't die. I needed to put everything on the table. It wasn't just my life and my happiness at risk anymore. Because she really was the only thing that mattered to me, and I needed to ensure that Lora would get to experience the life she deserved.

We remained on the overlook, hand in hand until the food arrived with no sight of Marshall. I hadn't seen him since the Beckle incident and I wondered if he was taking some much-needed time out.

I ate happily, left my tray on the shelf, gave Lora the routine goodnight wave, and retired to bed feeling determined to prove myself over the following days.

I developed an intricate plan of attack. I'd ask Lora to pair me with Tye in combat so I'd be more inclined to fight back. I would continue to push myself in each challenge. Of course, I'd only mutate if I really *had* to, but I'd certainly try harder and think smarter. I'd become a warrior of my own creation.

There was only one problem with my plan, and I didn't realize it until I awoke the next morning; by which time it was already too late.

I opened my eyes to a bright light shining above my head. It was the sun, beaming down from the cloudless sky. We'd been stripped of our barn and transported to an empty field at some point within the night and I didn't recognize my surroundings at all.

I wasn't the only one awake. We looked at each other with the same blank expressions.

"What the fuck is going on?" Zee was already out of her sleeping bag and pacing.

Lora was rummaging through the rucksack that had been left beside her.

Hail was still snoring.

I threw my pillow at him and he slowly opened one eye, letting out a low groan. "Somebody turn off the sun."

I watched and waited for something to click. Ten seconds later he sat straight up, his eyes wide. "Where has the barn gone?" He looked around and I shrugged as his eyes landed on me. "Did they leave us breakfast?"

Priorities.

I stood and stretched as the rest of the pack descended into quiet chaos.

Lora held a tablet in her hands. She read from the digital screen and the feeling I'd had about the training building to something returned, sending my stomach churning.

The new sense of normal, which had started to feel like home to me, had been ripped from under our feet and replaced with this vast emptiness.

We sat in the middle of a V-shaped valley with not so much as a tree in sight. The air was quiet, filled only with the gentle rustle of the wind through the long grass, and the hysterical voices of the pack demanding answers.

I took a deep breath of the icy morning air and closed my eyes, trying to capture the silence of the moment; because I knew that from here on out, everything was about to change.

I already knew the nature of what Lora was about to say as she read from the tablet in her hands.

"Lora, Tye, Indigo, Jayleigh, Hail, Ares, Teri, Diego, and Zee..."

She paused.

"Welcome to Phase Two."

Phase 2

YIELD

"verb,
-produce or provide (a natural, agricultural, or industrial product).
-to submit; to give way to arguments, demands, or pressure."

-Oxford Dictionary

CHAPTER
FOURTEEN

ARES

"Welcome to Phase Two." Lora held the tablet out so that we could watch the hologram that played. Dr White stood central, looking a fair few years younger than we knew him to be, although he still wore the same white coat and round glasses. "If you are watching this, then you have successfully passed Phase One.

"Phase Two is created to test everything you've learned so far in a mission-style challenge similar to those you will complete once you pass your training and leave The Farm. This tablet will provide you with updates on your next task, but how you go about the challenge is completely up to you.

"You have been provided with basic equipment in your backpack which you can use as you see fit. Breakfast and medicine will be provided, yet you will have to prepare your own meals throughout the day and build your own shelter. Camp must be set up before nightfall. If the sun sets before you complete the mission, or if you leave camp overnight, there will be repercussions.

"And, one more thing that you should know, is that you're not out there alone. Your rival pack is near, and only one pack will make it out of Phase Two alive. There are no rules. So, good luck and I hope to see you in Phase Three."

The tablet's screen turned black and it took a moment for us to gather our thoughts.

Only one pack will make it out of Phase Two alive.

It was us or them.

Either we'd kill the Veno pack to make it passed Phase Two, or we'd die trying.

My eyes darted around the area, expecting to see them appear over the hills surrounding us.

Lora started to fiddle with the tablet, trying to find direction on what to do next. I replayed Dr White's last few sentences over in my mind and tried not to panic, yet the more I thought about it, the more I panicked.

Tye was talking to Indigo and Omega 3, trying to reassure them. "This is what we were made for, this is the ultimate test…"

Jayleigh and Hail stood by my side, almost as though they were looking to me for guidance.

"I don't know what you're looking at. I don't do pep talks."

I backed up. "But, I'm all ears if either of you want to try."

"You knew that something was coming." Jayleigh pointed a knife at me and I held my hands up in surrender. Where had she found a knife? Did she always keep it on her person for safekeeping? "I trust your intuition. What are you thinking now?"

I tried so desperately to gather my thoughts but they drifted away with the wind. My mind was a mess. "Keep quiet... Avoid the Veno pack... Complete the missions as quickly as possible?"

"Amen to that," Lora chimed as she walked past us.

I smiled in response but she wasn't looking.

"Okay, fall in!" Lora ordered and the rest of the pack gathered around. "I've been searching for more details, but the only mission we've been given is to get to these coordinates by nightfall. I'm guessing that this is where we'll set up camp tonight. Pack your stuff, keep quiet, and let's get moving."

"What do we do if we come across the Venos?" Tye asked.

Lora's jaw clenched. "Fight for our lives."

We complied in an orderly fashion.

I wrapped up my sleeping bag and buried it in my backpack beneath a rope, wire, a bag of rice, a hand knife (presumably where Jayleigh had found hers), and various other items. I flung the bag onto my back and buckled up the straps to ensure that it wouldn't fall, and then tied the straggly ends into knots across my chest for good measure.

When I returned my attention to my surroundings, I found Lora watching with an amused smile playing on her lips. She attempted a more serious expression as she asked, "Alright there, Soldier?"

"Yes. Fine," I lied with a large nod of the head. "Are you?"

"Always. Thank you for asking." She lied too. I raised an eyebrow in question as she clenched her thumb, and then she quickly released it when she noticed me looking. "Nerd," she whispered as she walked past me, a little disrupted.

"No, but that's Tye's special nickname for me, you can't steal it…" The words died as she put more and more distance between us. I waited for her to turn back and steal a glance, but she didn't.

"You two are weird," Jayleigh interrupted my daze. I hadn't noticed that she and Hail had been standing so close.

I flinched and tried to pass it off. "You're a fine one to talk."

Jayleigh shrugged.

We headed out, following the map that the tablet provided. Tye took the lead with Lora, offering his assistance in any way that he could. "I'm good with maps if you want me to take over?"

"Thank you, Tye, but I think I'll manage just fine." Lora's tone was snappy. I wondered if it bothered her that I had worked out her coping mechanism? She was a very private person, after all. 'Maybe I don't want to be understood,' she had said. Did she find it intrusive that I had uncovered another of her secrets?

Or was I being selfish for thinking that this was about me at all? It was probably just nerves, we had no idea what Phase Two had in store for us. Leading a pack through a mission such as this would take a lot of organisation and responsibility. She was probably just stressed.

I tried to steady my racing heart as we walked. Every few minutes a sudden noise would remind me that the Venos were out here, too.

'*There are no rules,*' Dr White's voice kept flitting through my mind, sending my heart into overdrive once more.

We spoke only in hushed tones, keeping our eyes focused on the scenery around us. There was no place to hide if the Veno pack suddenly appeared from the hillside. I imagined them charging toward us in their reptile-like manner, ready for the kill. But my eye-darting was a waste of energy. We successfully made it out of the V-shaped valley within a couple of hours and arrived at a long but narrow lake. I had never felt so relieved to find trees.

"The coordinates are at the opposite side of the lake," Lora informed us. She removed her backpack and dipped it into the water. Everyone watched, baffled as to what she was thinking. "The bags float and they're waterproof. We can swim across the lake to save time, or go around and risk not making camp by nightfall. Group decision."

The majority voted to cross the lake until Teri stepped forward. "I seem to think that I can't swim."

My heart went out to her. It would be difficult for Omega 3, they hadn't yet been forced into the lake as I had on my second

235

day, and they couldn't remember their life before The Farm.

"I'm a strong swimmer." Indigo rested an arm on Teri's shoulder in reassurance as she volunteered to help. "You can use your bag to stay afloat and I'll swim with you for support. Swimming slow will still be twice as fast as going around the lake."

"Then, we all in agreement?" Lora asked for confirmation.

We started to remove our backpacks in reply.

The water was icy cold, but our clothes protected us up to the neckline. I tried my best to keep my head and hands out of the water when possible and used my bag as a float, pushing it out in front of me.

I felt a small sense of achievement as I started the swim, keeping up with the team. My stamina must have improved leaps and bounds in the past few weeks, or maybe it was just the floating backpack which made the job easier? Either way, I ended up finding the swim surprisingly enjoyable and somewhat relaxing until we reached the halfway mark, and then a noise brought me back to Phase Two and the consequences it carried.

I knew that sound only too well. I had been imagining and fearing it all morning. I grabbed onto my backpack to help me float in place and tried to splash the water.

The noise continued to grow louder.

Once I had the attention of the Titaniums, I held my hand to my ear in hopes that they understood my signal to listen.

The distant sound of ticking.

It took a while for the pack to understand that this noise wasn't just a cricket in the grass. It was the synchronized sound that always introduced the Veno pack.

"I can smell them from here!" A wild female voice cut through the air, transported by the wind.

The Veno pack laughed and yelled as they approached. They didn't worry about being heard because they weren't afraid of us, as we were of them. This was their playground.

"Hold onto your bags," I mouthed, hoping that the pack would understand me. I used my hand in a circular motion to gesture what I meant.

The Veno pack emerged from the woodland, making that awful half-cawing, half-rattling noise as they searched for us.

I grabbed my backpack tightly, wrapping my arms around it as I twisted upside down and submerged myself. The water felt sharp against my face. I held my breath, praying that the reflection of the clouds on the lake would be enough to hide us.

My legs started to sink and I let them fall; one less feature for the Veno pack to spot. I could still hear them yelling although their voices were warped by the water.

Everything suddenly seemed very still.

I opened my eyes and watched the sky dance on the surface. The world appeared less chaotic from this perspective, but the silence did nothing to calm my nerves.

We waited as the Veno pack scanned the area, several minutes passed and I struggled for breath, rising once for air before ducking back under and praying that the Venos hadn't seen.

The noise faded and the ripples in the water became erratic as members of the Titanium pack began to surface.

We gulped in oxygen and stayed quiet, looking around for any sign of the rival pack. We deemed it safe and continued to cross the lake to wait for Indigo and Teri on the cobbled shore.

"That was too close for comfort," I said as I took off my shirt and ringed the water out, knowing that it would take a while to dry at this near-freezing temperature.

Tye copied my actions, using it as an excuse to flex at Lora. I wanted her to seem unamused by his actions, to roll her eyes or grunt in disgust, but she didn't react at all when she looked at him. Instead, she turned to the group. "We need to get a move on. We've still got a fair way to go before we reach camp and we don't want any repercussions."

Only, two members of the pack were still crossing the lake. I was in the process of putting the shirt back on when we heard it again, sharing the same expression of panic.

The Venos were retracing their steps after losing our scent.

They were hunting us.

I remembered the way the Veno Alpha had charged toward me the last time he saw me and the fear took over. He would kill me if he had the chance.

In a fight or flight situation, I chose flight and sprinted for the forest to hide amongst the trees. I expected the others to follow, but the rest of the pack stayed put, ready to protect themselves and the two Titaniums in the lake or to die trying.

My heartbeat raced faster and faster as the ticking became louder and the Venos grew closer.

Tucked safely in the shadow of a fallen tree and a boulder, I watched the rival pack come into view.

The Titaniums stood strong, defending the lake as the two remaining hybrids slowly approached the shore. The Venos stalked the area. They spotted us with a quick jerk of the head, a momentary pause, and then charged forward with only one thing on their minds.

Kill.

My body froze over as the battle began and the reality of the situation sank in.

We were outnumbered nine to six, but I'd only have been a liability if I had stayed to fight. The Veno pack swarmed the Titaniums and swallowed them whole. The most experienced fighters struggled to fend off the additional Venos, doing twice the work.

We were at a complete disadvantage.

Through her blocks, Lora looked at me in desperation. She knew that I had abandoned ship, making the decision to save myself and leave the pack to it.

I couldn't sit by and watch this happen. I wouldn't. I wanted to help, but my body and my brain seemed to be at war with one another.

YIELD

I grabbed onto the branch of the fallen tree, trying to ground myself and escape the fear that kept me hidden in the woods. My eyes closed and I listened to the wind against the empty branches. It brought me a sense of peace; enough to think more clearly, at least.

I had been quick to judge Beckle for shutting down and hiding in fear when Donnah needed him most, and now I was following in his footsteps.

Beckle's actions resulted in the death of the person he cared about most (himself), and Donnah.

The same fate would await me unless I swallowed my demons and fought back. Only, I couldn't fight. I had watched the tutorials in training. I'd been on the receiving end of the attack. But it was like my body hit the power off mode whenever it came to fighting back.

I'd told Lora that I wouldn't fight, but in all honesty, the truth was that I *couldn't*.

"Loopholes." I reminded myself. It's how I had survived almost a month on The Farm. I just had to think my way out of the situation. *"There must be a way. There's always a way."*

My mind whizzed through everything I knew about the Veno pack and how I could use the information to our advantage. I took a deep breath, ran my fingers over the moss-covered bark one more time, and before I could talk myself out of it, I leaped from the forest and charged forward with the only weapon I had.

"Everyone stop!" I yelled as I neared the battle. Thankfully, nobody had been severely hurt yet. "What are you doing to yourselves?"

I recalled my past weeks of watching the Venos and picking out their strengths and weaknesses on the screen in the library. If there was one thing that I had noticed, it was that obedience was drilled into them like a drum.

Dickward turned to look at me as I spoke, slowly stalking his way towards me. I tried to get my words out before he could switch into attack mode. "We don't have time for this! The mission states that we have to make it to camp before sundown, and we're all going to face the farmer's repercussions if we carry on fighting."

Dickward stopped, staring at me in frustration.

"We will fail the mission," I continued. "We're just wasting time."

I backed up slowly as the Alpha yelled out, and the caw stopped the other Venos from attacking. They joined in the chorus, the sound nothing like I'd heard before. Chills covered my skin, and this time it wasn't from my damp clothes.

And then the Venos retreated without a word.

I collapsed onto the grassy bank and tried to rid myself of the sound which rang in my ears, burying my head between my legs. I felt sick.

The Titaniums collected themselves, bandaging up any wounds and recovering as Teri and Indigo made it to shore.

"Looks like I missed out." Indigo sounded genuinely disappointed and I let out a long-held, agitated breath. I would happily have swapped places with her.

Nobody would look at me as we gathered our belongings, but at least they kept their opinions to themselves as we set off in search of camp. I could imagine what they were thinking of me, I didn't need to hear anybody say it.

We'd been walking in silence for no more than five minutes when a growl erupted amongst the pack and we all jumped, still on high alert.

"Sorry," Hail said. "I'm just so hungry."

At the thought of food, my stomach replied to Hail's. We made the decision to stop for a few minutes and spear fish from the stream. We ate them raw, peeling the skin off with hand knives and gnawing at them as the map took us uphill, along an old dirt track which was now overgrown and uneven. The further we climbed, the more evident it became that my fitness had improved.

I no longer struggled with a heavy incline, but I focused on breathing exercises to give my mind something to focus on other than my mistakes.

"I'm sorry for running," I blurted when I couldn't take the silence a moment longer. Hail and Jayleigh looked at me, not expecting an apology.

"You came back." Jayleigh shrugged. "It was a moment of weakness but you redeemed yourself, and you probably even

242

saved a few lives in doing so."

"It's fine." Hail shrugged. Only, I knew that he was comparing me to Beckle. We had both let our fear consume us, but the difference was that I broke out of it and managed to help before it was too late.

But Hail was scarred and wouldn't see it that way. It would take a lot for him to move past the trauma and I became more and more worried about him with every passing day.

Nothing I had tried over the past few weeks could snap him out of the bubble of misery that he'd buried himself within. I knew that he was still feeling guilty for what he had done and it was eating him up inside.

So, as per usual, I tried to act normal around him, telling jokes, talking about sleep and food, everything that I knew he enjoyed, but I still couldn't get through to him. He needed more time.

At least the pack had moved on, even if they were still angry and grieving. They had come to the realization that this was Marshall's doing, and not Hail's.

"What do you think will happen if we don't reach the camp in time?" Jayleigh questioned, changing the subject and bringing me away from my thoughts. I had been so worried about the Veno pack all day that it really hadn't crossed my mind until this moment.

Jayleigh considered. "Repercussions... We'll have a time penalty on the next mission? Or there won't be any water near to the camp?"

I shook my head. "If the farmers are dealing repercussions then I can guarantee that we don't want to find out what they are. They won't go easy on us."

"Ares and his intuition again." Jayleigh smiled.

Hail remained quiet as though his mind was elsewhere. Or maybe he was just passed caring?

We reached the end of the track as the sun began to set and in turn, we started to slow, making a small circle around Lora.

"We're here," she announced, setting down her bag and placing the tablet on top of it. I felt a little uneasy with how open the area appeared. We would get the full front of the winter wind, maybe even a little snow at this altitude, and it was visible for miles. If the Venos were nearby then they'd be able to see us for sure. We may as well have painted a bullseye on our backs.

"I don't like it." I stood next to Lora and inspected the area as the rest of the pack got to work on setting up camp. We looked at the circle of red paint, marking the boundaries that signified the safe zone.

"Me either." She shook her head.

"Maybe we should keep going and-" I stopped when I noticed the look on her face.

"The mission ends here. This is where we're supposed to be." She pointed to the circle. "And so, this is where we will stay."

I nodded once in understanding. "Aye, aye, Captain... I'll, uh, go and find some firewood."

Firewood...

I regretted my words almost immediately as I walked away. Collecting wood was going to be a near to impossible task considering that there were no trees nearby. I groaned internally and ventured outside of the circle, noticing a small woodland a little way down the hill. I was sure that I could quickly get to the treeline and return by the time the sun started to set if I made a brisk jog, and so I scurried like a squirrel to collect twigs and small branches.

Find wood.

Return to camp before sundown.

It should have been a simple task, and it would have been if I had been paying attention, but I was too focused on rushing around to notice that I had a scavenging partner.

It was only as I bent to pick up a prize-winning log that I noticed movement further across the woodland and the clicking sound registered in my mind.

My heart hammered in my chest as I slowly glanced up.

Ten feet away stood Dickward.

He appeared motionless, unblinking, with his neck bent at an inhuman angle, his yellowing eyes fixated on me.

A creepy smile which will forever haunt my dreams crawled over his teeth as our eyes met.

"You're not getting away this time," he cackled.

CHAPTER
FIFTEEN

ARES

I started to back away slowly, hoping that if I didn't make any sudden movements then he wouldn't attack. It was doubtful but worth a try.

"Um, Steven…" that was his real name, wasn't it? I tried to recall. "I really don't think that you want to do this."

His head tilted in the opposite direction with one swift snap of the neck. He paused briefly and I wondered if it had hurt. "Don't I?"

His voice was raspy, as though he hadn't drunk anything in several days. It sounded like the words scratched at his throat.

I took another step backwards, retreating out of the tree line. I could see the sun quickly disappearing now.

"If you follow me, you'll be out of your camp parameter

when the sun sets." I used the same trick as this afternoon, if it had worked once then hopefully it would work again.

My life depended on it.

"Maybe it will be worth it, it'll be fun." He snarled his teeth like a dog, they appeared pointy as though they'd been filed down and I tried to shake the image that appeared in my mind of him chewing into my neck.

I shook my head, still slowly making my way back up the hill. "You're a long way from camp," I concluded, on the basis that I couldn't hear any other Venos nearby. "The farmers won't be happy with you if you set a bad example for your pack. They might even deal you more severe repercussions for purposely disobeying their orders."

Dickward stopped stalking me as he reached the edge of the woods and his attention snapped to the sun which was now setting behind the mountain, proving that my words were true.

His smile faded as he realised that no *'fun'* would be had tonight. The anger in his eyes was uncontrolled. "You just wait until tomorrow." He held onto the *'s'* a little too long for any normal human. "You're a dead man walking."

I continued to back up until he had completely retreated into the woods. Even then I moved slowly, the last thing I ever wanted to see was a mutated Veno hybrid. They were scary enough in their human state.

The clicking sound started to fade away as he moved further down the hill, and only when I was sure that he'd left completely did I sprint to the Titanium camp, almost tripping over my own feet and dropping several sticks in the process.

Zee, Lora, and Hail stood within the boundary of the circle, staring as I approached.

I unpiled the logs and collapsed onto the ground as my jelly legs gave way.

"Thanks for the help, guys." I almost didn't recognize my voice through its shaking.

"That was some scary-assed shit." Zee was still staring at the woods as though waiting for Dickward to return.

"You're telling me." I tried to laugh, I felt a little hysterical from the adrenaline rush. "Try standing ten feet away from him as he tells you that killing you will be fun."

"I'd show him some fun," she replied. "Why don't we ambush him now, whilst he's alone?" She picked up one of the sticks and studied it, then got a feel for the weight as she proceeded to use it as a staff, spinning it over her shoulders. "I'll spear him."

"That's not a good idea. I'm not sure about you guys, but I'd rather go into tomorrow's mission without any repercussions," Lora shut her down.

"For fucks sake!" Zee threw her *spear* into the grass in a tantrum and stomped off.

"She is one angry hybrid," I said through a shallow breath.

"She swears a lot," Lora agreed. "It makes you wonder if she swore before she came to The Farm or if she picked it up during hibernation."

Hail collected the firewood from me and left us to talk, giving me a knowing look as he walked away.

"How could she have picked it up in hibernation? We were asleep for fourteen years."

"Not asleep, really. We were in a simulation, so our minds were still learning."

My face fell blank. My knowledge of simulation was limited. "What? What does that mean?"

"Our minds were still active, so the farmers groomed us into the warrior mind-frame by influencing our dreams."

"Well, they didn't do a great job of grooming me," I joked. "How is that even possible?"

"We were semi-conscious the whole time. It was almost like a strange form of hypnosis, seeing things that weren't there and imaging whatever the farmers programmed. We were sent on imaginary missions and our results were recorded. Only when the farmers were happy with our results did they wake us up."

"That's crazy..." It seemed impossible. "But the farmers wiped our memories, so what was the point of training us through hibernation?"

"They only wiped our personal memories. The information we learned and the muscle memory still remains, which is how I know for certain that you were not concentrating in combat."

"And, we're back to that..." I sighed.

"You know the moves, you've learnt them before. The

muscle memory will still be there. You just have to coax it out of that enormous brain of yours."

"I think that my brain is probably pretty average-sized. I wouldn't say it's enormous, it's probably not even considered large-"

"You need to believe in yourself," she cut me off. "You'll die if you continue to run from danger. This is Phase Two, there are no rules, and Steven just pinned a target on your back."

"Like I need reminding…"

She cast her eyes to the sky and what had turned out to be a spectacle of a sunset. The sky had been watching us, and it celebrated the day's victory with streamers of pink and orange clouds. The sun had almost completely retired in exhaustion.

The majority of the pack had finished their tasks and congregated on the hill, watching as the last few minutes of light faded away. This was one of the finest moments we had shared, and it was one I'd always remember.

Beside me, Lora took a deep breath in and released it slowly, savouring the small glimpse of freedom. Golden hour suited her well. Her cropped hair blew gently in the breeze and I found myself watching her rather than the sunset.

I wanted to move closer, but I knew how she would react to any sort of physical contact, so I respected her wishes and stayed put. She must have felt my gaze because after a while she turned to look at me with a quizzical expression. "Do I have something on my face?"

250

"What? No. I was just-"

"I'm joking." She laughed, she knew exactly why I was looking at her but avoided addressing it. "You did well earlier." Lora nodded in the direction of the woodland where Dickward had interrupted my search for firewood. She spoke quietly to avoid disrupting the rest of the pack from the peaceful setting we shared. "And I'm not mad at you for running when the fight broke out, we both know how it would have ended if you'd stayed."

I nodded, unsure of how to answer.

Thinking over the day's events reminded me of how much danger I'd managed to get myself into; especially if I was still going to try to avoid mutating.

"I'm sorry that I didn't pay more attention during combat. You were just trying to help me and I threw it back in your face."

She shrugged. "Hindsight is a wonderful thing. I'll get Jayleigh to show you a few moves later."

It was a good idea. Jayleigh was quick on her feet and knew how to wield a knife as though it were a part of her body. She gave even Lora a run for her money.

A thought crossed my mind then, and I questioned if the reason I couldn't fight Lora was because she was the Alpha. We were programmed to risk our lives for her, to protect her at any cost, so of course, attacking would feel unnatural. Practicing with Jayleigh suddenly seemed ideal. I could put my theory to the test.

"So what did you tell Steven to get him to back off?" Lora

asked out of curiosity, referring to my run-in with the Alpha in the woods.

"You mean Dickward?" I corrected.

"Dickward?" She laughed. "Why do you call him that?"

"It sounds less intimidating than calling him the Alpha of the Veno pack." I shrugged. "And I think it suits him better than Steven, the long greasy hair, the strange eyes… I don't know. It just seems right."

"Okay." She didn't need any more of an explanation. "Then, what did you say to Dickward?"

I smirked. "I told him that I don't fight girls."

The rest of the pack turned around as Lora disrupted the silence with laughter. It was a beautiful sound, although not everyone seemed to think the same.

Tye appeared immediately. I was surprised that I'd actually managed to get this long alone with Lora before he butted in.

He dropped two dead rabbits and a squirrel next to my head and I took that as my queue to leave.

"What's so funny?" He jerked his head in my direction.

"I almost died, nothing new," I replied as I rose to my feet, trying not to notice the fact that Tye was squaring up to me. Now was not the time, nor the place.

"See you later." I patted his arm as I walked past. I knew how much it would annoy him.

"Yeah, you'd better run. Nerd!" he called after me, seething.

And to think that this was the same guy who had picked me

up and let me lean on his shoulder when I was injured. If he had known that I would interfere with his relationship with Lora then he would have left me in that coffin to rot.

I could still hear Lora laughing as I walked away.

Once the sun had vanished completely, we got to work preparing for dinner.

It was cosy but cold around the campfire. We wrapped ourselves in sleeping bags and cooked the food that Tye had caught together with some rice, scranning it as though we hadn't eaten in weeks.

Jayleigh helped me with some basic self-defence once our food had settled a little. She made several jokes about how Lora and I must have been making use of our time during training because I obviously hadn't learned a thing.

"I wish," I muttered as we got to work.

I tried to take it all in, fighting the voice in my mind which warned me that I was welcoming the anger. I took a deep breath and tried to calm myself as I repeated Jayleigh's moves, pretending that it was nothing more than a dance.

Soon enough, I was able to block a single fist to the face. Only the one though, the second caught my right cheekbone.

"I wasn't prepared for two!" I complained.

"My God, you take this way too seriously. Lighten up, have some fun!" She laughed and swept her leg underneath my feet in one swift motion. I didn't trust Jayleigh anymore. Her version of fun was the same as Dickward's.

Tye, Indigo and Zee laughed in amusement from the campfire as I took a tumble to the ground.

Climbing back to my feet quickly, I braced myself and tried to ignore my audience. "Again." I nodded, ignoring the pain and the embarrassment, just glad that at least I was able to think straight whilst I practiced with Jayleigh.

Once I nailed the move and the pack became bored of watching, Jayleigh moved onto a more advanced combination involving a counterattack.

I started to gain confidence as I progressed. She seemed impressed by my efforts, and I started to realize that maybe fighting wasn't so bad after all.

It was nothing more than a little friendly competition. But, in true Ares style, I ended up taking it one step too far, catching Jayleigh off guard and jabbing her nose which crunched upon impact. I leapt back and heaved into the grass.

She laughed through the pain. "That's more like it, Ares! Oh... it's bleeding."

I retched again.

"I'm so sorry." I tried to pull myself together but the sight of the blood made me queasy.

I'd done that. I'd hurt her.

I pulled a tissue from my bag and handed it to her to help it stop. "Does it hurt?"

"No, it's fine. Don't apologize, you did great!" Her voice sounded nasal through the bloody tissue.

We made the decision to turn in for the night after my fiftieth apology and her bleeding began to slow.

Diego had created a shelter out of the materials found in our backpacks. The make-shift tent seemed small for the nine of us, but Diego was proud of his creation and held out an arm as we entered. "Bienvenidos a mi casa." He welcomed us and Jayleigh swooned.

"God, he's so exotic." She fanned herself with the used, bloody tissue. "How long have you been speaking... Italian?" She lingered by the entrance to ask him.

I mentally face palmed as he replied, "Oh, I think I'm actually Spanish."

I nodded as the accent registered and tried to ignore the rest of the conversation as I set up my sleeping bag next to Hail, who was already snoozing in the corner, and then threw my backpack outside to make more room under the shelter. It was still too much of a squeeze for us all, so, of course, I struggled to sleep.

Hail was snoring into my right ear, Jayleigh pressed up against my left arm, and Zee was laying opposite me, kicking my feet with hers every so often.

The experience was exhausting, although not exhausting enough to knock me out, apparently.

And it seemed that I wasn't the only one struggling when a few hours into the night, I watched Teri scramble over the sleeping bodies to leave the tent. She ducked out into the night and I eventually fell asleep awaiting her return.

CHAPTER
SIXTEEN

ARES

I slept light.

The sound of movement awoke me the following morning, accompanied by the sound of pouring rain hitting against the plastic sheet. I peeled my eyes open to find a large dip in the center of the makeshift roof, full of water. It wouldn't take much more before it collapsed.

"Teri?" Lora's voice encircled the tent. I frowned, trying to summon the events of the previous day, and chilled by the remembrance of my run-in with Dickward.

Lora's voice cut through the rain again, and as my mind cleared the sleep which lingered, it dawned on me that didn't recall Teri returning to the tent last night.

I quickly clambered from the shelter, pulling my raincoat

from my backpack and proceeding to search for Lora and Teri. They had both vanished now.

I was in such a state of panic that I couldn't even muster the brainpower to fit my arms into the sleeves of the jacket, so I carried it as I searched.

After doing a round of the tent, I walked up to the corpse of the campfire where I found Lora standing at the boundary of camp.

"Lora?" I questioned, unsure if she had noticed me following her, or heard me approach over the sound of the rain. She didn't turn at the sound of my voice but continued to fixate on something beyond the borders.

I didn't want to look.

As I approached, I realized that the something was Teri. Or, at least, it used to be.

My heart stammered and my knees shook. "What happened?" My coat fell to the floor.

Lora was deflated. "I have no idea."

Teri's body lay at a strange angle, her skin pierced as though she had been used as a human pin-cushion. Her bloodshot eyes remained open, peering up to the sky, and the rain washed away the blood which had teared down her cheeks.

It was a gruesome sight.

Lora collapsed to the ground and covered her face with her hands.

I quickly dropped with her and scooped her up, holding her

tightly.

"Don't." She tried to push me away. "I don't want you to see me like this."

"Then I won't look." I pulled her in closer, as I had wanted to do for so long, but turned my head. "Crying is nothing to be ashamed of, Lora. It's not a weakness." I pulled one of her hands from her face and held it close to my chest so that she could feel my heart beat against her palm. "It's a reminder that you're human."

The sobs began in short bursts as she buried her face into my neck.

"She didn't deserve this," she whispered through the tears.

I shook my head. "Nobody does."

I found that I was crying too. I'd barely known Teri well enough to call her a friend, but she was a part of the pack. A member of the team. And even though I had taken Hail's advice to keep the Omegas at arm's length, I would still miss her.

"It's all my fault."

I pulled Lora away to reason with her. "It's not your fault at all. She left the boundaries after sundown, she knew that there would be repercussions."

I'd never seen such sadness in Lora's eyes. "I should have reminded everyone of the rules, I should-"

"Stop." I placed a finger over her lips, not wanting to hear any more of it. "Everybody watched the video and we knew not to leave camp. You can't blame yourself for this. Teri made the decision for herself." I pulled my finger away quickly. Now wasn't the time to consider how soft Lora's lips felt under my touch.

"You think she left intentionally?"

I didn't know what to think. "Possibly. Why else would she go?"

Neither of us spoke as we considered what could have been going through the Omega's mind. Did she feel responsible for the fight against the Venos, because of her lack of swimming experience? Had she hated life on The Farm as much as I did?

"It doesn't make sense." Lora wiped her tears with the back of her hand.

"Nothing here makes sense," I contributed. Lora returned to her spot on my shoulder as the rain continued to pour. I picked up my coat and opened it around the both of us, fiddling with the toggles of the hood so that it sat perfectly on my head.

A small snicker disrupted Lora's tears. "Thank you," she murmured against my shoulder.

"For what?"

She paused, not sure how to respond. "For being you." She snagged at my hood's toggle.

I looked at her, not fully understanding what she meant, "You're welcome." I smiled. "Although, I've lost count of how many times I've wished that I was like everybody else."

I tightened my arms around her.

"How do I tell everyone?" She spoke after a short while.

"I don't think that there's a right or a wrong way. Whatever we say is going to come as a shock, we just have to support them in any way that we can."

"We?" she questioned.

"Of course. You don't have to go through this by yourself."

She didn't reply, so I wasn't sure if she approved of my involvement. She'd spent so long absorbing the pressure alone, the idea of having somebody to lean on must have scared her. I followed as she stood, taking one last glance at Teri's punctured body, and then we descended back to the tent.

Tye stood at the entrance, watching as we approached but saying nothing.

He didn't need to.

His eyes said it all.

Dickward wasn't the only one putting a target on my back. If the Veno Alpha didn't kill me, then Tye would finish the job himself.

HIM

I had made the right decision to force the animals into Phase Two early. Seeing how quickly they were adapting and becoming real warriors was pleasing. It was a small relief, but I couldn't celebrate just yet, there was still a long way for them to go.

In a change of events, Tye was becoming a problem for the Titanium pack. They needed to work as a team now more than ever, and this one individual was threatening to destroy the peace.

Of course, the root of the problem was Ares; it always came back to Ares. But, until he shared the information that he'd learned with the rest of the pack, he had to be protected. He was the key.

"Amber," I called to the woman nearest the screens. "Give me Tye's report."

She scrambled to find the information, clicking through various apps and folders on her tablet. I was losing patience. The farmers here had only one job; to collect information from their designated hybrid and recite it back whenever I asked. I would have loved to be in their position, and I struggled to comprehend how such an easy task could take so long. "Today, Amber!"

Her eyes widened in panic and she read out the information with haste.

"You really should give them a break." A voice appeared in the doorway to the Observatorium once she was done and I didn't have to turn to recognize it.

"Daniel," I welcomed my uncle, I'd become a fantastic liar in his presence. "It's always a pleasure."

"How is Phase Two proceeding?"

Small talk. Urgh.

It had been weeks since he'd last made an effort to visit. We weren't close. We co-existed on The Farm with very little face-to-face interaction, so today's interruption came as a surprise.

"What are you doing here?" I didn't answer his question.

Daniel looked baffled. "Just checking in. Am I allowed to do that?"

The farmers buried their heads, pretending not to hear our family disagreement.

"You're allowed, but you've never bothered before so I don't see why you're pretending to care now."

"You know why," Daniel shot back. "And I'm not pretending. I do care, even if I'm not always in here to prove it. I have my own job to do, you know?"

I gave Daniel the silent treatment, turning back to the camera screens and pretending to be more interested in the animals than our conversation.

I didn't know how to cope with family stress.

It had been a long time since anyone had really been there to support me.

"Is that all I'm getting?" Daniel tutted and joined in watching the screened wall. We stayed silent for a few minutes as I made myself busy with the tablet on my arm.

"Launch the additional drones." I pointed at the techs who sat in the corner of the room. Both packs had now left camp and commenced with day two, and it was time to follow.

"Teri has gone," Daniel noticed.

"And you haven't," I replied and Daniel finally got the

message. I didn't turn to wave as my uncle left the Observatorium, but I sighed in relief.

I was better off alone.

That's what I was used to.

"Maybe I'll regret the way I treated Daniel in a few hours," I thought, but I didn't stop now to question if feelings had been hurt, I'd never been very good at caring, a trait that I'd inherited from Father.

I could only concentrate on myself and what would produce the best results for The Farm. Confident in my choices, I printed the plan for the next few days.

"We're pushing Phase Three up by a week?" My assistant questioned the paper, worried that there was a mistake.

"Desperate times call for desperate measures," I replied.

Only, I had been desperate three weeks ago.

Now, I was verging on hopeless.

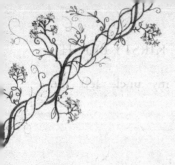

CHAPTER
SEVENTEEN

ARES

As expected, the news of Teri's death came as a shock to everyone. Nobody spoke as we disassembled the tent and packed the equipment away. I tried to answer their questions, keeping the attention away from Lora who still seemed shaken through her facade.

"Congratulations on making it through day one, Hybrids," she paused the reading, and I knew that she was taking a moment to think of Teri. "New supplies await you at Point A on the map, use them as you see fit. You must overcome all obstacles to make it to camp at Point B by sundown, and as you have already witnessed, repercussions will be dealt to those outside of the camp's boundary after dark. Good luck." Lora's face was as readable as a rock. She spoke quickly, and once she was done she simply shut down the tablet and walked away. "We leave in three minutes!" She yelled back to the group, glancing in Tye's direction for too long.

Hail gave me a look of confusion. I shook my head.

"It's been a rough morning."

"I've only been up five minutes. What did I miss? Other than Teri's... You know."

"I'll fill you in on the walk," I said. I didn't want anyone to overhear.

Two and a half minutes later, we started the journey to Point A to pick up our supplies. We set off down the hill, keeping an eye over our shoulder in case the Veno pack followed.

I had almost forgotten about Dickward's threat for a full half hour, but the it crept back into my mind as I stepped over the red line on the ground. I walked a little faster so that we overtook Zee and Indigo who were laughing quietly together, seemingly oblivious to the fact that the rest of the group were mourning and that the Venos could be around any corner. We caught up with Jayleigh.

"I bumped into Dickward in the woods last night," I whispered. Jayleigh freaked out at the thought of it. "I managed to get him to back off, but he told me that he'd kill me today."

Saying it out loud suddenly made it feel very real. I took another look back for good measure.

"Well, if that's not terrifying then I don't know what is," she replied.

"You're toast," Hail added and then paused. "Oh, toast... Smothered in butter." He held his stomach. "Stop it."

It seemed that being away from the barn was taking Hail's mind from everything that had happened recently. His mood seemed brighter than it had been in days. At least there was *one* positive to come as a result of Phase Two.

"Yeah, so I just wanted to say that it was nice knowing you both, thanks for everything, and I'll see you in the afterlife." I was only half joking.

"You're not going to die," Hail replied matter of factly.

"You just told me that I'm toast. There's no way I could fight him off, even if I mutated."

"What if you evolved?"

I shrugged. "I wouldn't know how to evolve. I've never done it. And it's a damn shame that I can't get any pointers from somebody who has."

Hail huffed.

I knew that I was pushing my luck. But even if Hail was mad at me for bringing it up, he couldn't be mad for too long because the odds had it that I wasn't making it to the end of the day. Too many people out here wanted me dead.

He stared at me for a long time and must have read how desperate I was somewhere on my face.

"Fine, I'll tell you. But only because," he paused for effect, "you're my only friend."

I couldn't believe his words.

Jayleigh's hands flew into the air and she started ranting about how she'd been there for him, day in and day out since he arrived, even if he didn't appreciate her company to start with.

We ignored her because we knew that it would annoy her.

"You mean it?" I was genuinely touched, I put my hand out so that he could do the handshake he loved so much.

"Yeah, Bro. For real."

"Can I at least stay and listen?" Jayleigh asked.

Hail shoved a hand in her face. "No, this is friend stuff. Get out."

He pushed her back so that she was no longer walking in line with us. When she started to protest, he got her into a headlock and messed up her plaited hair. "No, I'm joking, get in here." He wrapped his arm around her shoulder. "You're not quite on the friend level. But you're a Bro. Or a Broski, a Broskette? What would you rather?"

"Bro suits just fine," Jayleigh beamed.

"I'll be dead by the time you tell us," I reminded him.

"Okay, yeah sorry."

"Just let me have my moment," Jayleigh shut me down.

"The moments gone, *Bra*." I shrugged.

"Killjoy."

"So, what do you want to know?" Hail interrupted.

"Everything."

"What does it feel like?"

Hail smiled. "It feels like electric. Not like when Mad

Marshall tasers you. It's like energy running through your veins. Time seems to go slower and everything seems so clear. Your mind feels free and calm. You can control every part of your body, it makes you feel so... alive."

"As opposed to feeling dead?" I joked.

He held his hand out in front of his face as he spoke, imagining the energy in his fingertips.

"It feels good, Bro." He nodded.

"How do you do it?" Jayleigh asked, she watched Hail's arm in awe, as though she too could see the so-called electricity.

He shrugged. "I don't know, I've only ever done it after mutating. And I'm always so angry then, I don't take notice of what happens."

I thought back to the fight, which I had so desperately tried to block from my memory, but seemed to recall the certain revelation I'd had as Hail reached his darkest moment.

"It's Donnah."

Hail didn't respond. He tried to make his face as unreadable as possible.

"What do you mean?" Jayleigh asked.

"Well, whenever he thinks about her whilst he's in his mutated state, it mellows him and must release the hormones needed to evolve."

Hail frowned. "Hormans…?"

"Hormones…" I needed to simplify. "Getting angry makes us mutate. Feeling love whilst in the mutated state must make us evolve." I used my hands to help me explain. In one hand was anger, and in the other hand was love. "The emotions are on opposite ends of the scales so they balance each other out. It brings us back to a place between our human and animal state to reach a happy medium." I fused my hands together. "Like levelled balance scales."

"That kind of makes sense," Jayleigh considered. "So if I mutate and then think about what I love most, I'd be able to evolve?"

"Theoretically." I nodded.

"What do you love most Jayleigh?" Hail nudged her.

"Well I was going to say you but apparently we're not friends, so I'm going to have to say pizza."

"Oh... Pizza, I'd kill for pizza right now." We looked at him, both a little wary, especially now he knew how to fully harness his power. "But I'm on a killing ban, so I'm not gonna."

I wished that the whole world was on a killing ban, it would solve ninety-nine percent of my problems.

Ahead, Lora stopped at the crossroad, taking a look around for the supplies. A drone appeared, carrying a sling which dropped before us. We unwrapped the goods as it flew away, finding a new backpack for each of us containing equipment, a fully powered portable charger for the tablet, and a basket of fruit and bread.

I sorted through my new backpack, which was several times heavier than the last one, and tried to make room for leftover rice, my knife, the plastic sheet that we had used for the shelter, and my sleeping bag.

It was a squash but I successfully closed the zipper and fell back into line. Lora handed out the food, making her way down the queue so that everyone had an equal share.

I could see the anger in her eyes as she approached me. "What's up?" I held onto her elbow as she handed me my portion.

She shook her head, not wanting to elaborate in front of Jayleigh and Hail. "I'll catch you later."

I continued to watch her as she moved down the line. I'd never seen her so distracted. She had always been great at hiding her emotions from the rest of the pack, but the mask was slipping.

We started to walk as we ate and Jayleigh spoke between mouthfuls. "What the hell is going on between you two?"

I shook my head. "Nothing is going on between us. We have established mutual feelings, but we're not acting on them for the sake of the pack, and the rest of the world."

Jayleigh's mouth dropped and I witnessed the state of her half-chewed bread.

Hail began to sing into my ear. "Ares and Lora kissing in a tree, K-I-S-I-N-G!" He didn't seem to notice that he was missing a letter.

"Keep your voice down!" I tried to calm their excitement. "Nothing is happening between us, and nothing will until the war is over."

"But it might not ever be over!" Jayleigh seemed as disappointed as I felt.

"Too much is riding on us... Love is a distraction," I recited Lora's words.

"Bullshit," Hail muttered. "Love is a powerful force, it will always provide an answer."

We stared at him, dumbfounded.

"Have you been foraging again?" I questioned. It would definitely explain today's upbeat manner.

Jayleigh stared at him in disgust. "You make me sick sometimes, you know that?"

"I like to call it being in touch with my emotions," Hail defended. "At least when I evolve I'll have something to think about other than pizza."

Jayleigh threw her head back and laughed. "Yeah, I can't argue with that."

The pack started to gather up ahead. The stream next to us had dropped several feet and a cliff trailed our path. It connected to a much larger river, below the remains of a wooden bridge.

"We need to get to the other side of the river." Lora studied the map on the tablet. "But there doesn't seem to be any way around."

I stood at the edge of the cliff where, far below, it met the fast-flowing water. The bridge was in a state of no repair; rotten and unstable, with several pieces missing. It was unusable for sure.

"Can't we just swim across?" Zee questioned.

Lora shook her head. "The water is rapid. We can't risk being carried downstream and losing time trying to get back on the path."

"Diego, go and find a large fallen tree to place across the river," Tye commanded.

Diego cocked an eyebrow, his dry tone almost made his words humorous. "I can carry branches, a tree is pushing it too far. Idiot."

Tye frowned. "Who do you think you're talking to?" He squared up to Diego who was almost a whole foot taller.

That would have been a fight I'd love to watch, but I couldn't let them waste time. I was still too aware that the Venos were out there, most likely tracking us down as they made their way to the Veno camp.

"We were given supplies this morning. The farmers knew that we'd be faced with this challenge so I'm sure they'd give us something to help. Everybody empty your bags." I pulled out the contents of mine as I spoke. "Leave anything that looks remotely useful to one side."

Tye and Diego continued to glare, and then slowly backed away from each other. Tye threw his bag in my direction, not wanting to follow my orders, but knowing that my plan was the only sensible one we had. "Nerd."

I didn't object. He might start on me next, and that would

be another waste of time.

I left the rope out, it wasn't long enough to reach the other side of the river, but I knew it would come in handy. I watched as others started to set items aside, too.

One particular piece of equipment caught my eye. I wasn't sure what it was but it looked like an anchor, with four legs and a large loop at the end. No wonder my backpack had felt heavier today. Hail threw an identical item in my direction and a plan formed in my mind as I started to tie the ropes together. I also tied each end of the rope to a four-legged hook.

"We just need to find a way to hook this to the bank on the other side," I explained. "And then we can climb across. Jayleigh, you have the best aim. Try and hook this to the oak tree." I pointed to the old tree on the other side of the river. It had a low, sturdy branch ideal for the rope to wrap around.

She nodded once, trusting my leadership even though she doubted the plan. Jayleigh made throwing look easy, precision seemed to come naturally to her. I'd never seen her miss a shot.

The hook swung around the branch and the teeth perfectly snagged the rope. We yanked it to make sure it was sturdy, and then I took the second hook and tried to find a branch on our side of the bank to secure it. A short way down the path I found the perfect tree. It was slightly smaller than the oak meaning that we'd have to climb on a small incline, but it would have to do. I wrapped the anchor around the branch several times until the rope was taut, and then hooked it.

I jumped up to the makeshift bridge, swinging to make sure the rope could take our weight. "Diego," I motioned for him to do the same as he was the heaviest of the bunch.

He copied my motion and the rope remained strong. I mentally prepared myself for the climb, trying to calm my shaking hands. Of course, I planned on going first. I was the test run.

If I fell then I'd only have myself to blame. I tightened the straps on my backpack and tied the loose fabric across my chest for safe measure.

The rest of the pack gathered around to watch as I hefted myself up, wrapping my legs around the rope like a monkey. Seeing the river from this angle was a whole new level of scary. The drop was at least thirty feet, the water swirled and splashed beneath me as I started to cross my arms, one in front of the other, and pushed myself forward.

"It's like the rope of doom," I told myself. *"Just horizontal instead of vertical."*

If I could do that daily, then surely I could do this.

As one arm lifted, so did the opposite leg. I quickly realised that monkey traverse was a lot more difficult than it looked, especially with the elements against me. The rain battered down, making it difficult to see without getting water in my eyes and I struggled to grab at the rope, my hands slipping. To make things worse, the wind was doing everything in its power to get rid of me. I made sure that my legs were secure. If my hands let go of the rope, at least my legs could hold me up.

I was halfway across the river when the blood started to rush to my head and the dizziness kicked in.

I tried to bench my head up for a second, giving me time to release the pressure that being upside down had created, but the weight of the backpack pulled me back down.

The faster I crossed the river, the better.

The pack started to cheer as I neared land. As I hovered over it, I let my feet drop from the rope and lowered myself to the ground, knelt as the blood started to circulate in a normal manner again, and Hail followed my lead, jumping up to the rope on the other side.

I cheered as one by one, the team started to cross the river.

The plan was working.

Lora went last. She stared at me from the opposite side of the water with her hands on her hips. Her hair was slick from the rain and clung to her face and neck because she always refused to put her hood up. She looked fierce.

I waited for her to pinch her thumbs as she always did in high places. Only this time she didn't, continuing to stare at me instead.

I smiled, confident that Lora would complete this challenge like a walk in the park. Her strength was immense, and her mindset never wavered in challenges. She was prepared both physically and mentally.

She jumped up and started to cross the river.

Only, there was a problem with my plan.

I hadn't considered that the Veno pack would cross our path at this exact moment.

Tye heard them before anyone else as they made their way through the trees.

"No," he whispered.

His disapproval perked my interest, and as I focused in, beyond the sound of the river and the rain, I could hear them too.

That awful clicking sound sent fear shivering down my spine.

"Lora!" I yelled as the pack emerged from the trees on the other side of the river. "Quick!"

I wasn't the only one yelling.

She looked back to see what the commotion was about, to find that the Veno pack were approaching with speed.

The Venos were quick to act, gunning for the makeshift bridge I had built. One by one, they started to jump up to the rope, giving barely a meter distance between each hybrid.

I had tested the weight for myself.

I had tested the weight for Diego.

But I hadn't tested whether the rope would be able to hold Lora and the whole Veno pack.

The branch of the old oak started to creak and crack as more and more weight loaded on.

Lora looked back at me. Even upside-down her eyes seemed

assured and calm, but her glare held a certain concentration; less of annoyance or fear, and more of a need. She focused in, oblivious to the fact that they were closing in on her.

What was she trying to tell me?

I stared back, panicking for her safety. Shouldn't she have been trying to cross the rope instead of staring at me?

There were three members of the Veno pack on the rope with Lora now, closing distance as she broke from the trance and started to-

What was she doing?

I feared for her now.

The next series of events happened so quickly that I barely had time to process them.

She reached down to her foot where she had stowed her knife in her calf pocket. And then, as though God were creating a distraction for us, a flash of perfectly timed lightning erupted through the sky. Lora sliced the knife across the rope behind her in one swift motion.

"Branch!"

Her voice echoed around my mind as though I'd imagined it. But that was impossible. She dropped out of view and the rest of the pack scurried forward to see what had happened.

The force of the drop caused the branch of the old oak to give way.

It crashed to the ground and I leapt to take hold of the anchor that raced forwards, toward the edge of the bank. I clung

to the branch for dear life, knowing that Lora was still dangling on the other end, over the river. It pulled me toward the edge of the cliff and I dug my heels into the ground.

"A little help here!" I yelled as I continued to slip forward in the slushy mud that the rain had created.

Diego was quick to assist, grabbing the rope from further forward. One by one, the pack joined in and we reeled Lora up together.

A hand appeared and Tye helped her over the edge and back onto solid ground. Everybody crowded around her; offering assistance; telling her how badass she was; realizing that we had pockets at the bottom of our leggings.

I caught my breath, watching as four members of the Veno pack washed away downstream with the reckless tide.

Dickward remained on the bank at the other side of the river, glaring at us.

Any other time, I would have felt threatened.

I would have overthought the look in his eye and the fact that he was surely planning each of our slow and painful deaths, especially as his eyes landed on me.

The rain soaked down on us and the wind howled through the trees, pushing us to move. The weather was telling us to get going or else we wouldn't make it to camp in time.

But I really couldn't absorb anything that happened at this moment.

I was busy trying to calm myself.

Trying to recover.

I looked to Lora who read the astonished look on my face and gave me the small shake of the head which I had come to know meant *"say nothing"*.

I couldn't if I'd wanted to. I was speechless for the first time in a very long time.

The questions were building and building and never ceasing. It was only making me more anxious.

As we collected ourselves and pushed forwards to make it to camp, I was finally able to mutter the barely audible words, "What the... Crap?"

CHAPTER
EIGHTEEN

ARES

I walked in silence, trying to find an explanation for Lora's voice in my head. Had I imagined it? Was it just my subconscious warning me that the branch was going to snap?

Hours passed and I barely spoke. I listened to Jayleigh and Hail's pointless musings, switching in and out of the conversation. Somewhere along the journey, the storm gave way to a clear sky, and I reluctantly removed my hood, feeling as though my safety blanket had been ripped away. Of course, I knew that a hood wouldn't protect me from the Venos. If anything, it would become more of a hindrance in a fight, but something about it comforted me.

"What do you guys actually know about the war?" Jayleigh

asked and it perked my attention enough to draw my mind away from my worries.

"Not much," I replied, deciding to keep my answer short and sweet. They'd know if I was lying. The less I spoke, the better.

Thankfully, Hail lifted all of the pressure from me completely.

"It's close."

Jayleigh and I shared a look before turning to him in confusion, I noted his odd choice of words and pushed for an explanation. "What do you mean, close?"

"They're outside," he replied.

"Well yeah, I'd be a bit worried if they were inside." Nervous laughter came from Jayleigh's direction.

"No, you're not getting me," Hail huffed.

I raised an eyebrow. "We're not understanding, or you're not explaining yourself properly?"

Hail paused and realized that he was going to have to start from the beginning. "Okay. That night that I... killed Beckle, I ran away, and I could hear Marshall following and I thought he was going to kill me because he had a gun and he's crazy so I ran as fast and far as I could and-"

"Breathe, Hail," I reminded him, his voice was gaining speed as the story developed.

He took in a large amount of air before continuing. "And I ran right to the edge of The Farm, behind Mount Two, and somebody was standing on the other side of the fence, watching me."

I stopped walking.

An icy shiver flew from my toes to the small of my neck where it settled and made home for several minutes.

"Somebody, like a refugee looking for safety in The Farm?" I suggested.

He shook his head. "She tried calling me closer. She knew my name."

"How could she possibly know your name?" Jayleigh questioned, she'd stopped walking now too.

Hail paused. "That's not all. She had red eyes, and the smell just wasn't right, you know? Jayleigh, you smell like pineapples. And Ares, you smell like mint and freshly cut grass. Humans smell like salt…" He pulled himself back to the story again, "But this woman? I don't know. She smelt… dead."

Jayleigh's eyes reflected the same fear I felt.

"They're not human," I whispered Lora's words. Whatever Hail had seen beyond the fence sent alarm bells ringing. The farmers felt the same fear. It explained how quickly everything had escalated since that night. The challenges had stopped, and Phase Two seemed to have come out of nowhere.

"We have to tell Lora." I quickly picked up the pace of my walk. I didn't care what Tye thought, he could try to stop me but this was just too important.

"Why haven't you said anything before!?" Jayleigh yelled at

Hail whilst we marched to the front of the pack.

"I had just killed a guy!" He threw his hands in the air. "My head was a mess."

"Lora!" I yelled as we neared.

"Ares, we don't have time-"

"It's about the war. Hail saw a woman outside the fence."

Lora stopped, taken aback by the outburst. She seemed just as rattled as I was. We were the only ones who really knew how dangerous the situation could become. "What?"

"She was dead." Hail added.

I shook my head. "No, she wasn't dead." I shot Hail a look, insisting that he let me do the talking. "It was on the night of the fight with Beckle. When Hail ran away, he found the woman, she knew his name and tried to call him over whilst he was in his evolved state. He said that she had red eyes and she smelt dead."

She looked at the ground, I could see the gears turning in her mind. "Hail, what happened after you saw her? Did she run away?"

Hail shook his head. "Marshall was following me in a truck so I ran off and left her there."

And I hadn't seen Marshall since. Suddenly, I worried that the thing on the other side of the fence knew his name too.

Maybe it was just a coincidence.

Or, maybe another person had become a victim of the war that night.

"Okay." Lora continued to process the information, keeping

the panic from her voice. "It's more than likely that the farmers already know, but I'll contact them later to be sure. For now, we must get to camp."

I hadn't noticed that the sun had started to slowly sink behind the horizon.

"How much further?" I asked.

"Too far." For a second, there was a brief frenzy in Lora's eyes. She recovered quickly. "We're out of options. We have to run the rest of the way!" She ordered the pack.

Everybody took off after the Alpha's lead, twisting through forest, field, and track. The race was on, and the sun seemed to set much faster than it had the night before.

It was every man for himself. Those who weren't fast enough would be lost to the night and the repercussions it dealt. I couldn't let it happen to myself, I didn't want to end up like Teri. I pushed myself as though the Venos were chasing us, knowing that the consequences for not making camp in time would be just as severe.

We stopped as we approached a dried moat, spotting a deer with its leg caught in a clamp; yet another one of the farmer's challenges that we had no time for.

I collected sticks, poking the hunter's traps as I saw them buried beneath the autumn leaves. They snapped shut, breaking the sticks in half.

Each time I flinched back.

Once a path had been made clear, we continued the run.

Finally, Lora slowed and I could see the red paint on the ground marking where we'd be making camp tonight. We crossed the line and I doubled over, feeling nauseous; not from the run, but from the realization that the war was so much closer than I had anticipated.

They were right outside the fence. Anxious no longer covered it.

I lay down as the final members of the pack crossed into the safe zone, with only a few minutes of sunlight left to spare.

It took us a while to recover from the panic. I closed my eyes and tried to convince myself that, for now, I would be safe. I would live to see another day.

"Great job with those traps." Jayleigh gave me a hand off the ground once my heart rate returned to its normal pace.

"Thanks." My head spun as I stood and asked, "could you do me a favor?"

"Depends what it is?" she said.

"I really need to talk to Lora, could you distract Tye for a little while?"

"Oh, yeah. Of course. Better now whilst everyone is distracted in setting up camp. Are you planning a little hanky-panky?"

"Boom-chicka-wow-wow." Hail appeared out of nowhere, wobbling his head on his shoulders.

I rolled my eyes. "Nothing like that, I just have some questions."

"Okay." They didn't seem convinced. "Go and ask your questions."

"Thanks, guys."

Lora seemed overwhelmed as I approached. She rapidly typed a message onto the tablet and pressed send before I interrupted. "Bad timing?"

She looked around quickly and I knew exactly who she was searching for. "Jayleigh and Hail are distracting Tye. I just wondered if you were free for a moment, I have to ask about what happened this morning."

"Let's go down there." Lora nodded and motioned to a small lake at the bottom of the track, overgrown with shrubs, away from the hustle and bustle. It would hide us from Tye and the rest of the pack.

"What did you do?" I got straight to it with my questions, knowing that I didn't have long before Tye became bored with the distraction and decided to scout.

"I don't know what you're talking about." Her tone would have been playful if not shadowed by the stress of the day. But I was so serious, it had been driving me mad.

"So I didn't imagine your voice then?"

"You're not crazy," she confirmed. "Or maybe just a little bit." She pinched her fingers to give me an example as we walked.

Relief swarmed me. We reached the lake and I lay back in the damp grass, my whole body aching from the day's events.

286

"How is it possible?"

"Remember the time you asked Tim what our pack's trait was? Well, that is the trick of the titanium frog. They can manipulate each other's brainwaves. The farmers call it mind-jumping." Lora lay back to join me, tucking herself into my chest, her head resting on my shoulder.

I tried to hide my shock.

"Are you cold?" I wondered what had changed between us for her to suddenly want to cuddle.

"No."

The answer put a smile on my face.

"So... The frogs communicate? Telepathically?" I mumbled in disbelief.

"It's more of a sixth sense to them. It's their mating call." If she noticed my nerves then she didn't mention it.

"Do their eyes glow too?" I joked.

"Their whole body glows." At this point, she could tell me that they could fly and I wouldn't even bat an eyelid. "We're only able to do it when we evolve, harnessing the energy in ourselves makes us able to sense and harness the energy in other Titanium hybrids."

"That's ridiculous," I said, and I wouldn't have believed it if I hadn't witnessed it first-hand. "So you evolved earlier?" My memory was fuzzy; the lightning, the voice, the branch collapsing… "The lightning was you…"

She laughed at my revelation. "Yeah, there was no lightning.

When I evolve my eyes and hair produce a beam of light. I don't know why. It's like the energy is exploding from within me. I knew that the Titaniums wouldn't connect the dots because they've never seen an Alpha mutate before."

"I- I don't understand. Why do you keep it a secret that you can evolve?"

She sighed. "I have to. You need to discover how to mutate and evolve for yourselves. We're not the first Titanium pack ever created, and previous research shows that an Alpha teaching their hybrids doesn't always pay off. You need to discover, develop, and learn from mistakes. It makes for a better warrior."

"I knew that you were hiding more information from me." I poked at her. "So tell me, Alpha, what do you love?"

"Sorry?" Lora sat up in astonishment.

"When you evolve, you have to focus on what you love," I explained. "So what do you think about?"

"How long have you known how to evolve?" she questioned.

"Only today, I worked it out this morning."

"Who else knows?" She seemed both relieved and excited.

"Jayleigh and Hail. We were talking about Donnah, she is always Hail's catalyst. I put two and two together."

Lora closed her eyes and let out a long sigh. "I have waited three years for this day," she revealed and snuggled back into my chest. I didn't have the words to reply as her arm fell across my body. "And to answer your previous question, I've told you before that an Alpha's love for their pack is eternal. That is my catalyst."

"I'm a part of that pack, so does that mean you love me?" I joked.

"I guess it does." her smile faded as she leaned on her elbow to look into my eyes. I caressed her cheek with my finger, enjoying the way that her body felt against mine, and in the corner of my eye I noticed her squeeze her thumb between her fingers.

The moon appeared stark against her eyes. This time, her glance didn't seem conflicted, the usual longing replaced by a hunger that consumed both of us.

My finger dropped from her cheek to her lips, brushing over them in one small stroke.

The threat of us being together loomed over me for a split second. What would the farmers do to me for distracting the Alpha from her duties? What would Tye do if he found out?

"Tell me that this is a bad idea," I whispered against her.

She propped herself up and this time didn't interject. Instead, she replied through stuttered breath, "For once in your life, could you stop talking and kiss me?"

"Is that an order?"

Her eyes gleamed. "You bet your sweet little ass it is."

"You've been looking at my ass?"

"Ares-"

I cut her off, leaned forward, and closed the space between

us. I wouldn't allow this moment to escape me, despite my nervous chattering.

She didn't stop me as our lips touched.

Her kiss was warm like honey and I sank into it, slow, steady, and releasing the desire that had been building up for weeks. My hand found her face once more, tracing her cheekbone back until I reached her hair, running my fingers through it and holding her against my body.

She didn't protest as my tongue met hers.

It was right in every sense of the word. There wasn't much that I was sure of, but of this I was certain.

I finally felt as though I had found my place on The Farm. The hollow space in my heart had been filled in and cemented by Lora, and suddenly the world seemed okay. This is exactly where I was supposed to be.

The kiss was delicate, passionate; everything I'd imagined it would be.

Perfect.

Until it was cut short.

I could sense Lora's disappointment as scurrying footsteps made their way down the track, accompanied by the yelling of Tye's name.

The kiss reluctantly ended, pulling back with yearning eyes.

"Tye!" Jayleigh's voice sounded closer this time.

I struggled to tear my eyes away from Lora's, not wanting our perfect moment to end in this way, but knowing that it had to.

It was time to stop this stupidity.

I expected to turn and find Tye standing there, ready to drown me in the lake or start throwing fists, but instead I found Jayleigh and Hail with panic on their faces.

I was taken aback.

Tye was nowhere to be seen.

Lora was quick to stand, just as confused as I was.

"What's wrong?" she asked.

Jayleigh looked at me apologetically. "It's Tye, we can't find him anywhere."

Hail added, "He didn't make it to camp before sundown."

CHAPTER
NINETEEN

ARES

My heart deflated as the light in Lora's eyes vanished. "What? What do you mean? He was right behind me…" She drifted off as she tried to recall the memory. "Shit!"

She sprinted up the track and I stayed on her heels.

"Tye!?" She called, alerting the other hybrids that something was wrong. Very wrong. They began to join the search, hoping that he was busy hunting or sleeping, just anywhere within the borders of camp. I scanned the field on the other side of the red line, Jayleigh and Hail joining me because they knew for certain that he wasn't on our side of the boundary.

"Look!" Jayleigh pointed to a figure emerging from the gate across the field. Surely enough, it was Tye. He moved slowly, dragging his leg out behind him and stumbling from time to time.

Lora rushed over to see what Jayleigh had spotted, her whole body seeming to fold in on itself as she let out a winded gasp. "Everybody, stay put!" she ordered and quickly crossed the border.

What was she doing?

Was she crazy?

She knew the consequences of going out after dark, seeing first-hand what could happen.

She was risking her life by going out after Tye, and there was no way I planned on standing about to watch. Before I could talk myself out of it, I stepped one foot over the red line, and then the other, and pushed into a sprint. I didn't know what danger awaited us in the darkness, but I knew from taking just one look at Teri's lifeless body earlier today that the death would be painful and slow.

Tye called out to Lora as she reached him, relieved and astounded that she had come back to help. And then he noticed me trailing behind.

"Nerd?" he questioned as I came to a stop beside them and studied his wounded leg.

"Ares?" Lora seemed shocked. "What the hell are you doing? I told you to stay within the boundaries."

"And watch you two fight for your lives alone out here? Yeah... No thanks."

"I can evolve, Ares! I'm basically three hybrids in one body.

293

Go back to camp right now!" She seemed almost hysterical.

"I'm not going anywhere. There is safety in numbers whilst we're within The Farm's boundaries."

"There's no safety. Not here, nor anywhere. We will all face the consequences of being out after dark." Tye piped up, grunting as he collapsed.

We both turned to help him up. "What happened?"

"I was angry that you took my place at the front of the line, so I fell to the back and took my anger out on a tree." He glared at me whilst I tried to hide how humorous I found the image in my mind.

Poor, pathetic Tye.

I almost pitied him.

"When I turned back you were all running away so I followed, gaining distance as you paused by the moat. I didn't question why you had stopped, I was too worried about being left behind, so I ran straight through and got my leg stuck in a trap." He pulled the ripped fabric away to reveal chewed-up skin and a bone jutting out. "I mutated to unclamp the trap, and then I passed out for a while. When I woke up it was dark and I couldn't see anybody. I followed your scent in hopes that it would lead me to camp."

We slowly crossed the field, unable to move any faster due to Tye's injury. "I'm sorry that we left you behind," Lora apologized.

"It's his own fault!" I struggled to bite back the anger

caused by his stupidity. "He chose to stay behind and beat up a *tree*."

"Ares!" Lora snapped. "Have a little sympathy."

"Are you joking? He's so immature." The nerves were making me act out of sorts.

The sound of branches snapping behind us caused us to stop, turning slowly to find out what followed. But, nothing.

"What the hell?" Tye whispered. He had never appeared scared before, but now he seemed terrified, his whole body shaking.

"You two go on ahead. I'll check it out." Lora lingered.

This time I didn't argue back. I picked Tye up as we had done in our Phase One training, ignoring as he yelled out in pain, and made for camp.

"Stop whining," I muttered under my breath.

Tye grimaced through gritted teeth. "Why did you come back for me?" he asked as I pushed into a run. "You clearly don't like me."

"I get the impression that it's a mutual feeling. Besides, I didn't come back for you," I corrected, "I came to support Lora."

"Ha," Tye tried to laugh but it resulted in a painfully sharp intake of breath. "What a hero you are. At least her plan paid off."

"I don't think that *any* of this was part of the plan."

"Oh, no. My leg wasn't intentional, I'm talking about her

promise. She made me swear not to tell you but I can't stand it any longer."

"Shut up, Tye." I didn't care for anything he had to say.

"No, you followed her out here. You're risking your life for her, so you deserve to know the truth."

"What truth? What are you talking about?" My stomach twisted.

"Her plan to keep us alive, whatever it takes."

I rolled my eyes. False alarm. "She's the Alpha, that's kind of her job."

"No, but she knew that you weren't strong enough to make it in this world. She's been playing you this whole time, hoping that if you caught feelings for her then you would agree to mutate. You're no more special to her than the rest of us. She can't actually *feel* that way for us, it's impossible."

"Did you hit your head, Tye?" My pace slowed to a walk.

"Ares, listen," Tye tried to reason with me. "Alpha's are Gen 1's. We're Gen 2's. I'm not making it up when I say that we are basically a different species. First Generation hybrids are programmed to feel protective over their pack in a maternal way, to love them, but never to fall in love with them. Whatever she's told you is a lie. She's just trying to keep you alive because you're incapable of doing so yourself."

I paused as I remembered how distraught Lora had been upon finding Teri's body, blaming herself for the hybrid's death.

How coldly she had treated Hail for killing Beckle, but still sitting up all night with me in worry as we waited for Hail's return to the barn.

The way she dropped everything to come and save Tye.

And every single time she had bent her own rules, shared her secrets, just to keep me *alive*.

My stomach churned.

Could there be any truth in Tye's words?

"Tye?" Lora's voice cut through the air like a blade.

I turned quickly, dropping Tye on his leg in the process. "Is this true? What he said about Gen 1's feeling maternal love over Gen 2's?"

I felt sick.

"Please tell me that it's all some strange fever dream that Tye has conjured up from an infection," I pleaded.

"I only told him what you told me," Tye yelled back to Lora through his pain.

I couldn't take her silence anymore.

"Well?!" Sweat broke out over my skin and bile rose in my throat.

I didn't know what to concentrate on, the fact that I had just been a part of her plan to keep the pack alive; that our relationship had been nothing more than a ruse. A lie. A manipulation.

Or, the fact that she had just kissed me, despite apparently feeling maternal over her pack members.

'An Alpha's love for their pack is eternal.'

"Ares…" she started but never finished the sentence, looking between the two of us and unable to find an answer that wouldn't completely destroy me.

I yelled out, my heart feeling as though it were being squeezed between a metal bar clamp, closing in tighter, and tighter.

I didn't need an answer, the way that she said my name was enough.

The sadness quickly gave way to anger, and this time I had no reason to hold it back. I didn't care for Tye at all, he'd only made my life on The Farm more and more difficult with each passing day.

And Lora? All I'd ever wanted was to make her happy, and every moment we'd ever shared had been a lie.

What about trust? And our plans after the war? What about the house by the sea?

It had felt so real.

What about our last night in the barn, where we made a pact to fight for each other? To focus on the war now, so that we could be together later?

"Only, that wasn't exactly how it had played out, was it?" I realized now.

She had insinuated that she felt the same, but never really admitted it. I had guessed, and she had simply played along.

I felt cheated, I felt humiliated, and once again I felt fully and completely alone.

"*A lie…*" The words echoed around in my head, dizzying me. "*A lie.*"

"Ares, calm down." Lora held her hands out. "Now isn't the time to mutate."

"But that's what you want, right? Because once I mutate, I can learn to evolve and protect myself. And if I can protect myself, then my death won't be on your hands, like Teri, and Beckle, Shyla and Torn, and Zayne-"

"Ares, stop!"

"The truth hurts, doesn't it?" I spat. "Get out of my way!" I warned as I changed direction, heading away from camp with my blood boiling. "I can't even look at you right now."

"Where are you going?" she called after me.

"Anywhere. As far as I can possibly get from you! Just please, let me die in peace."

I didn't want to be a part of this anymore. I couldn't leave The Farm, but I certainly couldn't stay, either. Death stared at me from every direction and, just like Teri, I wanted to be rid of this world.

Lora's hand was around my wrist then, preventing me from moving any further. "I won't let you go." She clung to me, and that was the trigger. Before I could prevent it, my body fought back against Lora's grasp, twisting my arm around and then slamming the palm of my hand into her chest. She flew back several meters, my attack unexpected.

The power surged through me. I welcomed it.

"Ares, you…" her words faltered as she turned back and witnessed my mutated state for the first time. I glared at her, wondering if she could feel the hatred radiating from within me.

"Oh. Damn…" Tye joined in from the sidelines. "Dude, that's not normal."

I didn't care for anything that they had to say. My body lurched forwards, ready to prove that I didn't need anybody's protection. I wasn't as incapable as they all suspected. I didn't need their lies or their friendship. All I had ever asked for was their acceptance.

The anger burned red, it's all I could see. I became it. Lora charged forward as I made a beeline for Tye, wanting to make him pay for outcasting me. We were in this situation because of him and he'd have been better off dead, but of course, Lora was there, ready to claim her mother of the year award and protect her hybrids at any cost.

"This isn't you, Ares." She tried to hold me off, but I was stronger, more powerful, and unlike in my human state, I was able to break through the Alpha block which had previously prevented me from attacking her.

"You're right," my voice sounded different, empty. "Ares is gone."

Tye whimpered and scrambled back into the mud behind Lora.

"Come back to me, Ares," she pleaded through several failed attacks. She became almost predictable. I interrupted her lead, flipping her over my shoulder and pinning my knee into her neck so that she was face down in the mud.

"Well, this isn't familiar at all!" I laughed. "Impressed yet?"

"I preferred you when you didn't fight girls," she shot back.

Suddenly, she stopped squirming and the energy around me seemed to draw in. I recognized it as she evolved, and leaped away as the energy exploded from within her like an atomic bomb, sending me flying across the field.

Tye held an arm in front of his eyes as the light blinded him and the leaves rustled towards his face. He didn't see me coming. I picked him up, gripping his neck and squeezing. I'd waited for this moment for so long. Finally, no more jealousy.

"Who's weak now?" I laughed, Tye's legs kicking out from underneath him as I lifted him off the ground completely.

And then the world tumbled. Tye was back to the ground and I was rolling through the grass with Lora on top of me.

Her eyes were ethereal.

Mine were consumed by rage.

We continued to fight, oblivious to the fact that we were still in danger of the farmers' repercussions, but even in her evolved state, she couldn't out-strength me.

I didn't stop to ask questions, I didn't care anymore.

I didn't care about her, or the war, or what would happen to me.

"Guys?" Tye questioned from a distance but we paid him no attention.

301

"Channel the anger, Ares." Lora's voice appeared in my mind.

Ah, the power of the frog mating call. Pathetic.

I ignored her, casting her out. I wanted her to experience the same pain that she had caused me. She thought that she was doing good by me, keeping me alive and making me feel involved within the pack. But she had only made things worse. She had made me look stupid. She had humiliated me when all I'd ever wanted was to fit in.

I doubted I'd ever trust her again.

"Tye."

A voice I didn't recognize drifted across the field, echoing around us and silencing us all. Lora stopped fighting and for a split second my mind went blank. A chill crawled across my skin.

"Tye." It sounded closer this time; a whisper in the wind.

Lora scrambled away from me and towered over Tye to protect him as he tried to crawl forwards, towards the source of the voice.

I stood, the confusion distracting me from the anger.

Even the night animals had gone quiet.

"Channel the anger," Lora repeated to me as she studied the empty field. *"I know that you can't control it, but try to focus the energy elsewhere. On whatever is out there…"*

I wanted to laugh. Did she really think that I would still follow her orders? She had lost my cooperation and my respect. I wasn't hers to control anymore.

In all honesty, I never had been.

"I play by my own rules!" I yelled back, charging for them both.

Only I didn't quite make it.

"Ares." The whispers called my name now, attempting to draw me in. The mutant fought against the voice which threatened to take over my mind like it had Tye's. He tried to claw his way towards the sound, passed Lora, heading towards the source of danger.

"Ares."

I quickly spun to meet the source of the voice and punched out. My eyes saw nothing but my fist connected hard.

As the drone dropped from the sky, it became visible to the human eye. It crumbled at my feet, with four green arms protruding from the body like needles, and I quickly stamped on the drone to make sure that it would never fly again.

"Ares?" Lora's voice was sober.

"Stop, Lora!" I yelled. "I told you that Ares is... gone..." I looked up from the drone as the field became alight with red and revealed that the machine at my feet wasn't the only one.

Lora wasn't trying to converse with me, she was trying to warn me.

I was in danger.

We all were.

The drones stalked forward, calling out Tye's name as they closed the space between us. They were targeting him.

The shuffling alerted me that Lora and Tye were on the

move but I stayed put. I needed an outlet for this anger and taking down fifty drones sounded perfect. I didn't care if Lora and Tye made it to camp, and I didn't care what happened to me. The mutant was in control and my body charged forward. The drones buzzed around me like bees, I grabbed them from the sky, ripping the needles from their bodies and hurling them towards other drones.

I didn't stop; not until the field was clean of red light; not until my body felt bruised and exhausted. But I sure did feel alive.

I took down the last drone, wrenching the arms off one by one, green liquid pooling out of the robot. I held it in my hand and began to walk with no destination in mind; the world was my oyster. There was nothing that could stop me now.

But, as I crossed the field, everything began to spin out of control. My feet failed me. And then I saw nothing but the stars.

I lay there for a while, my body paralyzed, but I didn't seem to notice until Lora hovered above me. Her face was a picture of sadness. She picked me up and carried me back to camp without any objection from me. I tried, but I couldn't say a thing.

Once safe, she gently placed me onto the ground, telling everybody to back off and give us some space. She was crying, although I couldn't understand why, and it seemed that my mind was a little foggy, too. Jayleigh and Hail leaned over me with expressions of horror on their faces. I wanted to ask them what was wrong. There seemed to be so much sadness, and the anger slowly left my body like somebody had pulled a plug.

"Look." Jayleigh watched. "His eyes."

Lora leaned over me to check my pulse, and one of her tears landed on my cheek. "He's still with us," she confirmed.

Barely.

They set up the shelter around me and covered me in blankets. Hail and Jayleigh made small talk amongst each other whilst Lora disappeared.

"Where did she go?" Hail asked Jayleigh.

"Down to the lake."

My friends watched over me, never leaving my side, even as the aroma of cooked duck drifted across the camp.

"Do you want some? You really should eat." Diego suggested but they both turned him away.

"Ares would be making a joke right now about something I once said about turning down food." Jayleigh almost smiled.

"He'd be asking me if I'm okay because I never turn down food," Hail contributed.

And then silence returned.

Lora came back a little while later and my friends left to give her some privacy. She lay down next to me, the way we had done by the lake merely hours earlier, and rested a hand on my face.

Her hair was wet, and her clothes were damp. "Stay with me, Ares," she whispered. "There's so much I should have told you when I had the chance. You can't leave me like this…"

In her presence, I felt at ease. Even after all that had happened tonight, I felt most comfortable with her. My consciousness started to fade away, and it was okay.

I was safe now.

"Stay with me… That's an order."

CHAPTER
TWENTY

ARES

"He's awake!"

"Go and get Hail."

"Lora, wake up. He's awake."

The air buzzed with anticipation.

A weight lifted from my chest as Lora came into view. Her hair was wild, her eyes still half-closed. "Ares?"

"Hmm?" My voice felt harsh.

"Oh, my God, Ares!" Lora smiled so wide it lit up her face.

"Bro! Welcome back!" Hail waltzed into the tent and pushed Lora out of the way to make room for our handshake. I was starting to get the hang of it.

"Hey," I welcomed them, my mind still fuzzy. "What happened?"

They shook their heads in unison. "We'll talk later. Do you

want anything? Water?"

"Hey!" Jayleigh ducked into the tent. "I just grabbed you some fruit and bread. How are you feeling?"

I slowly tried to sit but my body took a while to respond. "Okay, I think." They watched with curiosity as I took the apple from Jayleigh and bit into it. "Why are you all staring at me?"

The three of them shared a look. "You don't remember what happened?"

"I remember... We argued," I replied to Lora, "and a lot of red. Drones? Oh, crap, I tried to kill Tye."

"Tye's fine," She reassured me. "The drones... not so much."

"Did I hurt anyone else?"

Lora hesitated before answering. "You broke my arm."

I stopped chewing in horror.

"Oh," I started. My stomach churned, and the guilt crept in. "Lora, I'm so sorry. This is exactly why I didn't want to mutate-"

"You don't need to apologize," she stopped me. "Thanks to you we managed to make it back to camp without too much trouble... Even if what happened before that wasn't so pleasant."

"So, I actually helped? By mutating?" I couldn't believe what I was hearing.

"Yes..." She seemed off, as though she were saying one thing and meaning another.

The fogginess surrounding last night began to clear, memories flashing before my eyes like scenes from a horror film,

308

and their discomfort as they witnessed me mutate for the first time.

"I'm not normal, am I?" Their silence was confirmation as each of them waited for another to break the news. "And, you didn't deny what Tye told me." I stared at Lora, waiting for an explanation. Her eyes kept flittering over Jayleigh and Hail as she tried to find the words. I stood, pulling several sleeping bags and coats aside, before ducking out of the tent. "I need to get some air."

"Ares!" Jayleigh called after me, alerting the pack of my presence.

Everybody stopped to stare.

"Nothing to see here, just your standard pack clown. Laugh all you like." I waved them off as I continued walking. Their stares lingered after me.

The sun was only just showing its face, slowly creeping up from behind the mountain. The frost still crunched underfoot. I found a fallen tree to perch on and watched the sunrise whilst chewing through the remainder of my apple.

Peace.

At last.

This was all I'd ever asked for, all I ever wanted. Was leading an uneventful life really so difficult?

My gaze fell to the lake, replaying Lora's kiss and the argument that had followed. How she had fallen asleep with her head on my chest last night, despite supposedly only feeling maternal love for other hybrids.

I'd broken her arm.

Or, the monster that lived within me had. That's what I would call him from now on; not an animal, but a careless, relentless, monster.

"Tim said that when a hybrid is super strong, like Diego, or has advanced hearing, like Tye, they are just lucky in the cards that they were dealt. Do you think that I'm just unlucky in how my hybrid basis affects me? Or am I genuinely a monster?" I asked as shoes consumed the melting frost from the grass, alerting me of his presence.

"Bro, you're not a monster. You're the nicest person I've ever met. Don't beat yourself up over this."

It was hard not to. I couldn't trust the thing that I became when angry. How could I live in constant fear of myself?

"Look at the bright side, you didn't kill anyone." Hail tried to comfort me. "I've been where you are. I killed Beckle and everyone was scared of me because of it, but they got over it eventually. If they can forgive me, then they can forgive you for losing your temper once."

"I attacked their Alpha and tried to kill one of the oldest pack members. They're always going to see me as a threat."

"Yeah." Hail was quiet. "It wasn't nice to watch, I'll give you that. But you saved them from the drone army, taking down the weapons so that Lora and Tye could reach safety. In the end, you risked your life for them."

310

I sighed at the memory. "Not intentionally. But at least my recklessness resulted in something positive."

The drones had attacked, the needles piercing my skin as they had to Teri, filling my body with God-knows-what. I was lucky to still be alive.

Lora had come back for me, retrieving my limp body, and carried me to camp with tears in her eyes.

I recalled the way that the three of them had looked over me the night before, as I lay on the ground, unable to move. "What do I look like when I mutate? How do you know that I'm different?"

"It's your eyes." Hail broke a twig from the tree that we sat on and played it through his fingers. "They glow blue. Not white like an evolved hybrid. I've never seen anything like it before."

"So, I really am just a freak," I muttered in defeat. "What do you think it means?"

Hail shrugged. "I don't know. But it could explain why you've always felt different to us. Because you are different, maybe you've always known it on some level."

I smiled at Hail's observation. He'd come a long way in the few weeks I'd known him.

The sun had completely revealed itself by the time that Lora called the pack to attention. I followed Hail back to the center of camp where the Alpha stood on a rock to make a speech. The crowd moved away from me, leaving only Hail and Jayleigh by my side.

"Yesterday was a lesson for us all," she started. "From losing Teri in the morning, to the events of last night. If we have learnt anything, then it's that the farmers don't want us out after dark."

"Why?" Tye interrupted, and a few others joined in.

"Because we've been lead to believe that the enemy is human." Lora started and I held my breath. This was it. She was telling them the truth. "But it's not. Hail saw somebody, or should I say something, on the other side of the fence. They appear human at first, but they have red eyes, smell like death, and have unusual abilities, beyond explanation."

Gasps surrounded us as the pack began to break down.

Lora held a damaged drone into the air for us to see. "These drones are supposed to replicate the thing that Hail saw outside of the fence." She raised her voice to quiet the chaos. "They call out your name and trap you in some form of hypnotism, and once you're under their compulsion you are no longer in control of your own body or mind. They draw you in. Once close enough…" she pressed a button and four arms appeared from the drone. "They attack."

I recalled how the drones had affected Tye as they'd called out his name, yet I could free myself from their compulsion thanks to the animal hormones that circulated my body.

"They can only control the human mind. That is why Tye was affected, but neither Ares nor myself fell victim to their call last night, nor Hail in his evolved state the night that he saw the

312

thing outside the fence. So if you ever get caught out after dark, you must lose the human part of yourself. We must evolve if we want to survive. It's why we were created; the farmers need us to be more than them. More than human. It's the only way of winning this war."

My heart sank as everything started to click into place.

The farmers weren't just trying to create the perfect warriors, they were trying to create soldiers immune to the mind control of the enemy. They pushed us and pushed us, at times to breaking point, so that we became used to mutating and ever closer to evolving. To help us. To save us.

And, all this time I had been searching for loopholes.

I'd been trying everything in my power to cling to my humanity in worry that mutating would only bring harm to the ones that I cared about most. But if I had clung to that belief last night and hadn't been pushed into mutating, all three of us would have suffered the consequences.

"Today's mission," Lora read from the tablet. "Locate goods stored at point A and return them to point B. Stay alert, stay positive, and stay safe. We leave in five minutes."

The pack began to disperse, everybody aware of their jobs by this point.

"And one more thing before we go." She regained our attention and we stopped to turn back. "You should know that I provoked Ares's attack last night. Do not shun him for my actions. Yes, his eyes are different when he mutates and we're yet to figure out why, but it does not make him any less deserving of a place within this pack. So stop staring at him, please. We're all on the same team here. We need to act like one if we want to make it through Phase Two."

I wanted to hide as everybody turned once again to look at me. I gave a small awkward wave of the hand which I was sure everybody was used to by now and walked away to remove the shelter with Hail and Jayleigh.

"How are you holding up?" Jayleigh asked.

"Fine." I nodded and confessed, "Although I feel nothing but pain and guilt every time I look at Lora. What about you? You look like crap, Jayleigh."

She stopped untying the rope and turned to face me. "Well, I was up all night looking after your sorry ass, wasn't I?"

"Really?"

She nodded and I was overwhelmed by the urge to hug her, dropping the plastic sheet in the process. Her eyes widened and she put her hands out in alarm. "Oh, and you're in my personal space. Okay." I stopped as she kept her hands firmly braced against my chest, warning me not to come any closer. "Respect the bubble, Ares."

"Not the hugging type?" I questioned.

She shook her head no and I offered a high-five instead.

"Phew." She pretended to wipe sweat from her forehead and laughed awkwardly.

"Sorry, I didn't think. You just don't know how much it

means to me that you would do that, both of you. I was conscious for a while last night, and it really did mean a lot that you stayed with me."

"It's what friends do, Bro." Hail nudged me as he passed. "No need to thank us."

"Lora stayed too, you know?" Jayleigh added.

I didn't reply because I didn't know how to feel about it. Any of it.

For a little while, I just felt numb.

I didn't want to think about what happened on the field; what Tye had confessed, and what Lora hadn't denied.

I could see that it was playing on Jayleigh's mind and when I didn't answer she continued. "What happened? Obviously, we saw you fighting, but how? Why? The last thing we saw was the two of you getting cozy by the lake, and then not even twenty minutes later you broke her arm and she flung you across the field."

I squinted my eyes shut because it hurt to think about it and put it off until we packed up and started the hike to Point A. It was several kilometers away so I had plenty of time to collect my thoughts and explain myself.

"Tye told me that my relationship with Lora was just a ruse to keep me alive, to give me something worth fighting for because Lora didn't believe that I could make it without her. To start with, I thought that he was jealous, that he was trying to hurt me because Lora had chosen me over him. But the more he spoke, the more it seemed to make sense. I've always thought that the whole situation between me and Lora was too good to be true."

Hail sighed sympathetically and Jayleigh opened her mouth to say something, but then decided against it. I raised an eyebrow to urge her on.

"It's just… Lora told me that she made a promise to herself the night that Torn died and Shyla was removed, and I guess Tye's story kind of fits. She said that she would do whatever it takes to make sure nobody else dies under her leadership. So I guess it could be true… I'm sorry, Ares."

I shook my head and took a deep breath. "You've not heard the worst of it yet. What do you know about Generation 1's and Generation 2's?"

"What?" They both looked confused, as though I were talking in another language.

"Yeah, it was the first I'd heard of it too. But apparently, all Alpha's are Gen 1's, and all other hybrids are Gen 2's. We're like a different breed of Titanium hybrid. But get this, Gen 1's are engineered to only feel maternal love over Gen 2's."

"Oh, ew, ew!" Jayleigh started to freak out.

Hail frowned. "I don't understand."

"Lora loves me like a son," I put it simply, and Hail's face folded in on itself in disgust.

"That's rank, mate."

"I know. I confronted her about it, and she didn't deny it."

"Well, what did she say?"

"Nothing. Just my name in an apologetic tone, but that was enough. And then I got angry and the rest is history."

"So, she's like our Mom." Hail was still trying to wrap his head around it. "But she's our age."

Jayleigh rolled her eyes. "She's not actually our Mom, idiot. But she feels protective over us in that sort of way, yes."

"But, you kissed."

I sighed. "I know. I'd rather just forget about it because it's just too confusing, and painful, and it's still making me feel a little sick."

"And, she cuddled you all night."

"I know! But somehow, I think I still love her, and I'm sure she feels the same."

Jayleigh and Hail shared a look.

"It's so wrong."

"I think you need to talk to her," Jayleigh added. "A proper talk. With no kissing or fighting."

It was true. I did, but I was scared. I didn't want a repeat of the night before; what if it really was just one big act to keep me in line and cooperating?

"Whatever it takes," I repeated and sighed.

HIM

"I need answers!" I yelled at the farmers as I replayed the footage of the drone incident. Over half of The Farm's drones had gone into that attack. There was no way that one hybrid could have been able to take them down alone, especially considering that Ares had been injected with nine needles; enough venom to kill two Titaniums. Teri had died from as little as two.

"Sir." Sandra held her hand into the air. "His body appeared to absorb the venom. It paralyzed him for two hours, but as he began to heal, his vitals returned to their normal rate and the toxins in his blood just... disappeared."

"He's a fucking hybrid, Sandra, not a magician!" I yelled.

This had been my one chance to rid The Farm of the troublemaker, yet Ares had managed to pull off the impossible once again, destroying The Farm's defense in the process. "And what about the eyes? Who has an explanation for that?"

The Observatorium remained quiet.

I flung a chair into the wall, making several farmers jump. *"Good,"* I thought, they needed to wake up. "Read me his Hybrid Basis." I clicked at Sandra.

"23% Arctic Wolf, 18% Titanium Frog, 6.2% Fennec Fox, 1.7% Raven, 0.2% Elk Deer, 0.% Leaf Cutter Ant, 0.07% False Widow Spider."

I clicked my tongue and wavered my head as I considered. Nothing struck me as out of the ordinary. The genes were from animals that I'd seen in hundreds of Titanium hybrids before.

It didn't make sense.

"They're approaching Point A," Mika announced.

I looked at the screens, but half of the cameras had been demolished with the drones. "Perfect," I muttered sarcastically. I couldn't even watch the climax of Phase Two in its full glory. I thought about moving other drones in place of the missing ones around Point A, searching for areas that didn't need the coverage, and that's when I noticed a camera to the far left of the wall which showed Daniel taking the lift to level -3.

"Shit."

I collected a few belongings and called forward my assistant.

"Distract Daniel," I ordered as I quickly poured two pills from the bottle in the top drawer and made a brisk exit, turning left for the stairs to the guesthouse to avoid meeting my uncle at the lift.

I ran through the tunnel, sure that Daniel would be nearing the Observatorium by now, and then proceeded to climb the stairs. Once I reached the guesthouse, I could take a truck to D16 and watch the end of Phase Two with a front-row seat.

And if Ares once again managed to escape death, I'd kill the little rat myself.

CHAPTER
TWENTY ONE

ARES

"Just around the corner!" Lora announced.

We rounded the hill, gazes dropping to the abnormally flat field which lay below. I assumed that at some point the farmers must have made the effort to manually level it; no natural occurrence could be so perfect.

Point A was at the far end of the field, behind a wall of Venos who were standing ready in an attempt to defend the goods which we had come to collect.

We descended into quiet mayhem.

The instructions on the tablet had hidden this small issue, and we were in no way prepared for battle. Dr White's threat loomed over us. It was us or them. Only one pack would make it out of Phase Two alive.

"Everybody, shut up!" Lora commanded. "Where is your

self-belief?"

The crowd silenced as we came to a halt near the gate on the opposite end of the field to the Venos. Nerves filled the air. My heart hammered against my ribs; I wasn't ready to face Dickward yet.

However, it was nice to finally put my brain to use for the good of the pack, rather than to hinder them.

"Are you ready to learn about evolving and loopholes?" I asked, a little more excited than I should have been. Between Lora and I, and the odd input from Jayleigh, we managed to form a solid plan. Scheming was our forte, and we knew that the Venos wouldn't stop to think about the consequences of their actions. We counted on it.

Strategizing our plan of attack would have been fun if not for the distant accompaniment of the Venos breathing. The tick resembled a clock and the longer we schemed, the more intense the sound became, and the harder it was to ignore. It imbedded itself, echoing inside the walls of my skull.

"Ares, under no circumstances are you to mutate," Lora finished. "As much of a weapon as you'd be on the field, we can't trust that you'll be able to control the anger and stick to the plan."

"That's fine by me." I let out a sigh of relief, glad to have a minimal part to play. I just had to find a way to ignore the ticking. It was starting to drive me crazy.

Final preparations were made. We dumped our backpacks at

the gate and began to stretch, and I found a moment to pull Lora aside quickly. It was now or never. Who knew if we'd make it to the other end of this?

"I don't know what's going to happen out there," I admitted, taking small sharp breaths. "But I need to at least know the truth before we go."

I recognized the look on Lora's face as she began to interject, "Ares-"

I didn't let her. I felt I was slowly spiraling into a haze of red and it was getting too much; the surprise battle, the events of the night before, the lies. I needed one thing to be sure of, a piece of truth to cling onto. "What we have is real, isn't it? I can't be imagining it."

She looked around, suddenly aware of how close we stood to the rest of the pack. "I can't do this right now," she shut me down, her mind elsewhere. "We'll talk later."

"But, I might be dead later." My heart dropped.

She snapped out of her trance with intense seriousness. "You won't be. Your evil alter-ego will make sure you come out of this alive. You're far stronger than the Venos, or any of us, and until we work out what makes you different, I need you to lay low."

"I'm good at laying low," I confirmed. "I don't want a repeat of last night."

"Just keep to the plan and we'll be fine."

"Keep to the plan," I confirmed. "We will be fine."

HIM

I waited for them on the hill above the field, encompassed within the depths of the trees, and noted that the view from here was much better than I'd have had on the screens in the Observatorium.

"Impeccable." I raised my flask to the corner of the field, knowing that a cloaked drone hovered there and that I was within shot of the camera. "Cheers. This one's for you, Daniel." I took a sip of the coffee.

The Venos gathered around the barrel, prepared for the Titaniums to come running in. That's how Phase Two usually went down.

The Venos would always follow their instructions, never straying too far from the item that they were told to protect, and then the Titaniums would attack in full force. A few of them would mutate because they were stronger that way, and the Alpha would evolve along with anybody else who could.

There would be bloodshed.

But in the end, the Titaniums always came out on top. The challenge was programmed to end that way. After all, the Venos only existed to challenge the Titaniums and push them to work harder; The Farm had no need for them after today.

Movement on the far end of the field spiked my attention and I rubbed my hands together.

"Here we go!" I waited for the pack to appear.

But only Lora entered the field.

She took her time, enjoying the walk as though it were a Sunday morning stroll rather than an attempt to ambush her rival pack. The Venos noticed her almost immediately. Some of them began to rush forward until realizing that the others were missing.

Lora stopped in the center of the field, willing the Venos to come to her, and surely enough, they took the bait. All at once, the pack rushed forward and left the barrel unattended.

"Stupid reptiles."

After closing half the distance, Steven paused and turned back, realizing that the barrel was free for the taking, but the other Venos didn't seem to care.

Lora smiled, waiting, and waiting. Once they were less than five meters away from her, she plowed her fist into the ground, conducting a beam of light upon impact. As she evolved, the Venos ricocheted back. And that's when the others attacked.

"Yes!" I cheered as though watching one of Father's vintage football matches rather than a gruesome battle which could only end in death.

Hail jumped out of the trees and onto the playing field, accompanied by two more evolved hybrids, Zee and Indigo, who swarmed the fallen Venos and the real battle began.

This took me by surprise.

Four evolved hybrids? This was more than I could have asked for. Phase Two had never accomplished so much. What would happen as a result of Phase Three? A fully evolved pack?

I could finally avenge my parents.

I watched as the evolved hybrids moved with precision and grace. They were one unit, the communication was clear, although not audible to the human ear, proceeding to use the Titaniums' greatest trait to their advantage. A silent army. They were a masterpiece.

But where were the others?

I didn't have much time to wonder before the sound of feet treading the leaves suggested that I wasn't alone in these woods. I retreated from my viewpoint and pressed my back into the bark of a tree, hiding from Ares and Jayleigh as they crossed the path below, flanking the perimeter of the field whilst the evolved hybrids created a distraction, and headed towards the barrel.

This wasn't how the battle usually played out.

I hadn't considered that watching at such close proximity could put me in danger, and I hadn't considered that they would plan their attack so carefully.

I halted my breath as the hybrids passed, waiting several seconds even after their footsteps disappeared before emerging from the hiding place and returning to the edge of the tree line to watch the show. The battle wasn't as exciting as I'd anticipated, one Veno was already dead, and it looked as though the rest

325

would be quick to follow.

My last hope for some entertainment was Steven; my secret weapon.

I had noticed early on that the Veno Alpha was particularly devoted to the farmers, abiding by every mission to the best of his ability without ever wavering. He never worried about the consequences, pushing past the danger, getting the job done.

I'd taken a particular liking to Steven, something about him reminded me of myself. I'd changed the challenges to favor him in the Alpha Arena. I'd even started to visit the animals daily to gain the Venos' respect. Soon, I had Steven completing small, inauspicious missions for me whilst the rest of The Farm slept. He tied up loose ends, like Shyla.

I ducked forwards, needing a clearer view, and pulled my sleeve back to reveal the tablet attached to my arm. I pulled it from the holder. Only, as soon as I'd unlocked it, what I presumed was a rock knocked the tablet from my hands and it bounced down the bank, stopping against the base of a spindly tree. Horror. I glanced across to the hybrid responsible and didn't hold back my disapproval.

"Surprise, surprise. Ares breaking the rules again. Go and finish your mission," I ordered.

Jayleigh appeared behind Ares after realizing that she had lost him somewhere further along the path. She reached a hand forward to place it on his shoulder but he flinched away, clearly annoyed.

"He's not worth it," she tried to reason with him, but Ares didn't listen.

"I'm not going to let you mess this one up for us." Ares approached me with determination. "The game's over, Marshall."

CHAPTER
TWENTY TWO

ARES

At first, I had assumed that something had died, but the closer I got to the source, the more familiar it became, and I realized that unfortunately, he wasn't as dead as I'd been led to believe.

And then it began to fade and I stopped, knowing that if Marshall was in these woods then it could only mean that he was getting ready to interfere with our mission. I'd not seen him in almost a month, and now he decided to show up when we needed it least.

I couldn't let all of our planning and hard work go to waste. I had to stop him before he stopped us.

Jayleigh held me back, fearing that I'd only lose control and end up mutating, but I knew that wasn't an option. I didn't want to kill Marshall, as much as I hated him, I only wanted to stop him from doing anything stupid.

I dropped my bag, rummaged for the rope, and proceeded to tie him to a tree; a fair punishment for his meddling, I figured.

"You've got to be kidding," he muttered. He didn't fight back which I considered odd, but I let it slide. Maybe Marshall was all talk and no bite? "You have no idea what you've just done!" His threats disappeared as we ran off to proceed with the plan.

I couldn't help but feel a little triumphant as we descended into the madness. It was the small victories which sometimes mattered the most.

I caught glimpses of Dickward through the trees, standing guard in front of the barrel and glancing in every direction. He could hear us as we closed the distance. Diego and Tye were waiting for us in the woodland across the field and emerged as Jayleigh and I took our positions.

Dickward didn't stand a chance.

We charged forward. Tye and Jayleigh - the most qualified of the four - were to put their combat skills to the test with any Veno who'd remained, whilst Diego and I were to keep on the down-low and carry the barrel back to the gate.

The barrel was strapped to a secure concrete base, which meant that we had to cut through the ropes before we could even consider transporting the asset, so we got to work. The faster we succeeded, the higher the chance of everyone making it out in one piece.

The barrel was full of water, and once free, we hiked it onto our shoulders. We tried to find an even balance of weight but quickly realized that our height difference was making things only the more difficult. We fumbled to find a comfortable position and ended up carrying it at waist height, Diego taking the lead.

"Good?" he questioned after a few meters.

"Good," I grunted in confirmation. And it was good. Everything was going according to plan. The evolved Titaniums were doing their best to keep the remaining seven Venos occupied without killing them, Jayleigh and Tye were holding Dickward's attention long enough for us to sneak past with the barrel, and there was no sign of Marshall, so I assumed that the rope was doing its job.

We moved as fast as possible, Diego taking the majority of the weight, until something flew across the field and knocked the barrel tumbling. Dickward screeched in victory, and between scrambling for the barrel and taking a look at what had knocked it, I realized that the Veno Alpha was mutating.

And, the *thing* that had hit the barrel and disrupted our escape was Jayleigh's limp body. She lay at my feet, unconscious. "Jayleigh!" I cried. We momentarily forgot about the mission and charged forward to make sure that she still had a pulse, although my heart was beating hard enough for the both of us.

"She's still with us," I reassured Diego who, for the first time ever, looked panicked.

"I'll take the barrel, you carry her to safety," he said.

"Are you sure you can manage?"

"I don't have a choice." He nodded towards Jayleigh. "We can't leave her."

I never planned on leaving her, I planned on getting help from the others. But if Diego thought that he could carry the barrel alone then I wasn't going to disrupt the plan. I helped him lift the barrel and then followed behind with Jayleigh in my arms.

She grumbled as her consciousness returned.

My mind wandered to Tye who was now fighting Dickward alone. I wanted to look, to make sure that he was okay, but the fear stopped me.

Jayleigh was the best we had.

If Dickward could knock her flying so easily then Tye didn't stand a chance, but there was nothing we could do. We each had a part to play and deviating from the plan would result in more death than necessary. We weren't here to kill the Venos, only steal the barrel from them, and so we vowed to avoid causing them serious harm unless our lives were put at risk.

Tye was at risk, sure.

But it was about time he got knocked down a peg or two. It seemed that yesterday hadn't been quite enough to do it. At least his leg had healed overnight.

I couldn't watch as we scurried up the fence line, mainly because I could hear the noise erupting from Dickward and it didn't sound pretty. I was scared to lay eyes on a mutated Veno

Alpha, and if I witnessed what Tye was up against, I'd only feel guilty for not helping.

In hindsight, Lora should have been the one to fight Dickward. She was the most advanced and experienced, but we didn't know that he would be the one to stay behind and guard the barrel, and it was too late to change to plan B now.

Ignorance was bliss until I couldn't ignore it any longer. Tye's scream cut across the field, deafening us all into motionless silence. I stared as he dropped to the ground, and that's when Dickward's attention turned on me.

Somehow, my brain managed to instruct my arms to safely place Jayleigh over the fence before my body shut down completely in fear. I had always imagined that a mutated Veno would resemble that of a monster, and I wasn't wrong.

Tim had laughed at me when I asked if we were werewolves as though it were completely out of the question, and whilst that may have been the case for Titaniums, I couldn't think of anything to better describe the Veno Alpha who now charged towards me on all fours.

His spine arched, seeming to have lengthened quite dramatically to enable his arms to reach the ground as he ran. Not that his arms were their normal shape. In fact, his whole body seemed out of proportion, larger on top. The iris of his eye narrowed, sharp like a snake, and scales formed over the small patches of skin which remained on his contorted face. His eyes were still yellow; still solely focused on me.

And at this moment, as the monster charged forward with only one intent, I realized that I had a decision to make.

It wasn't the choice of fight or flight, nor of how I would choose to die. It was a choice of defending or attacking.

Defending would result in him hunting me down and forcing the mutant out. I would try to fight it back, fearing my own inner animal as much as I feared his, and I would ultimately sacrifice myself. And, whilst I lay dying, Dickward would turn on the family I had built for myself, picking them off one by one as the life left my body.

Or, I could attack first.

I could force the mutant out instead of waiting for it to emerge and use the element of surprise to my advantage. He had no idea what I was capable of. Hell, *I* didn't know what I was capable of. But I knew that I was strong, as strong as Lora in her evolved state, and if anyone other than Lora stood a chance of taking Dickward down, it would be the monster that lived within me.

I didn't have time to consider my options. The Veno drew closer with each passing second and I acted in hopes that I was saving my friends, and tried to avoid considering the possibility that I may be the one about to kill them.

"Fear is a trick of the mind," I repeated Lora's words.

The Veno Alpha slowed as I started my run towards him, summoning anger and welcoming the feeling that took over as I lost control of my mind and body. I made the switch, and as I did so I thought of Lora, of my love for her; willing myself to evolve.

But all I felt was rage. She'd misplaced my trust. I couldn't focus on anything but that as the animal took over. The need to hunt. The push to kill.

Unlike Dickward, I didn't grow an extra twelve inches or develop scales or a snout as I mutated, but he seemed to notice the exchange of energy and the way that it danced blue in my eyes. We collided, the impact sending us both spiralling through the air and tumbling across the field.

"You've been keeping secrets." I gestured to his wolf-like frame as I smashed his head against a rock. "I'm ready now. Let's have some *fun.*"

He didn't reply. He hissed.

I didn't expect anything less.

Dickward shoved me off so that he could stand, towering over me. He was as intimidating as ever, but his extra height and weight made him slower to react, so I used it to my advantage. My body lurched forwards, catching him off-guard, and swinging around until I was on his back with my arm around his throat.

I recalled every encounter I'd ever experienced with Dickward. Every time he had tried to intimidate me, hunt me, and threatened to kill me.

No more.

The anger surged.

My legs gripped tightly at his ribs and squeezed. The Veno

screamed out as ribs started to crack under the pressure, and then I cut off his air supply. I used my free hand to pull the arm back further around his neck, and the Veno collapsed to the ground, rolling, trying to squash me.

And I should have felt squashed. My reflexes should have kicked in, forcing me to let go and scramble to safety. But I didn't seem to feel the pain that so surely consumed my body. I continued to squeeze as he rolled around until his body fell limp.

"What are you doing?!" The voice appeared so faint I almost thought I'd imagined it. "Kill him! End him now!"

I was ready to comply, but through the fog, I realized the voice wasn't talking to me, and I wasn't imagining it. The Alpha stopped fighting, not dead, but unconscious. And I suddenly registered the voice. My spare hand reached for the Veno's misshapen ear, pulling out a small bud. I was ready to launch it across the field and finish the fight, ending the Veno's life, until the bud spoke again.

"Ah. Hello, Ares."

I put the bud into my ear and glanced up to where I had left Marshall.

He stood at the edge of the tree line, no longer in ropes, and the tablet was fixed back on his arm as he clapped. The sound echoed around the valley, bouncing back and stopping the other Titaniums from fighting. Diego had almost reached the gate at the far end of the field, Jayleigh had woken from her place behind the fence and joined in helping him carry the barrel whilst Tye cradled his broken arm to his chest. Lora and the evolved hybrids had been dropping Veno bodies without causing them too much harm.

They looked puzzled as the sound swarmed around them. And then their eyes landed on me.

"What are you going to do, Ares?" Marshall questioned through the earpiece. "This is your chance to kill Steven, after all these weeks of torment. He's been hunting you, targeting you. This is your chance to put an end to it all."

I wanted to.

The animal tried to turn back to him, to finish what we'd started, but I forced my anger towards the voice as Lora had begged me to do last night. If I couldn't relinquish the energy, I had to redirect it.

Dickward didn't deserve to die. He wasn't the real monster here. He was a subject of The Farm, an experiment; just like me. He was just doing what he had to in order to survive his training.

We were one of the same.

If I was going to kill anybody today, it would be Marshall, and he realized it as I leapt over the fence and began the incline towards the woods. He disappeared into the shadows of the trees and left nothing behind except for the smell of sweat and coffee. I followed it.

"How does it feel Marshall?" I called out into the emptiness of the forest as I ran. "To be the prey for once?"

He laughed into the bud in my ear. "If you think that I fear you then you're a fool. I've encountered far worse than you."

"Then why do you run? Come and fight, like you force us to. Or are you too Beckle?" I taunted.

My ears picked up every sound; the blow of the wind, the approaching vehicles, the snaps of twigs, and the rustle of dead leaves with every step that he took. He led me back along the rabbit trail. The ropes that I had tied Marshall in earlier lay at the roots of the tree, cut with presumably a hand knife. As I studied them, I sensed a movement to my left and charged for it.

Marshall stumbled through the trees as though he were drunk. I chased him down the path, swerving through the branches and closing distance. Adrenaline fuelled me forward, and once close enough, I pounced.

Only he stumbled as I attacked, wavering away from me, and gravity pulled him down the bank and out of grasp. He fell from the woods, the forest spitting him out onto the field below. I pounded down the bank to reach him before any other Titanium could.

Marshall was mine.

I picked him up under the arms and shook, hoping that maybe it would knock some sense into him. He glared as he attempted to reach for his pocket in a last effort to save himself. He didn't say anything, and even as he revealed the taser, he never once took his eyes off mine.

I smiled, realizing where his confidence was rooted. That one little machine sourced his control, his confidence, and he believed that it would save him; that he would taser me and this would all be over.

But I had come a long way from day one. By now, I had spent enough time in my animal state to sense the energy within my veins, even if I was yet to control it, and it surged as he pressed the button, his eyes assured, steady, becoming wider and more panicked as the remote did nothing to stop me. I laughed at the helplessness in his expression.

"So much confusion," I snarled as he pressed the button again and I felt the small tingle of electricity against my skin. My body absorbed the energy. "I'm not like the others, Marshall. You can't stop me. Put the taser down."

Marshall dropped the remote. He scrambled now, feet kicking out, fingers trying to pry my hands open as they gripped his throat. I watched the hope leave his eyes and I squeezed tighter. "You can't do this. Do you know who I am?" His voice was barely audible.

"Ares!" Dr White's voice interrupted my madness. I had barely noticed the trucks pull up and the farmers unload, their weapons pointing in my direction. The pack stood amongst them. Lora was beside the doctor as he tried to ease me out of the animal state. "Think about what you're doing."

"Uncle Daniel!" Marshall called out in reply to Dr White's voice. "He's going to kill me, you have to kill him first!"

"Nobody is dying today." Dr White reassured Marshall. My mind twitched, but the monster didn't care for any of it.

Dr White's attention turned back to me. "We haven't been honest with you, Ares. And if you just put Marshall down, I promise to answer all of your questions. Every single one of them."

Marshall began to object. "You can't do that! I'm in contro-"

"Do you want to live or not?" Dr White snapped at him.

My mind fell in and out of focus, the information willing me to break through. I wanted to understand, I wanted to be free of the games and the lies, but I also *really* wanted to watch the light in Marshall's eyes fade away as I drained the life from him. And, the more he tried to wriggle free, the harder it became to ignore.

His skin was changing from pink to purple and the veins in his forehead held my attention, it was as though I could see the blood working harder the more he suffocated. For whatever reason, it amused me.

Enough to forget Dr White's bargain.

Enough to forget who I was and what I wanted.

Because right here, all the monster could think about was how best to kill Marshall. How to make him suffer the most before I relieved him of his desperate little life.

"It wasn't a lie!" Lora blurted out in desperation.

The trance-like state shattered as her voice cut through and regained my attention. My grip on Marshall weakened slightly as I turned to face her.

"I do have feelings for you, even though I'm a Gen 1 and you're a Gen 2." She walked towards us slowly, keeping my attention on her and not on the man suffering in my hands.

"And yes, in the beginning, I was just trying to keep you alive. I sensed that you had feelings for me. I formed a plan, but I knew after our first conversation alone that I was in trouble. I tried to fight the feelings, to deny them, and ignore them; knowing that it was wrong on so many levels. But, you are the one battle I cannot win, Ares."

She paused, as though noticing that everybody was staring and suddenly feeling exposed. She focused only on me as she continued. "I wanted to tell you the truth but I was afraid of what everybody would say. I thought that I'd lose their respect and that they might view me differently or judge me for how I feel because I know how disturbing it sounds and that it probably means I'm very, very ill. But it's true. I have feelings for you. I don't quite know how to describe it or know why I feel this way, but I *do* know that *this…*" She gestured to my grip on Marshall. "This… isn't you."

I looked back to Marshall, seeing him once again as another human being and not a piece of putty.

"I will understand if you kill him, believe me, we've all wanted to stand in your shoes at some point, but I know that you'll never forgive yourself. I know how much guilt eats away at you, it's one of the reasons I fell for you in the first place. I just want you to be sure about what you're doing because once he dies, there's no going back."

She was right. I never would forgive myself. And suddenly the colour of Marshall's face and the pulsing of his veins no longer amused me but made me feel nauseous. Marshall's body crumpled to the floor as my mind cleared and my body became mine to control once more.

"It's true?" I muttered as the truth sank in.

Lora smiled. "It's sickening, I know. I need to get myself checked out."

I felt weak all of a sudden, not from her words, but because my body had been worn out. Fighting Dickward, hunting Marshall down, I'd been tasered twice; it had taken its toll and I collapsed onto the ground.

I recalled the other Titaniums feeling the same exhaustion after mutating, so I wasn't worried about it. But, there was a haziness. My body felt light, as though I was in the air, being thrown around. People yelled. Lora screamed.

The dizziness cleared as commotion commenced, and once I came around, I realized that Marshall had turned the tables. He held me against his chest, a knife pressed against my neck, with Lora ready to attack and Dr White approaching with caution.

"I should have just killed you when I had the chance," I groaned.

"You should have," Marshall agreed.

Dr white walked slowly, holding his hands out in front of him. "Put the knife down, Marshall."

Marshall didn't move. "He's broken the rules one too many times, Uncle. You know that Father never allowed an animal to live for breaking the rules."

Uncle.

My mind jumped and I swallowed my regret. In my last counselling session, I had told Dr White that I thought Marshall, his nephew, was crazy. Of course, it was true. Marshall *was* crazy, but nobody would want to hear that about a family member.

And yet, the doctor still fought for *my* freedom.

"Daniel, Daniel, Daniel... Always showing up when I don't want you, never there when I *need* you," Marshall continued, waving around the hand knife he'd stolen from my calf pocket in a way that made me all the more uncomfortable with the situation. "Don't I get a release, too? When Mother died, you vanished for weeks. I picked up the pieces. I carried The Farm. And when you came back you expected everything to be okay? I was hurting too!"

"Marshall, please stop this madness! There is too much at stake!"

"You weren't there for me!" he continued. "For eight years I've been trying to keep myself together. Trying to recover from the murder of my parents. Do you know that I watched it happen? They locked me in the Observatorium to keep me safe, and on the screens, I saw that *thing* stalk in and take their lives. I saw everything! Do you have any idea how traumatizing it is to look at that screen? Every. Single. Day! Do you? Imagine leading

The Farm with Camera 72 staring at you, reminding you that you did nothing. You sat and watched."

Dread coated me as I made sense of the situation. No wonder The Farm was this messed up if Marshall had been left in charge for eight years, experiencing some kind of PTSD with no help from his uncle; the only family he had left.

"I-"

"Stop talking!" he yelled at the doctor. "I can't escape it. I can't even leave The Farm." Marshall began to sob. "You can hide away in your little room and pretend it never happened. I have to relive it." Marshall's sanity was starting to slip, his words began to slur as he returned to the intoxicated state he had been in earlier. "And you only come to check up on me when I've done something that you don't approve of. Let's take Donnah, for example..."

"You went about the situation wrong," Dr White interjected.

"I know that!" Marshall stabbed the air with his knife. "But I had to deal with the situation alone. I was tired. I wanted somebody else to experience the responsibility. Don't you see?! For once, I didn't want to be the one to make the decision! So I let Donnah decide for herself."

Hail broke the silence with a moan. I'd forgotten that the pack was listening in, now holding Hail back from both Marshall and Dr White. They were both as guilty as each other.

"I should have seen the signs... I should have been there for you instead of distancing myself from the world." Dr White sounded deflated. "You've always been so similar to your father, so strong, I thought that you were coping okay without them. I thought that you hated me, so I kept away."

"I do hate you," Marshall confirmed. "But I never used to. My parents never showed me any love. They only showed me how to run The Farm, and when they died I hoped that you might step up to the role. But instead, you blocked me out just like they did."

Dr White covered his face with his hands, the truth stabbing at his heart. "I'm sorry, Marshall. We failed you."

The madman stopped crying now, solemn all of a sudden. "Yes. Well, I've learnt to cope without a family."

The words were intended to hurt, and I wanted to feel sorry for Dr White but I couldn't help but feel like he deserved it. In my first days, I had wanted nothing more than to find my family, to feel as though I belonged to something other than myself, but I was starting to realize that even families were fragile; breakable. They were built on respect and trust, something which the pair beside me was void of. They were so far past it that they failed to see how lucky they were to have each other.

"So, what now? You're going to ask me to stand by and watch you kill Ares? For what reason? A release of the anger and resentment you've built towards me?" Dr White asked.

"He does seem to be your favourite."

"Favourite is a strong word. He is different, and coming

from a family of science, he perks my interest. I assumed that you would feel the same way."

"You assume a lot about me, doctor." Marshall held the knife against my throat, my body still too weak to fight back against him. "Let me remind you that not everything is about you."

"Your parents then? Your father's rules? Ares breaks them too often and you worry that your father wouldn't have let it pass, and so neither should you."

"He's watching me…" Marshall slurred. "I just want to make him proud."

"We all deserve a moment of madness in a world such as this." Dr White's words didn't fill me with confidence. "But I can assure you that killing Ares won't bring you any closer to your father. He's gone, Marshall. And for the record, you made him more proud than anyone, he just wasn't very good at expressing his emotions."

Marshall sobbed into the back of my head, the blade pressing deeper into my neck.

"Put the knife down, son." Dr White slowly crept towards us.

"I can't." He shook his head, the insanity returning. "I need this!"

"You don't know what you need. Let me help you." He tried to remain calm, his voice steady.

"Nothing you say can help me more than this will!" I waited

for the pain. "Every day since Ares woke from hibernation something has gone wrong. He messes up all of my plans, he is trying to destroy my work, everything the family has fought so hard to achieve. He is selfish, he is rude, and he just... won't... die!"

The doctor panicked, rushing forward as Marshall repositioned the knife. "You can't!" But Marshall didn't listen. The knife delved into the flesh underneath my chin. A sharp pain soared through me, choking me.

"He's your brother!"

And then the knife was pulled out.

Time slowed.

The silence that filled the air suffocated us both and the knife slipped from his fingers, free falling and landing at our feet. Marshall turned me around to look into my eyes and make sense of the situation. I stumbled and attempted to cover the blood which splurged from the gash in my neck. It was too late. "W-What?"

Uncle Daniel closed the space, hugging onto each of our shoulders as he repeated, "He's your brother, Marshall... Ares is your brother. Oh, dear Lord... What have you done..."

They caught hold of me as I collapsed.

CHAPTER
TWENTY THREE

ARES

Although exhausted, my body got straight to work on fixing the hole in my neck that my long-lost brother had created.

Lora's face appeared behind Marshall and Dr White's, and she pushed through to take a hold of my hand whilst my vision faded in and out of focus. They vanished completely as white heat injected my bloodstream, presumably the needle that the doctor pulled out of his pocket, and hopefully not the knife.

My body fell limp as I lost consciousness, but my dreams danced.

Flittering memories of Marshall and Dr White. Blurriness. Lora, the pack, back to my family, and the lies and the deceit. Every moment I'd encountered upon waking on The Farm.

Was I dying?

Pressure reigned over me. I was searching, in a state of semi-consciousness where my mind was free to roam.

And then I found what I had been looking for. A memory buried so deep, I plucked it from beyond the barrier.

The farmers hadn't removed our memories from before the metamorphosis, they had only made them impossible to access whilst conscious, but from this drugged state I could reach into the pool. I found a woman there, one I didn't recognise, bound in rope and fighting against the chair that she was tied to. I viewed her through a large window and another woman's voice appeared in my ear.

"It's okay." She willed me to step through the door next to the window, a comforting hand on my shoulder gently easing me forward. "You're not like the others, Ares. The answers you're searching for are in there. I'll be beside you every step of the way."

The memory faded as I reached for the door, and my eyes landed on Dr White as he fiddled with a strange plug which had been inserted into my hand. I felt at peace, although I couldn't understand why.

It certainly wasn't peace in finding my family, as I had expected I would feel. I had imagined a warm fuzzy feeling, a sense of belonging and familiarity. I knew that it would be a long time, if ever, before I could feel any sense of connection at all towards my brother and uncle.

Dr White had always been the kindest farmer, the most

respectful towards my thoughts and actions, but I wondered now if that was only because I was his nephew. If he had been kept in the dark as Marshall had, would he have acted the same? I couldn't forget his ignorance. I had asked him about my family and he gave nothing away, he saw how much pain I was in and he chose to discard it and lie.

At least I knew where I stood with Marshall. We'd both kill each other in a heartbeat. It was a mutual hatred, no lies. He had been straight with me from day one.

And I didn't even want to think about my parents, they must have been just as messed up as the rest of the family. Marshall was proof of that; I was proof of that.

Who could experiment on their own child? It took a special kind of desperation. But then, they had created The Farm for a reason. They were so scared of what existed beyond the fence that they built a facility to fight back, train their oldest son to take over, and turn the youngest into a monster.

"A monster who can't be controlled by the enemy," I reminded myself.

My mind wandered back to the story Hail told, about the woman beyond the fence, and I tried to imagine what we were up against. I recalled the drones, although my memory of that night was still fuzzy. The needles and the holes in Teri's body, and the blood that spewed from her mouth and eyes. The way that the drones called my name, attempting to take over my mind.

And my dream.

Only, it wasn't a dream, was it? The woman bound to the chair wasn't human, yet she had all of the answers that I needed.

I had to find her.

"Your mother used to sing that song," Dr White interrupted my thought process. "I'm surprised you still remember it." I hadn't been aware that I was humming anything at all. "I understand that this has come as a surprise to you, Ares. I'm prepared to answer any of your questions, no exceptions."

Laughter escaped me and I regretted it instantly. But I couldn't help it. He knew exactly what I wanted and how to twist me into cooperating. The king of bribery.

I had planned to give my uncle the silent treatment because I really was angry at him, and I knew that he could no longer be trusted. But he was willing to answer my questions in hopes that it could rekindle our fellowship, and although nothing he could say would make me trust him ever again, I wanted the answers. And so, I played along.

"Why did they hide me from Marshall?" I decided to start small. "Why didn't he know that I existed?"

Dr White fiddled with a monitor beside my bed as he spoke and it seemed as though he had prepared his speech, I wondered if the words were written somewhere in his folder.

"The first thing that you need to know about your parents is that they were very organised people. Of course, they had to be to run a cooperation such as this. But even before the war began, it was just a part of who they were. Your father had been promoted to Captain in the military the year before meeting your mother, who was a devoted and extremely successful biochemist. She had always been the clever one growing up and I often felt left behind in her presence, but she was truly wonderful.

"As you can imagine, the pair needed to be organised within their professions, and when they adapted The Farm into what it is now, everything was just as precisely planned. They would have one child who would take over at the age of twenty-five, assisted by Joe, your father, and Samantha would train the new generation of scientists. They had a backup for every scenario. In fact, there was only one thing that they hadn't planned for."

"Me," I finished.

"It sounds horrible, but yes." He sat on the edge of my bed. "Samantha wanted to train you with Marshall, but Joe said that it was hard enough training one child, let alone two, and he feared that you would distract Marshall from his studies."

"He sounds lovely," I muttered.

"He had his issues," Dr White agreed. "My advice to your parents was to train you as a scientist. And that was the plan for a very long time." My heart sank, I would have wanted nothing more for myself. "You were raised away from Marshall so that it wouldn't affect his learning. He travelled to another Safe-Zone whilst Samantha was pregnant, and then returned three months after you were born. You were raised in the infirmary by Samantha whenever she was able, and when she was busy, myself and my partner, Flynn, would step in."

He pulled the locket from his pocket once again, and this time I saw the people in the photographs with new eyes. My mother was naturally beautiful, with long brown hair, scattered freckles and a large smile. How had I not noticed the resemblance sooner?

"So Marshall was mainly raised by my father?" I questioned.

"Raised in a sense of the word," he confirmed.

"Have you ever considered that Marshall acts the way that he does because of his childhood?" It seemed obvious to me.

"I'm the psychologist in the family, of course I have. But he's not my child. And it wasn't my place to say or do anything."

"Is that what you said when our parents died and you abandoned him?"

My words lingered.

I don't know why I was now sticking up for Marshall, I still didn't like him, but suddenly it became very clear that we were more similar than I'd originally thought, only we coped with the lack of parental affection in very different ways.

"You left him to lead The Farm alone, before he was ready, knowing that he needed somebody to lean on at that moment more than any. As you said, you're the psychologist in the family. You should have known that he'd need you." My voice began to rise and my heartbeat beeped faster on the monitor. "But you abandoned him. Where did you go? Because you couldn't leave The Farm and he couldn't find you anywhere. Where could you possibly have gone-?"

He cut me short. "I was with you!"

Everything I was about to say disintegrated. Of all the excuses I had expected, this was the very last. "Me? Why were you with me?"

A small tear ran down the doctor's cheek and he gripped the locket tightly in his hand. "They say that losing a sibling is difficult, but losing a twin is like losing a part of yourself. I lost my twin and my partner on the same day. I didn't know who I was anymore, I didn't have anything left to fight for. The only family I had was you."

"And Marshall…"

"Marshall was a stranger to me, but you were the son I never had. I sat by your incubator for weeks. And you look so much like your mother, being near you was almost as though I was near her."

He wiped his eyes with a handkerchief which he pulled from his pocket. I wondered if he used it often. My heart mellowed a little, only, I couldn't understand his motives. How could he lie to me? Why would he keep it a secret?

"It was selfish of me and I should have been there for Marshall, but I figured that he was never really close to his parents and he had trained for this moment all his life. I never imagined that he would spin this far off the rails and start taking Joe's medicine, which is completely the wrong dosage and so far out of date that we're unsure the extent of his side effects."

I recalled the way he stumbled through the woods, the

dizziness and the slurring.

"How long has he been taking them?"

Ah, and now it appeared that I was worried for Marshall's health. I surprised even myself.

"Several months, according to Tim."

"Tim knew? And he didn't try to stop him?"

"Tim is Marshall's assistant. He knows everything that Marshall does, but that doesn't mean that Marshall listens to his advice. He doesn't listen to anybody except for the devil on his shoulder."

No wonder Tim always seemed so grouchy. He had to put up with Marshall's crap just as much as mine. I almost felt bad for giving him a hard time.

Almost.

"Where is Marshall now?" I questioned.

"He's with the medics. He won't be waking up for a while as we drain his body of the drugs and run a few tests."

"So, is he usually this crazy?" It seemed hard to believe that maybe the drugs had been influencing his decisions, bringing on the strange mood swings and hysteric laughter I'd witnessed on several occasions.

Dr White pursed his lips. "Anyone in his position would go a little crazy, I'm sure. But he was never this irrational." He looked down at the folder although his eyes didn't follow the writing. Was he blaming himself for all of the destruction Marshall had caused?

He was right to.

But I couldn't shake what Dr White had said about me. He was the closest thing to a father that I would ever know, and given time, maybe he could redeem himself.

"Why did you lie when I asked about my parents? You could have just told me who I was on day one and resolved all of this."

He shook his head. "I wish I could have, but I had to follow your mother's orders. She knew that you would be different to the others, and telling you would make you act differently. It would have alienated you right from the get-go. She wanted you to have a chance to be normal."

"How did she know that I would be different?"

"I'm aware that you know about the different generations of hybrid. You've been lead to believe that you are a Gen 2, to help you fit in with the rest of the pack. We assumed your differences would be subtle and they would go unnoticed. But obviously, we were wrong." Dr White shifted his weight. "You're not like the others because you're a Gen 3, Ares, the first and only one of your kind."

I frowned as the news began to sink in.

"Why would she purposely make me different? Why, if she wanted me to fit in, didn't she just make me a Gen 2 like the rest? This doesn't answer anything! It only gives me more questions!"

"That's a story for another day, Ares. For now, try to rest, think over the information I've given you and come to terms with that before you hear the rest."

"But I need to-"

"Stop!" He signalled a hand in my direction. "Believe me, you can't handle the full story until you've digested this."

I sat silently for a long while, watching the clock do its rounds. It was infuriating to know that Dr White was still hiding things from me, but the more I considered, the more I began to think.

"If I'm not a Gen 2, then it's okay for Lora to have feelings towards me. She's not ill."

"Correct. Lora is healthy and performing exactly as we expect a Gen 1 to act."

It was a relief to hear the words leave his mouth. All of this stupidity could be put behind us, I'd tell Lora and the rest of the pack what Dr White had told me, and they would understand why I always acted so differently. They had already witnessed enough to realize that I wasn't like them, now maybe they'd be more accepting in knowing that it wasn't in my nature to act like them, just as it wasn't in their nature to act like Lora.

Suddenly, all I wanted was to return to the barn. I wanted to hold Lora in my arms and tell her that everything was okay, she was fine, I was fine. Everything was going to plan. I wanted to make sure that Jayleigh had healed from the injuries that Dickward had inflicted on her, and welcome Hail with his handshake which I was now starting to get the hang of.

Dr White must have sensed the urgency and he stood whilst studying his watch, making a strange noise at the back of his throat. "I will answer your questions another day, but for now I'm needed in the Observatorium, what with Marshall away from his post and all. I'll have my people run some final tests and then you'll be free to return to the barn." He nodded once and turned for the door, and then paused.

"Here." He handed me the photo of my mother from the locket. "Keep her safe." And then he was disappearing through the door and down the cavern.

I studied the photo, just the size of my thumb, and spoke to it as though my mother could hear me. Who knew, maybe her ghost still lingered around The Farm.

"I wish that you were here. I've got so much to ask you..." I whispered and hugged the photo to my chest.

This was the feeling that I had been expecting to find upon meeting my family. The warmth and reassurance in knowing that I had once been loved, even if I couldn't remember it.

I tucked the photo into the secret pocket at my calf and zipped it closed as Dr White's associates entered the room. I expected them to run a few more tests, as my uncle had suggested they would, but instead, they quickly went about removing the needle from my hand and getting me to my feet.

The four farmers boxed me in as we left the hospital room, moving at a brisk walk. The hairs on the back of my neck stood on end as I figured that this wasn't protocol. I didn't recognize the farmers, but they lead me to the lift with guns in their hands.

Was this Marshall's doing? Getting his minions to finish the job?

The lift lurched into action and it didn't take me long to realize that we weren't rising to land, but delving deeper into the Earth, further and further down. The doors opened into a bunker, with sterile white walls and too many lights secured to a ceiling so high you could fit a full-sized aeroplane in the room. It was so bright that it was blinding.

Level -3 was in chaos.

The farmers scurried around like ants, hundreds of them, some heading down a corridor labelled "Weaponry", and others heading towards the "Infirmary". They didn't so much as glance in my direction as they led me down a large corridor tucked behind the lift and I wondered what was going on. This couldn't be normal behaviour for the farmers.

"Where are you taking me?" I asked the people leading me as we passed several doors. "What's happening?"

We descended more stairs, now surely several hundred feet underground. The stairwell lit up red, flashing in warning as a siren wailed.

We reached the bottom floor, abandoned. Minus the alarm, it was very still down here. As we turned the corner, I became aware of the windows lining the walls. One, in particular, caught my attention. It was empty, with rope strewn across the floor and a chair leaning on its side.

That's where she was. The woman from my dream. The woman with the answers.

I was briskly led passed the room, the farmers ignoring my questions about where she had gone and who she was.

We finally reached the end of the corridor and the farmers shut me inside, offering no sense of an explanation.

This certainly wasn't the barn. And where were my friends?

The siren echoed through the room as I turned, shocked to find that I wasn't alone.

The room was white, much like the rest of level -3, with a kitchenette in the corner, a couple of sofas, a coffee table and a door, to what I assumed would be a bathroom.

Marshall's bed sat against the far corner, the monitor bleeping peacefully against the violence of the siren. I crossed the room quickly, calling his name. When he woke, he was dazed, looking around with confusion.

"Marshall?!" I was almost relieved to see a familiar face.

He panicked upon realizing who I was, but after a second he seemed to calm down. "Ares. What's going on? Where are we?" He tried to look around but sitting proved difficult. Whatever Dr White had drugged him with must have made it difficult for him to move.

"A white room, kitchen, living area, bathroom. Down a long corridor of windows looking into smaller rooms. Red lights are flashing on the wall," I yelled over the sirens.

Marshall's eyes closed and a long sigh held him. The sedation was heavy. "The Safe-House."

My body ran cold. "Why are we in a safe-house? What's

going on?"

"Don't worry. This room is the safest part of The Farm. Daniel must have sent us here to save us."

"Save us from what?! What is going on, Marshall?" I was wracked with nerves and worry.

"The sirens only mean one thing, Ares. Pour us a coffee and read a book, it's going to be a long night. I hope that you kissed that girl of yours goodbye."

Even ill, drugged, and vulnerable, Marshall was still going out of his way to torment me. I grabbed his finger and began to bend it backwards, watching as his face twisted in pain.

"What is going on? Tell me now or so God help-"

"It's the Night Walkers!" he cut me off and I let go of his finger. For the first time, I saw genuine fear in Marshall's eyes; as though saying their name released a world of pain and dread within him. "It's the Night Walkers... They've breached the fence."

To be continued...

REVIVE
The Titanium Trilogy - Book 2

IT PAYS TO BE AFRAID OF THE DARK

Coming December 2022

Sign up to the
Kirsty Bright
Newsletter

Don't miss out on the next thrilling novel in the trilogy. Sign up to the author newsletter for first chapter reads, release dates and more!

For more details, visit
www.kirstybrightauthor.com

Love this book?
Make sure to leave a review!

With special thanks,

Kirsty.

#	TITLE		ALBUM
1	Two Face (Dark Version) Jake Daniels		Two Face (Dark Version)
2	Enemy - From the series Arcane League of Leg... Imagine Dragons, Arcane, League of Legends		Enemy (from the series Arcane League of ...
3	Something Like Me Chris Kläfford		Something Like Me - EP
4	The Middle Jimmy Eat World		Bleed American
5	Take on the World You Me At Six		Night People
6	Power Isak Danielson		Power
7	Too Far Gone Hidden Citizens, SVRCINA		Celestine
8	Demons Jacob Lee		Philosophy
9	Uprising Muse		The Resistance
10	Man or a Monster (feat. Zayde Wølf) Sam Tinnesz, Zayde Wølf		Man or a Monster (feat. Zayde Wølf)

Search

Yield (The Titanium Trilogy, Book 1) - Soundtrack

0:24   2:56

ABOUT THE AUTHOR

Kirsty is a British small-town girl with a big love for coffee and spicy food. She spent her childhood on the border of England and Wales, surrounded by vast countryside where she enjoyed horse riding and time outdoors with her family and friends.

She found herself drawn to the creative arts in her early teens, especially music, drama, and writing; and she still continues to sing locally from time to time. But reading or writing, with a candle lit and a mug of coffee in her hand, is where she finds herself happiest.